Come What May

Kevin Lee Swaim

PUBLISHED BY: PICADILLO PUBLISHING
COVER DESIGN BY: THE COVER COLLECTION
PROOFREADING BY: DONNA RICH
ISBN: 978-0692249215

10 9 8 7 6 5 4 3 2 1
FIRST EDITION
PRINTED IN THE UNITED STATES OF AMERICA

ACKNOWLEDGMENTS

Thanks to my beta readers. Your feedback was invaluable.

CHAPTER ONE

Tuesday

It was a warm September morning in Arcanum, Ohio. The wind whispered through the trees outside my bedroom window, and the smell of corn drying in the fields—almost ready for harvest—lingered in the air. I stretched and glanced at the clock on the bedside table before rolling over to look at my wife.

Stacie still slept. She faced away from me, the coppery skin of her neck glowing from the suntan she'd worked so hard to acquire. Our daughter, Lilly, wasn't yet awake, so I snuggled next to my wife, my lips pressed against the back of her neck. I kissed her gently. She stirred, her hand reaching back to cup my face and she breathed deeply. The smell of her—her skin, her hair—was intoxicating.

My heart swelled in that moment. I had everything I desired. A beautiful wife. A wonderful daughter. I was content. I knew how the world worked. I couldn't imagine a world where vampires were real. They were a load of nonsense, some work of cheap fiction that appeared in movies and dime-store novels.

I needed to get moving to open my diner. I gave Stacie one more quick kiss on the neck, then climbed out of bed and shambled to the bathroom. I did my morning routine: peeing, brushing my teeth, giving my face a quick once over with the electric razor, then looking in the mirror. I'm not a handsome guy, but I'm not bad looking, either. Pretty average, in most respects. Light brown hair, not too long. Brown eyes, not too deep-set. The next week would bring my twenty-eighth birthday, and the daily grind from the diner hadn't wore me down yet.

I turned on the hot water, letting it slosh in the old tub as it heated, before I turned on the shower head. We lived in an old farm house that dated back to the late nineteenth century. It wasn't much, but it was paid for—an inheritance from my father, like the diner.

I remember always working on it when I was a child, tearing away the lath and plaster walls, insulating it, putting up drywall, or running new pipes for the bathroom. We found traces of the original wiring when tearing up the bathroom floor, two cloth-covered cables running between the floor joists, evenly spaced by white ceramic insulators.

We modernized the bathroom last, my first year in college. It had a claw-foot cast-iron tub with a shower head and a curtain that hung from a metal hoop suspended from the ceiling. Stacie called it picturesque.

It wasn't like her parent's house in New Jersey, but she made due. Like so many other things, she gradually fell in love with Arcanum.

Soft light peeked through the bathroom window. I stripped out of my boxers and tossed them in the wicket hamper in the corner, then gingerly stepped in the tub, letting the hot water pound away at my body, working out the kinks. It felt good. I heard the bathroom door open and close, and then sensed movement in the bathroom. Stacie pulled the curtain aside and smiled at me.

"Mind if I join you?"

Of course I didn't.

I soaped her back with the lavender bath gel she liked. She sighed as I reached around, cupping her breasts. She leaned against me, pushing her body against mine, and it turned into a giggling bout of lovemaking, trying to keep from falling in the tub, careful not to wake our daughter.

Men always say their wives are beautiful, but in my case it's true. I was in college when I first saw her from across the quad, and my heart skipped a beat. I didn't think a woman could be so beautiful, with her long golden hair in tight curls and her pale blue eyes. Then, an hour later, we bumped into each other in history class. We were both freshman, new to campus, both living away from home for the first time.

I summoned my courage, said hello, and soon we were inseparable.

When my Dad died, we moved back to my childhood home in Arcanum and took over his diner. It was hard work, trying to keep the family business going, but Stacie helped however she could.

After our shower, I dressed hurriedly and kissed her forehead. "What's the plan for today?"

Stacie smiled, straightening my shirt. "The usual. I'll drop Lilly off at school, then be in right after. She has gymnastics tonight, so I won't be able to help."

I sighed. The evening rush was difficult by myself, but Lilly loved her gymnastics. I'd suffer through, for her. "I'll manage. See you soon."

I left Stacie to dress, and stopped by Lilly's room to check on her. She, too, had the same golden skin, the same golden hair and blue eyes. She lay in bed, still asleep. I leaned over and gave her a soft hug. She opened her eyes, barely enough to see, and squinted at me, her lips curling into a smile. "G'morning, Daddy."

I brushed the hair from her face. "Good morning, baby. Go back to sleep. You don't have to get up yet."

She hugged me fiercely, then her body went limp. "M'kay." She drifted back to sleep and I kissed her lightly on the forehead, too, and left for work.

I made it to the diner by 6:35, and the Coffee Crew members were waiting, parked in their pickup trucks in front of the diner.

Ralph, Bob and Earl, all farmers in their seventies, had been starting their day with coffee from the diner since before I was born. They greeted me with smiles and I ruefully opened the door to let them in. They took their usual seats at the table by the window and I started the coffee pot, the most important part of my morning ritual.

Coffee was the lifeblood of the diner. By 7:00, another handful of farmers would straggle in, waiting for their cups. Truthfully, I didn't make a profit on the coffee, but it served as a glue to bind the community together. The men would leave by 10:00, off to their farms, but a few would be back for the lunch special. Their adult children would swing by for the supper special, bringing their own children.

It was a tight-knit community and I loved every bit of it.

I took the cups from the stack against the wall and placed one in front of each man, pouring their coffee while listening to their morning banter. Earl complained about the weather, commenting on the light drought while working the brim of his John Deere hat, Ralph and Bob chiming in, keeping the conversation going.

"You farmers are never happy," I said, topping off their cups. "It's either too much rain or not enough."

Bob smiled, his tired brown eyes crinkling in the corners. "Kind of like running a diner," he agreed. "You never get what you want. Always got to make do with what you have."

I snorted. "Speak for yourself, I have everything I've always wanted."

"That's because you've got a good looking woman," Earl said with a knowing smile. "Don't take that pretty young woman for granted."

I couldn't help but laugh. "I won't."

* * *

I went to the back and pulled out my ledger. As I went over the numbers, I had to acknowledge the diner wasn't a fountain of profit. Sometimes it seemed we barely scraped by. I checked the updated price-list from my wholesaler and my heart sank. Prices were rising, but the economy made it tough to pass the increases along to my customers.

We were passing from 'barely scraping by' and headed to 'the panic' stage. I shook my head. I couldn't afford to hire another waitress. Stacie wanted more time with Lily, but it wasn't possible. If Stacie actually drew a wage, the business would quickly go under. The only thing keeping us afloat was my fourteen-hour days and her free labor.

Barely.

I put the ledger back and hustled outside to get coffee for the other farmers that showed up at 7:00, stopping long enough to greet them with a few kind words, then got busy cooking Mrs. Hamm's eggs and toast.

At 7:15, the door opened and Mrs. Hamm entered. She was a kind woman, matronly, and served as the town librarian. Every weekday at 7:15 the bell above the door would tinkle and she would enter, setting her purse on the counter as she ordered two scrambled eggs, over easy, two slices of toast, and black coffee. She would eat, delicately, occasionally answering a question from any one of the farmers, before leaving to open the library at 8:00. She'd been eating at the diner, the same meal, for over forty years.

I had her plate ready, her coffee steaming, when the door opened.

"Mrs. Hamm," I said.

She smiled. It took twenty years off her age. "Samuel."

She took her seat at the counter and was almost finished with her toast when the door chimed again and Stacie entered, Lilly in tow.

All the men smiled at Stacie, asking her how she was. She smiled back. I noticed then, when she smiled, how it warmed the room. The farmer's smiles grew brighter, their backs a little straighter. Mrs.

Hamm turned and nodded, her own smile taking another five years off.

Stacie had that effect on people.

She stepped to the counter and whispered, "Lilly forgot her homework in your office."

I nodded and went to my cramped office to retrieve her binder, buried under the notes from my wholesaler and my ledger. I dug it out and returned to the counter, passing it to her. She smiled, then turned back to the diner. Her smiled faltered.

"There never seems to be many people here, anymore," she said softly, brow furrowed.

I shrugged. "There'll be more for lunch."

"I hate to say this, but it seems more of your regulars are dying off, like Ned O'Malley. Or, getting their coffee at the Casey's on Main."

Ned was a friend of my Dad's, a regular customer, who died the month before after a short bout with pancreatic cancer. Everyone was careful, never mentioning his name, almost as if they hoped it would somehow protect them.

"Do we have to talk about this?" I whispered. "Shouldn't you take Lilly to school?"

She gave me a quick hug. "Sorry," she breathed in my ear.

The Coffee Crew was teasing Lilly about her long curly hair. She smiled happily and ran to Stacie, grabbing for the folder. "Thank you, Daddy!"

I picked her up and gave her a bear hug. "You're welcome, little girl. Now off to school."

Stacie left with Lilly and I waved goodbye.

I had no idea what was coming.

* * *

Lunch was over and the diner had cleared. I took a deep breath. The lunch rush used to fill the diner, but now it meant five paying customers and Earl, who had stayed over from breakfast.

I watched Stacie out of the corner of my eye as she cleaned the tables with a cloth and a bucket of soapy water. Her face was troubled, and I knew she was worrying about the declining finances.

I came up behind her and she turned, the scowl slowly fading. She finally managed a half-hearted smile.

For the first time, I noticed that it never made it to her eyes.

I reached out to brush the hair from her face, curling it behind her ear. "It's going to be fine," I said. "I promise."

She nodded. "You're a good man, Sam Fisher. You don't have to keep reassuring me." She moved to the next table, picking up the dollar bill that Earl left and placing it in her apron pocket. She was washing the tabletop when the door opened and the bell tinkled.

We both turned to look at the couple who entered the diner. The man was mid-thirties, with fine blond hair and a sunken pallor. The short black woman had kinky hair in a style that hadn't been popular since the seventies, her black skin tinted bluish-white, like it had been powdered. They both wore sunglasses large enough to obscure their eyes. They were strangers to Arcanum.

If I had ever seen them before, I would have remembered.

Stacie turned to me and raised an eyebrow, then went to seat them. I scrubbed the grill top, making sure it was clean, watching Stacie hand them menus.

She came back to get silverware. "There's something weird about those two," she whispered.

"You mean the sunglasses?"

She took a deep breath. "Yeah, and something else. They smell funny."

That gave me pause. "Sweaty? Like, no deodorant?"

"No. They just smell...*funny*."

She took them their silverware and I pretended to inspect the oven, trying to catch a glimpse of what had Stacie so spooked.

Stacie asked for their order, but they remained silent, their expressionless faces following her movement, then the man spoke.

"You're Fisher?" His voice was raspy and he had a lisp. It sent a shiver up my spine. The hairs on my arms stood on edge, like a static charge, and something in the back of my brain sent a warning signal. The rational part of my brain said everything was fine, but the primal part was screaming. The man was dangerous.

Stacie nodded. She turned back to me, unsure of what to do. I reached under the counter and grabbed the short wooden club that belonged to my father. When I was a kid he told me he kept it there just in case, and that someday I would understand.

Now I understood.

I gave her a shrug, glanced meaningfully down at the counter, then back up. She attempted to smile, then the black woman grabbed Stacie's wrist, quick as a snake, and yanked Stacie to her.

Stacie yelped in pain and pulled back. I heard the bell over the entrance tinkle and there was a flash of light, then a man's voice.

Then nothing.

CHAPTER TWO

My head felt like it was exploding, and the blood pounded in my ears. A pinprick erupted behind my left eye, and I gasped for air as my legs buckled. I grabbed the chair in front of me to steady myself.

The last I remembered, I was behind the grill, but now I was in the dining room with no idea how I got there. The place was empty, the couple gone. Their table lay on its side, and the table next to it as well. Chairs were strewn about the room, some upright, and some on their sides. Silverware littered the floor.

Stacie stood in front of me, and I saw her jerk. She turned to me, eyes slowly coming into focus. "Sam?"

I looked down at my empty hand. The wooden club was nowhere to be seen. "What happened?"

She trembled as I wrapped my arms around her, holding her tight. She choked out a sob. "I don't know. Something's not right."

I nodded. I knew what she meant. Something felt wrong inside, an impending sense of doom, and my insides were twisted in knots. Then I noticed the stain on the white linoleum. "What's that?"

Stacie stepped closer. "I don't know. It looks like ash." She dropped to her knee and touched it with her finger, then pulled back, grabbing a cloth from her apron and rubbing furiously at her finger. "It's greasy. Something was burned there."

I dropped as well and sniffed. There was a smell akin to burning meat, but under that, something else. I remembered when the freezer went out during a hot July day and my father asked me to empty it. A piece of steak fell under the freezer and rolled to the back, then thawed over the afternoon. By the next day, when I found it, the smell was unbelievable. The heat from the condenser had caused the meat to spoil at an accelerated rate. It was beyond rancid.

The stain on the floor smelled just like that spoiled piece of meat.

"Sam?"

I turned. Stacie's voice was tinged with panic. It made my heart skip a beat. She pointed to the clock, eyes wide. "It's 1:42," she said. "That can't be. I just looked at the clock a minute ago. It was 1:20. It can't be 1:42. There's twenty-two minutes difference. It just can't be."

I struggled to remember the last time I had looked at the clock. "Maybe you got it wrong? It was probably 1:40." Even as I said it, I knew that wasn't right.

She turned, eyes blazing with anger. "I'm *telling* you, it was 1:20. You always do this. You dismiss whatever I tell you. It was 1:20," she said stubbornly, lower lip quivering.

"I'm not dismissing you." I tried to put my arms around her and she drew back, almost stepping in another pile of ash.

She turned her blue eyes to me as the panic gave way to fear. "What the *hell* is going on?"

I grabbed the table and pulled it upright, then picked up a pair of chairs, rearranging them. Stacie never cursed, not even when Lilly wasn't around. I knew she was upset, but it didn't seem she wanted me near. "I don't know. Let's just clean it up." I picked the silverware from the floor and headed to the kitchen, dumping the forks, knives, and spoons in the sink, and filled a five-gallon bucket with soap and water. When I came out, she was kneeling on the floor, dabbing at the ash. I handed her the bucket and a fresh set of towels and joined her until the linoleum finally came clean.

As clean as it was before, at least.

I rearranged the diner, putting all the chairs and tables back in position. Stacie had emptied the bucket and refilled it. "I think we got it all," I said.

She knelt and scrubbed.

"Stacie. It's clean."

She scrubbed harder, then threw the towel against the floor with a wet thwack. She turned to me, eyes fierce. "It was *1:20*."

* * *

The school day was almost over when Stacie left to pick up Lilly. The diner was back to normal. I still didn't know what happened, but my anxiety was finally lessening.

Lilly burst through the door, ahead of her mom, and rushed to greet me, her Dora the Explorer backpack bouncing wildly. "Daddy, Daddy, guess what I learned about today?"

I grabbed her and swung her up in a bear hug. "What's that?"

She leaned in and whispered. "I learned about a pre'tor."

I laughed. "I think you mean predator."

"That's what I said. Pre'tor." She pursed her lips, frowning. "Sometimes you don't listen."

Stacie entered behind her, glancing at the spot on the floor where the ash had been. She inspected the diner, looking for something out of place, then turned and offered a faint smile. "Honey, daddy only hears what he wants to. You should have learned that by now."

I set Lilly gently down on the floor. "Don't listen to Mommy. She's just grumpy today. Now, go sit in the corner and do your homework."

Lilly nodded solemnly, then skipped to the corner. She pulled papers from her backpack and started on her homework. I leaned in to Stacie. "Give it a rest, will you?"

Stacie pursed her lips, then looked away. "Let's just get through the evening."

I nodded and started the evening prep. The afternoon passed quickly, and before long we had our usual group of customers. The diner was busy. There were old friends, a high-school boy and girl on their first date, and a young couple who just moved to Arcanum whose daughter stopped to color with Lilly.

The diner emptied after the evening rush, and Stacie gathered up Lilly's things and prepared to go. Lilly rushed to me and I gave her another big hug. "Okay, baby, Mommy's taking you to gymnastics. I'll see you soon."

Lilly smiled. "See you later, alligator."

I hugged her and took a deep breath, the scent of her hair still strong from her strawberry shampoo the night before. It erased the last of my unease. "After 'while, crocodile."

Stacie took off her apron, folded it carefully, and took Lilly's hand. I noticed the worry in her eyes. "How soon can you close?"

"An hour and a half."

She frowned. "That long?"

I shrugged. "I have to clean the grill and run the dishwasher. Besides, you won't be back from gymnastics until then." I leaned in and gave her a quick kiss. "Everything is fine," I whispered. "Stop worrying."

She started to speak, then bit her lower lip. Lilly waved at me as they left, and I waved back, then flipped the sign in the front window to CLOSED.

* * *

I drove the deserted streets of Arcanum, heading north to our house on the edge of town. Street-lamps cast muted pools of light, and my car passed slowly from gloomy oasis to oasis. It wasn't the first time that I noticed the town, the aged and washed-out houses, the lack of traffic. Arcanum was barely hanging on. Most of the younger kids moved to Cincinnati, Cleveland, and Dayton for jobs. Only those without skills or a college education stayed in Arcanum.

I had only moved back because my father left me the house and diner. But, as I passed house after house with peeling paint, the streets still cracked and potholed from the previous winter, I knew the town was getting worse.

Stacie was right. The town was dying and the diner would never be as full as it was in the eighties and nineties. If the house and diner weren't already paid for, we would be virtually bankrupt.

I pulled my Nissan into the white-rock driveway next to the house, behind Stacie's old Taurus parked in the garage, the door still up. The streetlight in front buzzed, and the meager light cast long shadows between the house and the garage, all the way through the back lawn to the wooden shed at the back of the property.

The house was dark. Usually the kitchen and living room light spilled from the side windows, but it was black as night inside and there was a stillness that I found unsettling. The lots on the north end of the town, past the school, were large and my neighbors' houses were at least two-hundred feet in each direction, with tree-lines in between.

The September sky was inky black, and the moon hadn't yet risen. The heat had finally tapered off to something more bearable, but I didn't hear the window air conditioner struggling to keep the house cool.

There was something else, as well. It took me a moment to realize the cicadas in the trees were silent. Unusual, since they had been chittering away for the past week.

I entered the house through the front door and flipped the switch on the wall. The overhead light blazed on and I saw a long dark streak across the living-room floor, heading to the kitchen. The smell hit me, something dark and foul.

I stared at the dark streak, wondering what it could be. "Stacie? Lilly?" I walked forward until my foot almost touched it.

With a growing sense of dread, I realized what it was.

Blood.

I want to say that I did something heroic, that I reacted as a man would, with strength and courage.

That would be a lie.

My tongue was thick inside my mouth, my heart hammering in my chest. Something terrible had happened and I had no idea what to do. My hands felt cold as ice and my legs trembled as I approached the kitchen. I heard a high-pitched keening and knew it was Lilly.

I rushed forward. There was a shape sitting at our kitchen table and a smaller shape sitting on it.

"What's going on?" I shouted, my hand frantically searching for the kitchen light switch. When I finally managed to flip it, my mind reeled.

A young man with dark, unkempt hair sat at my kitchen table, his face smeared with blood, caking the goatee on his chin. He stared at my daughter, who sat on the table in front of him. Neither turned to look at me.

Stacie lay on the floor, face-down in the trail of blood. Her flowery yellow sundress was coated, turning the yellow horrible shades of orange.

She was so very still.

I heard a man's voice behind me. "Silas? You want I should hold him?"

I whirled and found a fat man towering over me, grinning. He, too, had blood smearing his face. His tongue darted across his lips, snake-like.

"No, Jimmy," the man at the table said. I nearly wet my pants at the sound of his voice. "Sam is going to sit right down at this table, aren't you Sam? No fussing, now."

I turned back to the man at my table, his eyes like black pools, and there was a tugging sensation, like I could fall into them. I knew, in that instant, that I wanted to. I lurched forward and he turned his eyes away, the hint of a smile on his face. The man behind me placed his hand on my shoulder. I tried to twist away, but the hand was like a steel clamp, squeezing so hard I thought my bones might break.

The fat man used his grip to guide me across the kitchen, and I found myself sitting at the table across from the young man, Silas. The door to the back porch opened and an older woman stepped in, the bottom of the screen door banging against Stacie's head.

Stacie didn't move.

The woman glanced down, then back to me. "This him?"

Silas nodded. "Go back outside. Help Cassandra."

The woman nodded, looked down at Stacie, then sniffed the air like a dog. She shook her head, her short platinum blonde hair barely moving, then stared at me with a mixture of anticipation and something else.

Silas turned back to me. "Forgive Pearl, she's hungry." He took Lilly's hands and held them in his. "Lilly was keeping me company until you arrived. Isn't that right, Lilly?"

Lilly nodded.

I reached for her and felt a stinging slap across my hands. I turned to see Jimmie, grinning, his hand held high.

"Now Jimmie, there's no need for that. Sam, I have some questions for you. Sam!"

I turned to him. I kept hoping to wake from a bad dream, but the young man just watched me with his black eyes

"I don't know what's going on," I managed. "What did you do to my wife?"

Silas's eyes flicked toward Stacie. "I was hungry. Jimmie, too." He turned back to me. "You want to know who we are and why we're here. But, first a question for you. Are you Samuel Fisher?"

"Y-Yes," I stammered.

"Good. This is very important. Your father's name was Mark Fisher and your mother was Karen Weaver?"

It didn't seem real. "Yes."

"That's very good. I'm Silas. And you've met Jimmie and Pearl. Cassandra is outside, guarding the house. There, now we know one another. I have just a few more questions, if you don't mind. What did you do to Bill and Esmeralda?"

"Who?"

"Bill and Esmeralda. They paid you a visit this afternoon. What did you *do* to them?"

I had no idea what he was talking about. "I don't know any Bill or Esmeralda. Please, I need to help my wife. She's bleeding."

Silas laughed, high and unpleasant. "Oh, she *is* bleeding. Give the man a cigar, Jimmie. He's either a liar...." Silas cocked his head. "Sam, I'm going to kill you. Know that right now. I'm going to kill you and you can't stop me. But, whether I kill this little girl of yours? That's the question, isn't it? Do you believe that I will kill you?" He reached across the table and put his hand around my throat and I felt the same iron grip I had felt from his man, Jimmie.

"I believe you," I gasped.

Silas laughed again. He released me and I sank into the chair.

This was crazy. My wife was dying, or maybe already dead, and there were maniacs threatening to kill me and possibly Lilly. None of it made sense. "Just tell me what you want. Do you want money? You can have everything. I'll give you everything. The cars? Take them. Just take them and go."

"I don't want your *things*," Silas said patiently. "I *want* to know what you did to Bill and Esmeralda. Did you stake them? Did he teach you?" He cocked his head again, but this time he had a peculiar look on his face.

I recognized that look. It was fear.

"I don't know what you're talking about," I said. "I don't know who you're talking about. Who is *HE*?"

There was a rough voice behind me, filled with anger and disgust. "*I'm* he."

* * *

In the doorway to the living room stood a man, his face wrinkled and weathered like old shoe leather, his long gray hair pulled into a ponytail. I couldn't begin to guess his age, but got the impression it was closer to eighties than sixties.

But, that wasn't the first thing I noticed. The *first* thing I noticed was the black leather patch over his right eye. The second was the brown leather duster. The third was the shotgun in his hands. He watched us with a face as hard as granite. "Hello, Silas."

I turned back to Silas and Jimmy.

They stood so still they looked like statues. Silas frowned. "Hello, Jack. I take it you're responsible for Bill and Esmeralda?"

The old man glared at him. "You best be leaving, boy."

Jimmy shifted slightly.

"Don't, Munzinger," Jack growled. "You move again, even an inch, and your insides are gonna be your outsides."

"Now, Jack," Silas said, voice cool, "if you kill Jimmy, I'll be forced to kill this little girl. What about dear old Sam? Do you really want to risk that?"

The old man snorted. "Trying to distract me? Waiting for Pearl or Cassandra? They're not coming. They're bound."

None of their words made sense. "I don't know what's going on," I said, "but leave me and my family out of it. I need to get my wife to a hospital." I started to reach for Lilly and Silas raised an eyebrow. That was all it took to make my momentary courage fade.

The old man looked at me with his tired eye. "I don't think your wife is going to make it," Jack said softly. "I'm sorry about that. I truly am."

"Are we going to sit here all night?" Jimmy interrupted. "He's *just* an old man."

Silas shrugged. "You ready to die, Jimmy? Don't underestimate him. He's a survivor. Isn't that right, Jack?"

There was a long silence, then Jack spoke. "What are you playing at, Silas? How do you think you're getting out of here?"

"You can't take us both, Jack," Silas said. "Not even on your best day."

"Don't count on that. Munzinger is soft. He won't put up much of a fight. As for you? You'd be surprised."

Silas licked his lips, a ghost of a smile on his face. "Well, well, well. Isn't that an interesting turn of events. Oh, how the mighty have fallen. How does it feel, Jack? Tell me. I'm fascinated."

Jack's eye narrowed. "Take Munzinger and leave. You're done here."

Silas laughed again, the sound not even remotely human. "I'm going to have to say *no* to that. Tell you what, I'll make you a straight up deal. You can have the boy or the girl. Your choice."

"Last chance," Jack said quietly. "It's just you and Munzinger. There's no way you both leave here."

"That might have been true, if Cassandra and Pearl were truly bound," Silas said. The door behind him opened and Pearl entered, with another woman, a brunette in her early thirties. They both glanced down at Stacie, then back at Jack.

I turned and saw a big rawboned man with cowboy boots and a shiny belt-buckle standing behind Jack. "You haven't met Ben, have you?" Silas asked. "I found Ben just a few months ago. He was more than happy for the gift."

Jack didn't respond, he just cocked his head. "I'm sorry about this, Sam," he repeated.

I barely had time to register the words before Jack moved.

I say moved, but that doesn't do the word justice. He was a blur, bringing the butt of the shotgun up and into Ben's nose. I heard the sickening crunch, and I used that moment to turn back to Lilly, reaching for her. My hands were on her shoulders when Silas grabbed her and yanked her away. I heard the roar of the shotgun behind me and then Silas shoved the table toward me, hitting my sternum like a sledgehammer. I went backwards so hard my chair shattered and I found myself on the floor, sliding through the trail of Stacie's blood.

The shotgun roared again and again and I turned and saw the man, Ben, on the floor, gasping in pain, blood oozing from a smoking wound to his chest. Jimmy grabbed the barrel of Jack's shotgun and Jack swung it around to Jimmy's chest and pulled the trigger. A cloud of blood sprayed from Jimmy's back, coating me, and Jimmy sank to his knees. The two women, Cassandra and Pearl, jumped forward, over my kitchen table.

Nobody can move like that.

I watched, horrified, as they brought Jack to the ground. They clubbed him in the head, but he got one foot under Pearl and kicked. She went flying into the air, blasting through the ceiling and up into Lilly's bedroom on the second floor.

My heart skipped a beat.

Nobody is that strong!

Impossibly, Jimmy was struggling to his feet. I grabbed the remains of the wooden chair and prepared to swing it at his head when I heard Silas laugh. I turned and he held Lilly in his arms, her face slack, her eyes empty, and Silas opened his mouth wide. Inside his mouth I saw a second set of teeth, long and pointed, and I screamed as he bit down on Lilly's neck.

Her eyes widened. "Daddy," she managed, and then her eyes rolled up, head pitching forward.

Silas turned, Lilly firmly in his grasp, and fled through the kitchen's back door into the night.

CHAPTER THREE

I struggled to stand as my feet slipped on the blood-soaked hardwood floor. Hands grabbed my arm and I turned as Jimmy came at me with the same second set of teeth. I tried to pull away, but he held me tight, then lunged toward my neck.

I don't remember plunging the remains of the wooden chair toward his chest, but I felt the splintered edge crunch as it rammed into his breastbone. There was an electric surge through my arms and the remains of the old oak chair slid straight through, like soft butter, and out his back.

Jimmy's eyes widened and he gurgled, arms flailing, and I felt heat rise from his body, like a blast furnace. I fell back and watched as he burst into flames, the fire erupting from under his skin, burning white hot as his body consumed itself.

It took only seconds before his body and clothes were reduced to a grease-stained ash heap on the floor, a sickening smell that filled the room, mixing with the smell of gunpowder and death.

I felt a ripping, and, for the briefest of moments, I saw a cloud of wispy gray smoke rise from the ash before it slammed into me. I'd once touched a live wire replacing a wall outlet. This sensation was a thousand times more intense, and it didn't stop. I convulsed and my head whipped back and forth, pounding against the refrigerator.

In the background, I heard a man's voice, Jack's voice, roaring in pain. I turned in time to see the brunette, Cassandra, clawing at his stomach, her fingernails curved and thick like an animal's claws.

Jack's face was contorted in rage. With blinding speed he grabbed the woman by the head and took her to the floor, slamming her so hard I felt the vibration through my body. He stood and threw her backwards, across the room, where she hit the wall, the drywall breaking around her as the wall bowed outward.

She rebounded, but Jack pulled a foot-long wooden stake from his duster and rushed forward. He caught her in the chest and I heard her howl, then she burst into flames, shaking violently and scrabbling for the front door.

She didn't make it. Within two steps she dropped to the floor, her body disappearing in a flash of light that momentarily blinded me, then she, too, was reduced to a stinking pile of ash.

Jack turned to the man on the floor. He dropped to one knee and impaled Ben with the stake and I felt the impact as the stake sank completely through Ben's body and through the wood floor below. The body burst into flames, like the others, but burned more slowly. His cowboy boots kicked uselessly. He turned to me and I watched in horror as his eyeballs melted like wax inside his skull. He thrashed as he burned, making horrible squelching noises, but the fire kept burning and in seconds he was no longer a man, but another pile of ash.

I heard a crash of glass from the second floor and in a blur Jack pulled a massive revolver from under his duster, aiming at to the stairs in the corner.

A siren wailed in the distance. Someone had called the police.

Jack cocked his head, then put the revolver away. I tried to say something, but my mouth wasn't working. He strode across the room, through the ash and blood, and looked down at me, an unreadable mix of emotions on his face. "We have to leave."

I tried to speak again, but my body shook and my teeth chattered, even though I wasn't cold. "Can't. Stacie needs help."

He leaned to me and grabbed my hand, squeezing tight. "Your wife is gone," he said gently.

"Stacie—"

He shook his head. "It's too late for her. We have to go. When the police get here, they'll find her dead and covered in blood. Who do you think they'll blame?"

I shook my head. I knew our town cop, Elbert Morrison. My father had gone to school with him. "I'll tell them what happened."

Jack grunted. "You'll tell them what? You were attacked by vampires?"

"Vampires? There's no such thing," I said. Then I looked behind Jack, at the piles of ash on the floor.

It *couldn't* be.

"Son, we're going." He picked me up like I weighed nothing and threw me over his shoulder.

"Lilly—"

"She's gone, too. You have to come with me. Once the cops have you, you're dead. Silas will find a way. I know it seems crazy, and I know this pushes the limits of what you believe, but if you want to live—if you want to save your daughter—come with me." He stopped to pick up his shotgun, then we were outside.

I tried to speak, to beg him to turn around, to plead for help. I needed to save my wife. She *couldn't* be dead.

I tried, but failed. I was tired. I knew Jack was right. Stacie was dead. There was too much blood. No, I had seen things that burned to ash, things that killed my wife and left her dead on the floor.

Something else had happened, too, when I killed Jimmy.

Jack took me outside, threw me in the back of his pickup truck, shut the topper door, and started the engine. He roared out of town and I felt my body slide from side to side as he turned, my head slamming into the sidewalls, then I fell asleep to the steady hum of the tires on pavement.

God help me, but I fell asleep.

* * *

I woke when the engine stopped and felt the truck shake as the door slammed close. I opened my eyes and stared at the underside of a truck topper, light gently streaming through the darkened windows, the smell of gas and oil thick in the back of the truck.

Memories of what happened flashed through my mind, my wife's dead body on the floor. So much blood! My daughter screaming. Silas. Jack. Vampires.

It couldn't be. I must have been dreaming.

I tried to sit up and the pounding in my head forced me back down.

Not dreaming.

Maybe I was going crazy.

"You awake in there?" Jack asked from outside.

My tongue was dry. "I'm awake," I croaked.

The back of the topper opened. "Good, get out."

I slowly lifted myself up to my hands and knees and crawled to the back of the truck. The light was bright and burned my eyes. I squinted, blinking away the tears, and saw the Shell sign in the corner of the parking lot, the gas pumps behind us. It was still dark, but the lights glared around us.

I climbed over the tailgate. When my feet touched the concrete, my legs buckled, but I felt Jack's hand grab me, holding me upright.

"Steady. You've been through a hell of a lot. Focus on walking."

I nodded. "Doesn't matter. I'm crazy. This is all some kind of hallucination."

Jack let go and I collapsed to the ground, my face slamming into the concrete. "Ow."

"That feel like a hallucination? Now get up, people will notice." He hauled me up like I was a child. "You need food. You'll be like to starving by now."

Starving? How could I think of food? But, before I could even complete the thought, my stomach growled and I felt a ravenous hunger.

I followed him into the Apollo Mart and watched as he poured a 24- ounce coffee. He grabbed every pack of beef jerky off the shelf next to the coffee machine, handed them to me, then grabbed a fistful of Slim Jims and dozens of bags of peanuts. "You thirsty?"

I licked my lips and nodded.

He went to the back and got a two-liter bottle of Coke from the refrigerator against the wall, then went to the front where he paid for the gas and food.

I followed him outside, shaking my head. "Who are you?"

"Get in the front, Sam. We have a lot to talk about."

I glanced between him and the Apollo Mart. "Where are we?"

"Mahomet, Illinois."

I blinked. "Illinois?"

"Get in the truck. We can talk while I drive. Unless you'd like to walk? Maybe call the cops? Tell them all about how you think you're losing your mind, because you saw some things that you just know are impossible. Sure, then they go to your house, find your wife and all the blood. What do you think happens? What do you think they'll believe? Now *get* in the damned truck!"

I eased myself into Jack's truck, a late seventies Chevy. He got in, glanced over to me, snorted, and before long we were cruising west on I-74, eating up the miles as we rolled through the night.

"Who are you? What happened back there? Why did those maniacs kill my wife? What are they?" I had many more questions on my mind, but Jack stopped me with a raised hand.

"Eat the jerky. You need protein."

I wanted to ask why, but my stomach growled. I've been hungry before, but nothing had ever prepared me for the body-gnawing hunger I suddenly felt. A complete, gut-twisting, empty-to-the-core hunger that threatened to consume me. My hands shook as I opened the pack of jerky and started gulping it down, barely chewing.

"Slow down, you'll make yourself sick. Drink."

I opened the ice-cold two-liter bottle of Coke and washed a quarter of it down. I had never tasted anything so sweet, and the icy fizz burned all the way to my stomach, like a golden liquid syrup. I tore open another bag of jerky, eating and drinking, burping occasionally.

Jack looked over. "They're vampires, Sam."

I stopped chewing. "That can't be. Vampires don't exist."

"They *do* exist. Can you think of anything that explains what you saw? Look, I know this goes against everything you've been taught, but vampires are real."

The old man didn't appear crazy, but his grasp of reality was clearly slipping. "What, and werewolves are real, too? I've seen that movie with that girl and that boy."

Jack's hand snapped out and cuffed me in the side of the head. I almost dropped the Coke bottle. "*Jesus*, what was *that* for?"

"You think I'm joking? They just killed your wife. Vampires are *real*. They're monsters. Silas is a vampire. It's not like the movies. That's a bunch of make-believe horseshit. Vampires exist. You saw them with your own eyes."

"But why me? Why Stacie?"

"Because I killed Bill and Esmeralda yesterday at your diner. I made you forget and that's why you don't remember."

"Come on, how did you make me forget?"

Jack sighed. "For Christ's sake, kid. I tracked Bill and Esmeralda to Arcanum, then followed them to your diner. They were going to kill you. Your wife, too. Only, I killed them first."

I felt the jerky start to come back up. "That's why there was ash on the floor." The sickening realization of what he said hit me. "You brought them to my *house*."

Jack shook his head. "It shouldn't have happened like that. I didn't sense any of them. I thought Silas sent Bill and Esmeralda as scouts. If I'd known Silas was near, I never would have left you. By the time I figured it out, it was too late." He stopped and took a ragged breath. "I'll never forgive myself for that."

The lurching in my stomach slowed and the hunger came back. I wolfed down another bag of jerky, then started eating peanuts. "Why am I so hungry?"

"It's the change. You killed your first vampire. The first one is always the hardest."

"What change?"

"Aren't you tired? You should sleep until we get home."

"Where's home?"

"Iowa. Now sleep."

I started to tell him I wasn't tired, but my eyes drooped. I tried to fight it, but a bone-weary exhaustion fell over me and I drifted into a dreamless sleep.

* * *

Wednesday

When I awoke, the sun was beating through the truck window, more late-July than early-September. Jack was listening to the radio, barely loud enough to be heard over the throaty roar of the engine. It sounded like Texas swing, scratchy, and in mono. I realized he was listening to an AM station. I couldn't think of the last time I'd heard AM radio, and certainly not the haunting song that caused Jack to sway his head.

"Bob Wills," Jack grunted. "Waltzing in Old San Antone." He turned to look at me with his remaining left eye "Feeling better?"

We were going up and down hills, the trees and grass a vibrant green, with depths I had never noticed before, and the stalks of corn that dotted the hills were a yellowish white that seemed to glow from within. I blinked, looking around. "Where are we?"

"Just went through Belle Plaine a few miles ago. We'll be home soon."

I considered that. "Where's home?"

He shrugged. "Toledo, Iowa. You feel better?"

Strangely enough, I did. Physically. The hunger was gone and my head felt clear. Then it hit me. My wife was dead. My daughter was taken. By vampires. I gasped for air.

"Deep breaths," Jack said, "I know how you feel. It's hitting you all at once."

I remembered.

I remembered the two in the diner, the man, Bill, and the woman, Esmeralda. They were going to kill us, and then the doorbell tinkled and Jack entered. Esmeralda snarled at him, her mouth drawing back, exposing fangs. She jumped, knocking tables out of the way, but Jack grabbed her and smashed her into the linoleum.

The man lunged at me and suddenly a wooden stake erupted from his chest. He fell to the floor and burst into flames. Jack stood behind him, then Esmeralda was on Jack's back. I beat at her with the short club in my hand, so scared I couldn't even scream. Jack grabbed the club from my hand and jammed it straight into her mouth. I heard the crunch of teeth and bone and she dropped to the floor, spasming. Jack pulled another stake from his duster and spiked it into her chest and she burst into a white-hot flame, leaving nothing behind except for a greasy pile of ash.

Jack gave me the once-over. "You two okay?"

Stacie turned to him, her face frozen in fear. "What just happened?"

Jack smiled. "Nothing to worry about. They won't be bothering you again."

"Who *are* you? What *were* those things?" I asked. "They looked like people but they burned like torches."

"Vampires, Sam." Jack turned to Stacie. "Don't worry, you won't remember a thing." He smiled and pattered her gently on the shoulder.

She stared at him, unblinking. "I won't remember a thing," she repeated.

I couldn't believe Stacie was agreeing. "What?" I asked. "How could we forget something like that? How do you know my name?"

Jack turned to me and I felt the pull in his good eye, like I was sinking, and I heard him say, "You won't remember a thing, either."

I jerked as the memory ended, like I had just relived it.

I was back in the truck. I turned to Jack, and I felt my mouth drop. My heart was pounding. "Jesus Christ. That was *you* in the diner!"

"Remembered, did you? I didn't expect it to last, not after what happened last night. At least you understand, now. Vampires *do* exist."

I leaned back against the seat.

Jack drove through the rolling hills, finally turning onto a loose-rock road, a dusty red cloud trailing behind us. He continued on until turning onto a dirt road a hundred yards long that led to a house nestled against a hill.

The house had seen better days. The white hardboard siding was stained and missing in places, the windows streaked with dirt. The grass stood three foot high, a field that stretched from the front of the house all the way to the loose rock road.

He wheeled the truck to the front of a large machine shed that butted up against the hill and triggered a remote control. The door rumbled sideways and he pulled the truck inside, the door rolling closed behind us. The inside was utterly black. Jack turned off the truck, and I heard him open the door, then close it. He must have flipped a switch because the overhead lights blazed on and I saw that it wasn't just a machine shed.

There were at least 5 different vehicles, from a black Camaro, to a mid-80's Ford Econoline van, to a dark blue Crown Victoria. A newer Ford F-150 pickup sat in the corner, next to a vintage Indian motorcycle.

The back of the machine shed was fitted with a complete machine shop and mechanics bay, including lift. The entire wall was lined with rolling tool chests, pegboard fixed against the wall above them.

Jack opened the back of the truck and pulled a long steel toolbox from the back. It was at least four feet long and he carried it like it was made of Styrofoam, but I had the distinct memory of it sliding against me as we left Arcanum and I knew it weighed more than an adult man.

He placed it against the back wall, filling the empty hole in the line of toolboxes, then opened it and took out the shotgun he'd used at my house. He stood waiting patiently as I got out.

My eyes darted around the shed. "What is this place?"

"My garage. Follow me." He opened a steel door in the back and I followed him through. We walked down a concrete tunnel, then he stopped and pulled a key from under his shirt and unlocked the massive steel door. We entered and he flipped a switch and I stood, gaping.

It was a concrete room, forty feet long and thirty feet deep with a domed ceiling twenty feet high. There were racks of guns of every type, from handguns and rifles, to shotguns and some that I couldn't place. A whole wall was devoted to knives and swords, and they glistened in the light, shiny and sharp. In the middle of the room was a long workbench, a vice on one end, and more toolboxes.

"Holy hell, Jack."

He turned to me, expressionless. "This is my armory."

Something on the far wall caught my eye. "Is that a rocket launcher?"

He smiled. "RPG." He pointed to a steel door at the far end of the room. "That leads to the basement."

He laid the shotgun down on the table and took off his leather duster, draping it over the other end of the workbench. Now that he had removed the duster, I could see that he was dressed simply in heavy black work boots, faded denim jeans and a faded denim shirt. He had a holster mounted on one hip and a shoulder hostler under his left arm. He took the massive pistol from the shoulder holster and set it on the bench, then a semi-automatic from the hip holster joined it. From his left leg, he unstrapped a knife with a foot-long blade and placed it on the bench as well.

"Let's get something to eat. It'll give me a chance to answer some of your questions."

He led me through the far door, down another concrete tunnel, and into the basement of the house. He stopped at a giant stainless refrigerator, grabbed a pair of paper-wrapped steaks, and led me up the stairs to a surprisingly clean kitchen. The steaks were huge, at least 40 ounces each, and I watched as he heated an enormous cast-iron skillet on the stove, then unwrapped the steaks. He took a tub of butter and coated the bottom of the pan, then began to fry the steaks.

He pointed to the cabinet next to me, and when I opened it, I found it full of Jack Daniels' bottles.

He grimaced. "The next one."

I opened the other door and found plain white plates. The kitchen held a square wooden table and he motioned to it. I set the plates on the table, and he finished the steaks, carried the skillet to the table, and plated them. He put the cast-iron skillet back on the stove, then opened the kitchen refrigerator and brought a six pack of Miller High Life to the table, along with silverware from a kitchen drawer.

"That's a lot of steak," I managed. The meat smelled amazing, and I felt my stomach growl.

Jack nodded. "Trust me. You'll manage."

I looked down at the steak, oozing grease and blood. "I like mine well done."

"Not anymore you don't." He cut into his steak and took a bite, then opened a bottle of beer and took a deep slug. "I'll start simple. Name's Jack Harlan. I was born April 23rd, 1868."

It was the last thing I expected. 1868? "That's impossible. That'd make you, what, over 140 years old?"

Jack sighed and took another bite of his steak, chewing slowly. "This'll go a lot easier if you spend less time telling me what's possible and more time listening. I killed my first vampire in 1909. I was forty one years old." He paused. "Eat your steak."

"What? Oh." I took a big bite of the steak. It tasted like ambrosia. "Oh my god, this is amazing."

Jack nodded. "Iowa beef, a mix of corn and grass, corn for the fattening and grass for the flavor. No growth hormones, no antibiotics. You'll find you have one hell of an appetite for the next month, thanks to the change. It'll settle after that."

I stared at him, a mouthful of steak. "Why? What's the change?"

He handed me a beer. "Drink this," he said. "As far as the change, let's start with the basics. Nobody knows what vampires really are or where they come from. They've been with us since the beginning of history. It's not like a disease of the blood. More like a disease of the soul. When a vampire feeds, it can choose to put some of itself into the human. If they put enough in, that human becomes a vampire."

I felt the steak lodge in the back of my throat. "I'm going to become a vampire?"

Jack snorted. "When you kill a vampire, some of its—call it essence—is absorbed by the killer. When you killed Munzinger, you got a dose of his essence. It's called the change. The first kill is always the hardest. It does things to the body. You'll feel like your starving. You'll like your beef rare. But, it also makes you stronger. Faster. You'll have better vision, better hearing. The aging process slows."

"That's why I'm so hungry?"

Jack nodded. "You're changing. And, you can sense them now."

My mind raced. "If that's true, then why didn't you know Silas was at my house?"

"Magic."

I laughed. "Magic? You're kidding."

Jack tossed his empty beer bottle into a trashcan next to the table, twisted the top off another, and cut another big piece of steak. He held it aloft, slowly turning the fork. "I don't know how he did it, but it had to be magic." He popped the steak in his mouth, chewed, then washed it down with half the beer. "Son, the world is a strange place. There's things out there you wouldn't believe. Silas found a way to shield himself. Don't ask me how he did it."

"Why did he attack my family?"

Jack paused, then chugged down the rest of his beer. "You have to understand, vampires have to feed. It's what they do. I've tracked Silas for longer than you've been alive. I kill his younglings every chance I get, but he turns new ones. He'll keep at it until I finally put him down for good."

"You're going to keep looking for him until you find him and kill him?"

Jack turned to me and absently scratched at his eye-patch. "Yes."

"Good. When do we start?"

Jack tilted his head back, regarding me. "Whoa. What do you mean, *we*? You almost got killed yesterday."

"He's got my daughter. I have to save her."

He let out a sigh. "I'm sorry to say this, but your daughter is gone. If he hasn't killed her already, he's keeping her for a meat treat."

"A what?"

Jack shoved his plate away. "A meat treat. He'll keep bleeding her, over and over, until she finally turns or until her heart gives out. I'm sorry about that. I should have gotten there sooner."

"It's not your fault. If you hadn't saved us at the diner, I'd be dead now. If you couldn't tell Silas was near, it's not your fault he killed Stacie and took Lilly. We have to find her. We have to save my daughter!"

Jack looked at me as if I'd lost my mind. "You have to face some hard facts. I know this hurts, but you're not going to see your daughter again. Even if you could find her, and that's a big if, what would you do?"

"I'd kill Silas and rescue Lilly. That's what I'd do."

"You don't even know what you don't know," Jack said sadly. "You think you could kill Silas? I've been hunting him for years and I know what I'm doing. You? It would be a slaughter."

"I killed one vampire already! I saw what you did to those other two."

"You don't understand. You got lucky with Munzinger, and the other two were younglings. The woman? Cassandra Lantier? She disappeared a year ago from a park in Omaha. She wasn't strong enough to put up a fight and that dumb cowboy was turned less than a week ago. Vampires get stronger as they get older."

"What about the two in the diner?"

"Bill was turned ten years ago, the woman thirty. Silas has older children, much older. Like Pearl. He turned her in 1937. I would have a hard time killing her in a straight up fight. But Silas? I've killed a lot of vampires, Sam. At the start, it was pure luck. Then I learned. And the more I learned the more careful I got."

"You're afraid to help me?"

He pulled his plate back and stabbed at his steak. "Fear doesn't come in to it, son. They're predators, plain and simple. Apex predators. Normal humans are outmatched. A vampire hunter, if they've managed a kill, has a better chance. If you've killed enough of them, absorbed enough essence, you stand a chance against a youngling, if you're careful. If you kill even more than that, a youngling isn't much of a challenge. But an *old* vampire? Silas doesn't have one or two old vampires, he has dozens. I have to take the kills where and when I can arrange it. To go after your daughter, it's madness. Maybe, if the conditions were right—"

"So there *is* a chance?" My heart soared. "If the conditions are right, you'll help me?"

Jack took another bite of his steak and finished off his beer. "If we trained you up. If we could find your daughter. If she's still alive. If the conditions are right. But that's a lot of ifs, son. I have other responsibilities."

I fought back desperation. "I can learn. I promise. I'll do whatever it takes."

"You will?"

And like that, Jack was moving. He knocked the kitchen table aside and grabbed me. I tried to pull back, but he ripped me from the chair, slamming me to the floor, rolling me onto my stomach. I tried to stand, but his grip was like iron. I screamed as he sank his steak knife a quarter of an inch into my neck. I jerked back and forth, but he held me down, as easy as an adult holding a child.

"That was just a steak knife," he growled. "A vampire would have fangs in you by now, draining you. This isn't a game. *Do you understand?*"

I struggled to roll away, to get up. "What the hell?"

Jack yanked me up by the neck, completely off the ground, then dropped me in front of him, his one good eye glaring at me. "You learn what I teach, you do what I tell you, and maybe—just maybe—you won't get yourself killed. You want to save your daughter?" His good eye stared at me and I felt a sinking in my stomach, a twisting vortex that threatened to suck me in, like I had with Silas. "First you have to learn to save yourself. You're going to have to listen. You're going to have to follow orders. Can you do that? Will you obey?"

I fought against the weight of his gaze and the sensation of falling eased. "Yes, I'll obey."

"Good." He picked up his fallen chair and sat down, opening another beer. "Finish your steak. We'll clean up that puncture wound when we're done."

I looked down and saw that blood had trickled down my neck and onto my shirt. The puncture throbbed in time to my heartbeat. "Shouldn't we clean it or something?"

Jack gave me a hard look. "That's just a flesh wound. It'll be fine. First lesson. Never turn down a meal. You never know when you'll get your next one."

CHAPTER FOUR

Jack finished his steak and led me to the bathroom, a small room off the kitchen. Like the rest of Jack's house, it was simple and stark in its furnishings. The wound was still bleeding and he pulled a tackle-box from under the sink.

"Take off your shirt."

I peeled off the blood-stained shirt and handed it to him.

He pitched it in the trash can between the toilet and the shower-stall. "This is going to sting."

He rubbed the wound clean with an alcohol pad and I winced. "Do I need a tetanus shot or something?"

He smiled, but it didn't make it to his eye. "You're changing. You'll find you don't get sick anymore. Hold still."

I watched in the mirror as he dribbled a clear liquid over the bloody hole. It burned. I saw a wisp of steam rise from the wound. "Ow, sonofabitch! What is that?"

"Superglue. Water thin. Glues wounds, but the water in your blood causes it to set quick, generates a lot of heat. It's cheap and you can find it anywhere." He wrapped my neck with gauze. "That's to keep it clean. It'll heal fast." He led me to the west bedroom, opened his closet, and tossed me clothes. "These should fit you, or close enough to it. When I get a chance, I'll get you some more your style."

I looked down at the worn denim pants and shirts, his cast-offs, apparently. He found a pair of well-worn leather boots and tossed them to me. "The spare bedroom is at the end of the hall. You'll have to sleep on the floor, I don't have another bed. Never had a visitor, come to think of it. Now, let's talk vampires. Forget everything you've seen or heard. Vampires thrive in the dark. They get weak in the sun. That's how I could take the two in the diner. They'll move around in the day, but they don't like it." He sat down on the bed and slowly peeled off his boots, then tossed them in the corner. "They don't have to be in direct sunlight. Just as long as the sun's up."

"Why is that?"

He shook his head. "Don't know. It just is. Now, you saw that stakes work. Has to be a wooden stake. And before you ask, I got no clue about that, either. A wooden stake kills them. Silver hurts them, too. I use a lot of silver bullets or silver shot. Silver purifies. Works with most magical creatures. Same with fire. If you can set a vampire to burning, they'll burn like a candle. Won't necessarily kill them, but sure as hell weakens them." He slumped back on to the bed. "Okay, kid, that's enough for tonight. Tomorrow we'll start. Right now, I have to sleep. I'm feeling my age."

I looked at him, his long gray hair shot through with white, the deep crags in his face. He looked tired. I took the extra clothes and headed for the hallway, but when I reached the door I stopped and turned back to him. "Jack?"

He didn't even open his eye. "Yeah?"

"Why do you do it? Kill vampires?"

He sighed and for a moment I thought he was asleep, then he turned to me and squinted his good eye. "It's what I am. Now sleep. You'll need your energy tomorrow."

I found the spare bedroom. It was small and empty. The walls were a stark white, the floor carpeted in a design popular when Carter was in office, though it looked brand new. I sniffed. The room smelled old, the air stale. I sighed and took the clothes Jack gave me and hung them in the closet, where I found a spare set of blankets.

I laid the blankets on the ground and made a temporary bed, wadding a sheet into a pillow for my head. It was late afternoon, but I was exhausted. I closed the door and shut my eyes, but my mind kept drifting back to everything I'd seen, to what Jack said, before sleep finally claimed me.

* * *

Thursday

Sunlight beat against my eyelids and I grudgingly opened them to find the light streaming in through a dirty window. I heard noises from the kitchen and staggered to the bathroom where I took care of my morning business, then found Jack frying eggs in the cast-iron skillet in the kitchen.

Jack didn't turn around. "Still hungry?"

I thought about it. "Yeah, actually."

Jack plated six of the eggs and loaded my plate with a half loaf of toast. "One of the benefits of the change. You don't have to watch what you eat. There's butter on the table."

I sat. The eggs were crusty on the edges and soft in the center and they tasted thick and rich. I slathered butter on my toast and began wolfing it down.

Jack joined me with his own plate and I watched him pour coffee from an old fashioned percolator. He poured me a cup and I drank. It was good, better than I'd ever tasted. I poured cream from a pewter pitcher on the table and took another sip.

The coffee was amazing.

Jack smiled at me. "Tastes good, doesn't it?"

I nodded, sipping the coffee. "Part of the change?"

"Yes. Tell me, how do you feel? Take a moment to think before you answer."

"I feel great, actually." Then I remembered Stacie, dead on the floor, and I frowned. "I shouldn't. My wife is dead. And Lilly's been taken. How can I sit here eating?" I shoved the plate at him. "My whole world has been turned upside down. I ought to be freaking out."

"I'm going to tell you a secret. Life moves on. What happened to your parents? Are they still alive?"

I sighed. "My mom died when I was four. Car wreck. I don't even remember her. My dad died when I was twenty-one."

Jack nodded his head. "Do you remember when your dad died? You probably felt a great sense of loss. But you got over it, didn't you?"

I hated to admit it, but he was right. "Yeah. I still think of him, though."

"Of course you do. That's natural. But probably not like you did after he died. Were you with him when he passed?"

"No, I was at Ohio State. It was right before graduation. He had a heart attack in the diner. There was nothing anyone could do."

Jack nodded. "Must have been hard."

"He was always there for me," I said. "Without my mom, well...we only had each other. He was my best friend. He worked really hard to make sure I could go to college. When I went away, I think it really hurt him. After he died, I inherited the diner and the house. I talked Stacie into moving back to Arcanum. It felt like he might just walk through the door at any minute. I know that sounds crazy...."

Jack shook his head. "Not at all. That's what loss feels like. It can drive you crazy. But, you got over it. You built a life with your wife and daughter and eventually you moved on. You'll get over the death of your wife, too. You're still in shock. Your body doesn't know that, though. It's like an engine that's racing. All part of the change. Don't worry about it, don't try to rush it. Just learn what I teach, and when the time is right, you can deal with the grief."

"What's the plan? How long before we can go after her?"

Jack watched me with his good eye, sipping his coffee. "You have a lot to learn. Where did I leave off last night?"

I had a sinking feeling in my gut. "Jack, how long will this take?"

"Oh yeah," Jack continued, like I hadn't spoken. "Daylight. Daylight makes them weak. Crosses don't work, that's just a myth."

I sighed. "Well, what about garlic?"

Jack squinted his good eye. "Makes your breath smell. Doesn't do shit against vampires."

"Holy water?"

"Touchy subject," he said with a shrug. "There *is* a type of holy water, blessed in the right way, that burns a vampire. Too hard to get. Better to use a shotgun with silver buckshot. Holy ground is the same way. They can enter a church with no problems, unless it's been blessed in a certain way. So don't go thinking you can hide in a church and save yourself. You'll just wind up dead."

I nodded slowly. "I get it, Jack. They're hard to kill. But they *can* be killed. Right?"

"*Anything* can be killed," Jack said. "You just have to find the right way. Now go put those dishes up and let's get to work. How are you with guns?"

I spent the rest of the morning finding out I didn't know anything about guns.

Luckily, Jack did.

I learned the difference between single-action pistols and double-action pistols, semi-automatics and fully automatics. I learned about pump shotguns and semi-automatic shotguns. I learned that there were more calibers of ammunition than I ever thought possible and that Jack spent a fortune on silver bullion only to melt and make his own ammunition.

Jack pointed to the wall of the bunker and the enormous array of handguns. "You can't go wrong with any of these, but for you, maybe a simple .45 might be a good start." He pulled a gun from its display and handed it to me.

It was heavy, with a short barrel, wooden grips, and looked like something a cowboy might have worn. I picked it up and was surprised by how heavy it was. The gun felt…substantial.

"That's a Colt .45, single action." He took a leather holster from a rack and fitted it around my waist. "You only have six shots. In the old days, you'd only have five. You never kept a round in the chamber under the hammer. It might accidentally discharge. But, when you're going up against a vampire, that's the least of your worries." He put the gun in the holster. "How's it feel?"

"Awkward." I walked around the bunker. The weight of the Colt slapping against my thigh was irritating.

"You'll get used to it. Now, a gun like this, you have to cock it and then fire. Try it."

I nodded, then pulled the Colt, cocking the hammer with my thumb. It was a slow and clumsy draw. I holstered it, then tried again with the same result.

"It takes time. I want you to practice every chance you get."

"Wouldn't it be easier to use a shotgun?" I tried pulling the Colt again. It felt painfully slow.

"We'll get to that. Let's go shooting."

We left the underground bunker and Jack led me to the top of the hill, where he had set out a table. There was a square wooden target thirty feet away, the outline of a man inked on it. He showed me how to load the Colt and I put the gun back in the holster.

"Pull slowly, up and out," Jack instructed. "Don't thumb the hammer until it's clear of the holster, you could shoot yourself in the leg. When it's clear, raise it to hip level and pull the trigger. Don't worry about hitting the target, just practice the movement."

I did as he instructed and the pistol roared in my hand. Downrange, the bullet nicked the edge of the target, the report of the Colt echoing like thunder.

"Good. You're going to practice that motion. When you're done, we'll start working on accuracy."

I pulled the gun and fired, again and again. The shots were mostly wild, but occasionally I'd hit the target.

Jack kept up his instruction and soon I was regularly hitting the wooden square.

I turned to him. "It would be easier to hit if I could aim at it."

"When you're in a real fight with a vampire, you won't have time to aim. You'll have to shoot on instinct."

I spent the rest of the day practicing firing round after round. By the time the sun was sinking into the west, I was able to put a bullet in the target's chest, more often than not.

Jack nodded, approving. "Not bad, Sam."

"It's funny, but it's like everything slows down and I have all the time in the world."

"That's the change. Now, it's time for supper. I'm hungry."

* * *

We were almost finished eating when Jack's phone rang. He went to the other room to answer it and I heard him talking in hushed tones.

He came back to the kitchen. "I have a job," he said. "You stay here and keep practicing. I should be back in a couple of days."

I perked up. "Where are you going?"

"St. Louis."

"I want to go."

His good eye opened wide. "You have no idea what you're doing. You'd be a danger, to me and to yourself. You could get us both killed."

"I'm sure you could use backup. Haven't you ever had help before?"

He shook his head. "Out of the question. You want to help, and that's good. In a few months you might be ready to wait in the truck. Right now, I need you safe."

"Jack, I can wait in the truck. I may not be great with a gun, and I might have only killed one vampire, but I can sit in a truck. What if you need someone to drive? Surely I can do that."

He cocked his head and I could see he was considering it. "If you come with me, you do as I say. You stay in the truck and don't do anything stupid. Like get yourself killed."

I stood. "I can do that."

He grunted.

We loaded the Chevy with the toolbox full of weapons, all freshly stocked with ammo. Jack found an old leather duster and handed it to me. "Keep the holster and Colt. Here's a box of silver ammo." He passed me the box and when I took it, he grabbed my hand. "This is just in case, you understand. You're *staying* in the truck. The duster has loops for stakes, but you won't need it because you'll be where?"

I grabbed the thick wooden stake. "In the truck." I found the series of loops inside the duster and laced the stake securely in place. "Who was that on the phone?"

"People have my number. People who know about monsters. They call me when something happens. They called because children have been abducted in the past two days."

"Children? Like, teenagers? Or, like little kids?"

He gaze was steely. "Little kids, Sam. There's a chance they're still alive, so we go in tonight, as soon as we can. They claim it's one vampire. But, just in case, you'll be in the truck."

"I got it, I'll be in the truck."

He nodded. "I must be crazy to take you with me."

We headed west, into Toledo, then turned and headed south on 63, through Tama, on the way to St. Louis. Jack drove, pushing the truck well past the speed limit and the hills rolled by in the dark.

"Jack? If we find these kids, can we go looking for Lilly?"

He stared at the road. Finally, "We don't even know where she is. I've made a few phone calls, but no one knows anything. I've got people looking, people I trust. If we hear something, I promise you I'll do whatever I can." He turned to me, his face hard, shadows from the dashboard light dancing across his face. "You have my word."

I thought about saving Lilly. "Jack, what if he's turned her?"

There was long silence. "They can't be saved. That's a fact. I tried. Years ago. It's…complicated."

"Tell me."

"When they turn, they're full of bloodlust. They feel hunger. You've experienced just a taste of what it feels like for them. It consumes them, twists them. Twists their mind. They can't tell right from wrong. They lose their morality. They just feel hunger. You don't know monsters, Sam. You haven't experienced it. They'll turn on their friends, their spouses, their loved ones…."

I considered his words. "They're all like that?"

He nodded. "Yes. But, if they live long enough, and I'm talking decades, mind you, the hunger lessens. If they reach that point, they can control the urge. It's rare, though. There's a sheriff in Wyoming, I worked with him once. I got a call, rode into town and I felt him in my head. He has a *presence*. He's old, the oldest I've met. Why he settled in Wyoming, I'll never understand. He's got control of the hunger, but I still didn't trust him. We tracked the vampire down to a motel. It was a youngling, maybe six months turned. A man in his late fifties. The sheriff killed him, but only after the vampire had taken a teenage girl. I saw his face, the young girl lying dead on the floor. He wanted to feed." Jack paused, his hands gripping the steering wheel tightly. "I could feel it. I worked with him to stop the youngling, but I still didn't trust him. Afterward, he told me it was a good thing I didn't trust him. He knows what he is. Even with all those years, even with his control, he still hungers."

"What does he feed on?"

Jack shook his head. "He's got himself a young wife, a nice woman named Alma. She keeps him sated. He said it took him over five hundred years to learn that kind of control. Still, I stay out of his territory, just in case."

I thought about that. "How many are like him?"

"Damned few. There's one like that in New York. One in Chicago. Maybe a couple out west. They try to keep the population down. They have a place in the world and they don't like younglings messing it up. They send me tips, to help thin the herd. The church helps when it can."

I was taken aback. "The church?"

He nodded. "We have an understanding. Leave it at that."

I kept going over everything that happened. "What's your story, anyway?"

Jack grunted. "What story would that be?"

"How did you learn to do this? How'd you wind up killing vampires?"

Jack turned to me, his hand easily guiding the truck without looking at the road. "It's a long story and not something you need concern yourself with." I felt that weight behind his eye, a sinking in my stomach. "Get some rest, boy. You need it."

* * *

Friday

It was three in the morning when we pulled into a parking lot near the Mississippi river. I lurched awake, my breath catching in my throat, before I realized I was still in Jack's truck. I looked through the side window at the surrounding neighborhood. Even in the dark I could make out the bombed-out landscape, littered with weed-covered parking lots, where factories and warehouses once thrived.

Jack pointed to a three-story brick building a block away.

"There it is." He got out, leaving the keys in the ignition, and quietly opened the truck topper. "Can you feel it?" he whispered from the back.

I looked around, confused. "Feel what?"

He opened his duster and stuffed the shotgun under it. The nearest streetlights were blocks away and cast a dim glow over the deserted streets. He came to the passenger side and stared at me with his good eye. "It *should* feel like something wrong. Like evil. Close your eyes and reach out with your mind."

I looked around. "I don't feel anything."

"Close your eyes and *concentrate*," he snapped.

I sighed but closed my eyes and waited. I heard the rumble of trucks on the bridge over the Mississippi, far in the distance, and the sounds of the City, not far away. I could even hear the faint rumble of jets, a deep roar that was more vibration than sound, but I couldn't discern the direction.

Then I felt *it*.

The skin on my scalp tingled and I shivered. There was a weight to it, a pressure behind my eyes, and a profound sense of...wrong. That's what Jack said and that's how it felt. Something wrong. It clashed with everything I knew of the world, with life, with hope. It wasn't evil, exactly, but it was definitely a close cousin. My heartbeat kicked up a notch and my bladder tightened. I felt a wave of dread, and I pulled Jack's old duster tight against my chest.

"Jack? I'm pretty sure I sense it," I whispered.

He nodded grimly. "Feels like you're about to piss yourself?"

"Yes," I agreed.

"There's a vampire near. Don't depend on that feeling to save your life, but don't ignore it, either. Stay here."

My throat constricted, and suddenly I was glad to wait in the truck. Whatever was out there in the dark was something I wasn't prepared to face. My day of target shooting wouldn't save me against that primal force. It wanted to eat me, to drink my blood and take my soul.

Nothing wrong with waiting in the truck.

Jack strode across the parking lot, the duster making him look for all the world like a cowboy in an old western. He approached the dilapidated brick building, quickly opened the door and entered, closing it behind him.

* * *

It was only moments after Jack entered the building that I heard a scraping near the back of the truck. I craned my neck, looking in the side-view mirror, but I saw nothing.

I rolled down the window and the cool air felt good against my skin. I poked my head out, looking around, trying to figure out what caused the scraping. There was a sudden movement as a hand grabbed Jack's old duster, and, with an inhuman strength, twisted it tight against my chest and yanked me through the open window. I slammed into the concrete hard enough to knock the wind from me. I gurgled, trying to catch my breath, panicking as my lungs refused to work.

I blinked, looking up at the face I knew so well. My wife stared back at me.

"Miss me?" Stacie asked.

My heart leapt. "You're alive!"

Stacie smiled, but it wasn't like any smile I had ever seen on her face. "Not so much, honey."

She swung her hand and her nails, as hard as steel claws, gouged great chunks of flesh and blood along my cheek. I gasped in pain and tried to duck, to shield myself, and the palm of her hand struck my face hard enough to make my teeth rattle.

She straddled me, glaring. "You left me on the kitchen floor," she hissed. "That's not 'husband of the year' material. Silas gave me the gift. That's your fault!"

Her eyes bore into mine and I felt the weight behind them, the same sinking feeling that I got from Silas, but somehow I managed to resist.

"I'm so sorry, Stacie. I didn't know. It was so crazy. I didn't mean to leave you there. But, Silas has Lilly. We have to get her back!"

Stacie threw her head back and let out a peal of laughter. "I've got Lilly. Don't worry, she's safe with me. I promise. Cross my heart and hope to die."

The realization settled in my stomach, a hard knot right in my center, accompanied by a cold wave of nausea. "My god, Stacie. What have you done?"

"What have I done? Why, I've got our little girl and she tastes so sweet. I can't believe how hungry I am and there's nothing better than a child's blood. You wouldn't believe it, Sam. You can't understand. It tastes amazing. It's like liquid pleasure. It's better than sex. Better than anything."

I couldn't believe what I was hearing. "This isn't you, Stacie. You love Lilly. You'd never hurt her."

"It's the gift, dummy. It changes your perspective. Oh, how I love our daughter, it's like a cold drink when you're dying of thirst. It lights up your insides."

I shook my head. This wasn't like *my* Stacie. My wife would *never* do such a thing. I tried again. "Listen to me. We can find a cure. I *promise*. We have to get out of here. We can be a family again, but you can't hurt Lilly. Where is she?"

Stacie slammed my head against the concrete and everything went blurry. "She's not here, Sam, but don't worry. We'll be a family again. After I turn you, we'll get her. We have to be careful not to kill her, but we can feed whenever we want. You'll understand after I give you the gift."

"Listen to yourself," I pleaded. "Feed off her? She's our daughter! I don't want *any* gift."

I heard the muted roar of Jack's shotgun from the brick building, then again and again.

Stacie giggled. "They're going to turn him. Once Silas has made him one of us, everything will be different." She wiped the blood from my cheek and licked it. Her eyes rolled back and she arched her back and I recognized the look on her face. It wasn't just pleasure. It was orgasmic. "There's so much you don't know, Sam. It'll all make sense soon enough."

There was shouting from the brick building, a series of crashes, the sounds of things breaking and shattering, then the muffled reports of a handgun.

My stomach clenched as I realized she would do it. She was going to turn me into a vampire.

I jerked upright and slammed my forehead into her nose. There was a crunch of bone and she shrieked. I whipped back and forth like a wild animal, flinging her from me. I managed to get to one knee and was reaching for the Colt when she grabbed me by the legs and swung me like a baseball bat into the passenger door of the Chevy, collapsing it. I bounced off the truck and slammed into the concrete.

Everything went dark and fuzzy. I thought I might vomit, and when I managed to focus my eyes, Stacie crouched over me. "You're such an asshole, Sam. You think I wanted that life? Living in that shitty little town, working in that shitty little diner, married to a man with no ambition?"

I saw her fist coming and tried to roll my head. It slammed into my chin and I blacked out. When I came to, she was slamming the back of my head into the concrete, each impact causing an explosion of stars before my eyes.

"Ss—sorry," I said. "I'm sorry."

She scrunched her face in disgust. "I'm going to give you the gift, even though you don't deserve it. You didn't make anything of your life, maybe you'll make something of your death."

She opened her mouth wide and the ivory fangs erupted from behind her teeth. When she sank them into my neck, it was a white-hot branding iron against the skin. I screamed, desperately kicking at her, trying to make her stop, but she latched on harder. I tried beating at her face but my strength was fading. My hands were clumsy and so very heavy. I couldn't seem to make them work.

I was tired. I was drained. I was dying. It didn't sound so bad. Just close my eyes and let go. The pain would be gone. I would live again, as something else, joining my wife and daughter.

What harm could it do?

The roar of the handgun brought me back to reality and I saw Stacie spinning away. I turned toward the sound of the gunfire. Jack loped across the parking lot, his left arm dangling at his side, his right clutching his massive pistol. He fired again and Stacie let out a banshee wail, then she was gone, moving in a blur. I struggled to sit up and Jack was by my side, lifting me up and shoving me through the window, into the cab of the truck.

Everything was fading, but I heard the squeal of tires as Jack peeled out of the parking lot, the gagging smell of burning rubber in the back of my nose. I tried to clear my throat but the smell wouldn't leave.

I swallowed, over and over. "I stayed in the truck," I managed.

"You did," Jack said. "Just like you were told."

He was driving, hell bent, and the streets soon ran together before my bleary eyes as we rocketed through St. Louis.

Jack kept glancing my way.

I licked my laps and finally asked, "What happened?"

"A trap. Silas and Pearl were waiting. I tried to get some holes in them, but they got away." He glanced down at his side. "I think they broke my arm."

"Jack? I'm hot." I closed my eyes, as a throbbing behind my temple kicked into high gear. "I'm on fire. Why am I so hot?"

"Vampire venom. She was trying to turn you."

I thought about what Stacie said. "I'm going to die?"

Jack grunted. "Not if I can help it. Try and catch some rest, we'll be there soon."

Rest sounded good. I wanted to sleep.

My body hurt. Everywhere.

My wife had tried to kill me, to turn me into a vampire. I couldn't get my mind around that. She wasn't the woman I knew.

Then I remembered my daughter. Somewhere, Lilly was alone, probably wondering what happened to her Mommy and Daddy.

My skin was burning and my body was aching and everything went black.

* * *

I opened my eye. I was looking at a stone ceiling. I took a deep breath and realized that my everything hurt.

I rolled to the side. I lay on a cot in a room the size of a cafeteria. Mine was but one in a line, empty cots on both sides, army blankets tucked tight, all neatly made. An old fashioned lantern cast a flickering light against the stone walls, and I heard voices behind a massive ironclad door. The room smelled like wet earth and mold, but it was better than the smell of burning rubber.

I took a choking breath as the memory hit me.

Stacie had tried to kill me. She might have succeeded if not for Jack. I groaned and struggled to sit up, lightheaded, then sank back down to the cot, head spinning.

The door creaked open and Jack entered, his arm in a white cotton sling, and he was joined by a priest in his mid-fifties.

"Where am I?"

"You're in the sub-basement of the Cathedral Basilica," Jack said, then pointed to the priest. "This is Jameson."

The priest stepped forward. "How are you feeling, Samuel?"

"I feel like I just got the shit beat out of me."

Jack sat down heavily on the cot. "You're infected, Sam."

I looked at him. "I'm fine, Jack. I feel pretty sore now, but I'm going to be all right."

Jack shook his head. His face was hard and grim. "You're dying."

My tongue grew two sizes too big for my mouth. "What?"

The priest cautiously approached the cot. "You'd be dead already, if Jack hadn't scared off the vampire."

"It wasn't a vampire," I protested. "That was my wife."

"Your wife, the vampire," Jameson corrected. "It's too late, you've got the venom in you. Judging by the stain on your soul, you've got a couple of days. Maybe less." He shot a sidelong glance at Jack, then back to me. "I'm sorry. I'll pray for you, but there's nothing I can do."

Jack turned and glared at the priest. "That's not true and you know it, padre."

The priest took a halting step back. "It's beyond my ability. You *know* that."

Jack stood and the priest shrank back. "You called me in. You helped set the trap. That makes it your responsibility." Jack's right hand was clenching and unclenching and I thought he might smack the priest.

Jameson's face softened as he shook his head. "We didn't know. The children were taken. All the signs pointed to a youngling."

"The children were dead by the time I got there."

The priest's faced turned ashen, the pale skin almost white against his sandy-blond hair. "I'm sorry, but I didn't know it was Silas." He turned to me, eyes full of sorrow. "It doesn't change anything. I can't help."

"What will it take?" Jack growled.

"Even if I had the power, I don't know how," Jameson explained.

"What about Buehl?"

Jameson shook his head. "He's been dead for twenty years, Jack."

"Hendrick?"

"Cancer, two years ago."

"There's *got* to be someone," Jack said.

"There's only one that I know of," Jameson said, chewing at his lip. "Lewinheim."

"Lewinheim?" Jack turned back to me. "Not Lewinheim. Surely there's someone else."

"There isn't," Jameson insisted. "He's retired, living in Peoria. I haven't heard from him in two years, but he *is* still alive."

"How old is he? Ninety?" Jack snorted. "Would he even have the strength to perform the ceremony?"

"You're one to talk. As for the ceremony, it's just not done anymore." Jameson's gaze swept from Jack to me. "It's hard. You know that. The church has changed. They don't keep with the old ways, the traditions. I can place a call to the Vatican, but it might be weeks before we get an answer, and there's no guarantee that they won't ignore it. Samuel doesn't have that much time."

"It's worth a shot. I'm not going to let him go without a fight."

I reached forward and grabbed Jack's hand. "Hey, I'm right here."

Jack looked at me with his good eye. "You don't know what's coming. You won't just pass, you'll be in agony, and when you die, you'll wake up changed. You'll be one of them. You saw your wife. What was she?"

I started to deny it, but he was right. "She wasn't herself," I finally said. "She was...like an animal. Primal. She said things to me. Things she would never say."

Jack nodded. "Their humanity dies when they die."

"Jack? She wanted to turn me. She said we could feed from Lilly. How could she think such a thing?"

Jack shook his head sadly, his face pale. His good eye turned to me, then quickly looked away. "She's not your wife, not the way you remember her. I tried to tell you. When they change, everything you loved about them is gone. Just...gone." He turned to Jameson. "Get me Lewinheim's address."

CHAPTER FIVE

I was sitting up on the cot, my head against the hard concrete wall, when Jameson knocked on the door.

"Jack's bringing the truck around. Let me help you." He placed his arm under mine and helped shoulder some of my weight.

I staggered up. "My legs don't feel right."

"Son, I'm hoping Jack can save you, but you have to understand, it may not work."

"What are you saying, Father?"

He sighed. "I'm saying you have to consider your options. If it comes down to it, do you want to be reborn as one of those *things*?"

He helped me up the narrow stone stairs to the basement, my hand gripping the banister tightly to help shoulder my weight. "Father? What's with the cots?"

Jameson glanced back down the stairs and shook his head. "Vampires are a plague," he said. "The church has struggled to contain them, to kill them when we can, but they've gotten smart. They hide the bodies. When we find one of their victims, one they haven't killed or given the gift, we try to help them. We bring them here, try to heal them as best we can. We counsel them before we send them back into the world. When a vampire feeds from them, it does something to them. Weakens them. Not just physically. Once they know the monsters exist, they never truly overcome it."

I shuddered. "It damages their souls."

The priest bit his lip, then nodded. "Exactly. Tell me, do you know how old Jack is?"

I nodded. "I do, Father. He told me."

"Did he tell you anything else?" Jameson asked, watching me intently.

"I'm sorry, Father. I don't understand."

Jameson sighed. "Did he tell you why he has hunted Silas for so many years without killing him?"

I shook my head. "No, he didn't."

The priest sighed again. "Very few humans manage to kill a vampire. Even fewer manage to kill a dozen vampires. Jack's killed more vampires than any other hunter. Ever. He said you killed Munzinger. How did it feel?"

I didn't understand Jameson's point. "The change?"

"Yes, the change."

"It hurt."

He nodded. "I imagine it did."

He helped me up the stairs to the main floor. I felt a pressure in my head and I knew—without looking—that the sun was almost directly overhead. As we approached the door, I looked through the window and saw Jack sitting in his truck, waiting.

Jameson put his hand on my shoulder. "If the cleansing works, be careful."

"Of what?"

"Jack. He hasn't aged a day in twenty years. Look, there's some kind of history between him and Silas. He's chased him for a hundred years and still hasn't caught him. Plus, with all the vampires Jack's killed, it's done something to him."

A chill run down my spine. "You think he can't be trusted?"

Jameson put his hands on my shoulders. "Most of the church remains unaware that vampires exist. We keep it that way for a reason. The world doesn't want to know that we're at war. Twenty years ago I would have said the forces of good were winning. Now, I'm not so sure. The vampires are gaining ground, and we don't have enough hunters. The few master vampires who have overcome their blood-lust keep the younglings from multiplying, but it's not enough. Those of us who are aware of the threat help the hunters when we can, but the hunters tend to disappear or wind up in the morgue." His eyes narrowed. "Jack is special. Effective." Jameson paused. "There's always a price, Sam. What Jack is and what he's done, I think he's paying the price. Don't pay it with him."

I nodded. "Thanks for the help."

"I wish I could have done more. I wish I could have saved those children." He glanced out the window at Jack waiting patiently. "I'm praying for you. Save yourself and save your daughter. Then, find some place to hide and raise her, far away from vampires. But, if the cleansing doesn't work? You will have to make a choice. Go with God, son."

* * *

My eyes opened when I felt the truck stop. It was mid-afternoon and Jack had pulled his Chevy in front of an old brick building in downtown Peoria. The seedy neighborhood and the lingering smell of the nearby Illinois River provided a one-two punch of unpleasantness.

I rubbed at the crust in my eyes. "What is this place?" I asked.

"Retirement home," Jack answered. "Peoria used to have a thriving priesthood, but the population shrank and when they built new churches elsewhere, they started sending the old and infirm priests here. Come on, we have to talk to Lewinheim."

I pushed against the door, but it was wedged shut. Jack came around and yanked on the handle. The door opened with a squeal of metal. I staggered out and he forced it shut. I stopped to stare at the dent in the side, the dent my wife had made with my body.

"Sam!"

I nodded. "Right. Lewinheim."

We entered through the front, the glass door stained with years of grime. The place was almost deserted, except for the old nun at the front desk. She was dressed in a gray wool dress and a matching gray habit, and sat listening to headphones plugged in to an ancient Walkman cassette player.

"I haven't seen one of those in years," I said.

The nun didn't look up. "State your name and your business."

Jack stepped up to the battered oak desk. "Jack Harlan to see Edmund Lewinheim."

The nun looked up, saw Jack's arm in a sling, then turned to me. The gouges in my face had scabbed over nicely, but they were grotesque. She gave us a look usually reserved for finding something stuck to the bottom of one's shoe. "What happened to you two?"

Jack shrugged and cocked his head. "Car wreck."

The nun eyed us suspiciously, then picked up a phone and spoke briefly. She hung up and turned her disapproving glare back to us. "Sister Calahane will escort you. Wait here." Her gaze lingered on us, then finally dropped as she went back to listening to her headphones.

I turned to Jack, who just rolled his eye. Apparently we were no longer worthy of the nun's attention.

Soon, a young woman opened the door to the right and beckoned us in. Sister Calahane was about my age, creamy skin broken by a mass of freckles, and dressed in a simple brown skirt and nun's headdress. She was attractive, but her tight-lipped face could scare children.

She inspected us. "You are here to see Father Lewinheim?"

"We are," Jack said.

"How do you know him?" the Sister asked.

"Edmund and I go back," Jack said softly. "I've known him for many years."

The Sister's gaze was hard and appraising. "He's not well. He's not to be disturbed with trivial matters."

Jack smiled unpleasantly, then crossed himself. "As God is my witness, it isn't trivial."

The Sister stood motionless for a brief moment. I thought she would turn us away, but she finally opened the door. "Follow me."

We followed her through the building and up four flights of narrow stairs to a door with Lewinheim's name on it.

"He may not remember you," the Sister cautioned. "He's still strong for his age, but his mind wanders."

She knocked softly on the door before opening it and ushering us in. The room was simple; stained plaster walls, a few nondescript photos of flowers and trees in a misguided attempt to liven up the room, a bookcase brimming with old books to one side, and a bed against the far side.

It smelled of the old and infirm, the smell that instinctively makes people want to move on before they are forced to confront their own mortality.

I hate that smell.

Father Lewinheim sat on a burgundy recliner in the middle of the room, a Bible in his lap. His eyes were closed, his face slack.

The liver spots on his face were attempting to merge with the liver spots on his bald head. His wire-rimmed glasses were skewed and ready to fall off. I started to speak, but Jack gave me a look and I stopped.

The Sister approached the old man and gently nudged his arm. "Father, you have visitors."

The old man snorted and opened his eyes. It took them a moment to focus. He turned his head and offered a weak smile. "Hello. Do I know you?"

Jack stepped forward. "It's me, Ed. It's Jack."

The old priest looked to the Sister. "I'm sorry. I don't remember any visitors today. Who is it?"

Sister Calahane clucked her tongue. "Father, you need to use your other glasses."

The priest fumbled at the table next to his chair, then swapped his reading glasses for his other pair. He turned back to Jack, eyebrows raised. "Jack? Is that you?"

"How've you been, Ed?"

"My goodness, you look so young. It's like you haven't aged a day. How many years has it been?"

"Been a few," Jack said. "You doing okay in here?"

The priest nodded, and it was full of sadness and resignation. "I'm old. I don't have much left in me. I'm just trying to find peace before I go." He held up The Bible. "I read when I can. Pray as much as I can." He turned to me. "Who's the boy?"

Jack turned to the Sister. "Can we speak privately with the Father?"

Sister Calahane started to speak, but the priest interrupted. "Callie stays, Jack. She knows."

Jack turned to the Sister who stood, who stood her ground under Jack's gaze. "I don't know what the good Father has told you, but I'd prefer to speak in private."

The Sister matched his stare. "The Calahane family has always struggled against the enemy, and I've helped Father Lewinheim with his journals for the past year."

Jack turned back to the priest. "She knows everything?"

"Not everything, Jack. I've kept my word. But everything else? She's right, there's been a Calahane in the fight for hundreds of years. Her uncle was a friend of mine, I asked him if there were any Calahanes that could help me with my journals, and he sent Callie." There was a long pause where the old man worked his jaw before speaking. "And her sister, Katie."

Jack squinted at the old priest. "You trust her?"

Lewinheim nodded. "What's wrong with the boy? I can sense the evil in him."

That was news to me, and I started to speak, but Jack put his hand on my shoulder. "His name is Samuel and he's been bitten. He's got venom in him. I scared off the vampire that did it..."

The Sister sucked in her breath as Jack spoke the word, vampire, but the priest shushed her.

"But it was too late," Jack finished.

The priest beckoned me closer. I approached him cautiously. He made the sign of the cross, then closed his eyes. "I can feel it, Samuel. You're dying."

"I don't feel like I'm dying," I protested. Even as I said it, I knew that was wrong. I felt *something*, a lingering sense of illness or disease. I didn't want to admit it. I didn't want it to be true.

No sense in lying to myself.

The old man's eyes snapped open. "You're dying. If you're with Jack, then you know what comes after." He turned his attention back to Jack. "What do you want me to do?"

"Can he be cleansed? Jameson told me that the church isn't doing it anymore. You're the only one that I know who's still alive, Ed. You have to help him."

The priest shook his head slowly. "I can't do it. I just don't have it in me anymore. Time has wounded us all. Everyone except for you. You still fight. You never caught Silas?"

"No."

"Did Silas do this?"

"Indirectly. Silas turned Sam's wife. She bit him."

I knelt next to the old priest. "Sir, I know you don't know me, but if there's any way you could help, I'd appreciate it. She's got our daughter, Lilly. She's feeding from her. I have to help my daughter. If I turn, I'm afraid she'll die."

The old priest closed his eyes and tears streamed down his cheek. "I'm sorry, Samuel. I just can't. I'm not strong, not like I was. I'm just a feeble old man. There's nothing I can do."

Jack's voice was like iron. "I've been hearing that a lot, lately. Is this what the church has become? Do you remember what I've done?"

Lewinheim nodded slowly. "I remember, but it's not that I don't want to help. I *can't*."

"I can," Sister Calahane offered.

The priest glowered at her through his tear-stained eyes. "Hold your tongue. You *cannot* help and you *will not* help. You don't know what you say."

Jack hand shot forward and grabbed the woman's, lighting fast. She struggled to pull away, but he held her tightly. He leaned in close, his eye scanning her face, then pulled back. "She's of the blood?"

"Yes," the priest said, "but she's just a child."

The Sister scowled. "I'm twenty-six, Father. I can make my own decisions."

"No you can't," the priest said. "It's dangerous. You don't know, Callie. You don't understand."

"I've read your journals," she protested. "Besides, if this young man doesn't receive help he'll become one of them. I can perform the ceremony."

"No, Callie. I won't allow it."

Sister Calahane shook her head sadly. "I'm sorry, Father, but it's my decision. I have the faith, and I have the strength, and I have the blood."

I stood, watching the exchange, but I had no idea what they spoke of. "What's that mean, the blood?"

Sister Calahane hugged then old priest and then turned a disapproving glare upon me. "You don't need to know. I have the means to perform the ceremony. That's all you need concern yourself with. But I won't risk my life for nothing." She turned to Jack. "I want something from you, Mr. Harlan. I want you to find my sister, Katie."

* * *

"What happened to your sister?" I asked.

Sister Calahane lips quivered, then she finally spoke. "She was taken two months ago. She lived here, working for the diocese, but she...lost her way. She disappeared, and I strongly suspect she was taken by a vampire."

"Your sister was a Sister?" I asked.

She nodded. "She's my twin. We took our vows together." She paused, then turned to stare out Lewinheim's window. "Do you know what that means? To lose your twin? We've been inseparable since birth. When she rejected the church, she didn't just reject Christ, she rejected me. She knew I was helping Father Lewinheim with his journals. When she read the truth about the vampires, she wasn't horrified. She was intrigued. I think she went looking for a vampire, and I fear she found one."

Jack took a half step toward her, but she turned and stopped him with a withering glare. He tipped his head, but the look on his face was grave. "Sister, if she went looking for a vampire, she's probably turned by now. Or worse. I don't mean any disrespect, but there's little hope."

The Sister glowered at him. "I know who you are, Mr. Harlan. I know what you do. You kill vampires and you don't care much for the living. I need to know the truth. She's my sister."

Father Lewinheim spoke up. "Truth is a funny thing, Callie. All my life I wanted to know the truth, but what good did it do me? I might have been better off remaining ignorant."

Her face softened. "Don't say that Father," she said. "You saved people."

He nodded slowly. "A few, yes. But Jack did the real work. He's spent his life killing vampires. You don't know anything about him."

"I know what you put in your journals."

"I didn't record everything in those journals," he said. "Those are just a fraction of what I know and what I did. You haven't seen a vampire, you haven't felt them, in your mind. Performing the ceremony isn't as simple as saying the words and having the blood. It will change you. It stains you." The old priest trailed off. "And the truth you seek? You may not like it."

Sister Calahane turned to me, eyes blazing. "You want to save your daughter? I want to know what happened to my sister. Why should my needs be less than yours? I'll help you, but you must promise to find my sister first."

"We may not have time for that," Jack said.

She turned back to the window. "Then I suggest you hurry."

CHAPTER SIX

Jack drove us to the address Sister Callie had given, a small apartment in a complex near the McClugage Bridge. Jack knocked politely on the door and we heard a man's cursing. "Yeah, who is it?"

"Is this Daryl?"

"Yeah," the voice cautiously replied. "Who's asking?"

Jack gave me a hard look and I almost felt sorry for Daryl.

Almost.

"We're looking for someone," Jack said, surprisingly calm. "Katie Calahane. You seen her?"

"I don't know her, man. You got the wrong address."

"We just need to know where she is. You sold her some stuff, right?"

"Look, I told you, I don't know her."

I grabbed Jack's arm. "We're not cops," I offered. "We're not trying to cause trouble." I motioned to Jack, who reluctantly withdrew a stack of hundreds and waved it in front of the peephole. "We'll pay for the info. Her sister just wants to know where she is, that's all."

There was a long pause. "You guys PI's or something?"

"Or something," I said. "Look, a thousand just for an address. That's not too much to ask. You're not involved. Nobody knows we got it from you."

There was another long pause. "Like I said, I don't know nothing. Hit the bricks, fool."

"Son, we can do this the easy way or the hard way," Jack said. "You'll like the easy way a whole lot better."

"What you gonna do, talk me to death, old man? Now take your crusty old ass out my building."

Jack turned his good eye to me. "The younger generation gets stupider every year." He pulled his arm back and with a tremendous amount of force slammed the palm of his hand against the door. It blew inward, the door-frame exploding as the lock-plate ripped away. There was a thud from the inside and we found Daryl sprawled on the floor across the room. He was holding a nickel-plated revolver and trying to bring it up on us, but Jack stepped in and pulled his massive revolver and trained it on the man. "If you even think about using that pistol," Jack said, "think again. I could literally blow your hand off. Clean off. You understand?"

The scrawny young black man cowered against the dirty white carpet. "I don't know nothing, man. I'm telling you, for real. Whatever you got going on with him, I don't want no part of. Serious, man. I'm *not* part of it."

"You know where Katie is," I said. "Tell us."

"Look, I just deal a little weed, that's it. Then this dude shows up, he wants me to sling some meth. I'm not down with that, but that dude?" He shuddered. "He's scary, man."

There was the sharp smell of ammonia and Daryl's pants showed a spreading stain across the crotch. "Daryl, did you just pee your pants?" I asked.

"I didn't want to do it," he blubbered. "Didn't want to. He *made* me. Then that chick showed up, she didn't know nothing about nothing, I thought she was looking to get freaky. I sold her some weed, but she was looking for something else. He found out about her, wanted the hookup. I ain't seen her since. God's honest truth."

"What's the man's name?" Jack asked.

Daryl shook his head. "He'll kill me, man. He'll find out, somehow. He knows things. He ain't…right."

"Tell me his name, son, then get out of town for a few days. He won't be a problem after that."

"You think you can put him down?" Daryl asked, incredulous. "One old man with a bad arm and some Opie-looking motherfucker?"

Jack holstered his handgun, stepped forward, and picked Daryl up by the throat with his good hand. He wasn't even straining. He glared at Daryl, and his voice was full of malice. "You give me his name and address or I'm going to start cutting on you and I'm not going to stop. There won't be a piece of you big enough left to identify."

I grabbed Jack's arm. "Jesus, Jack. He's scared to death," I pulled on his arm, but it was firm as steel and didn't waver. "He's just a small time pot dealer," I continued, pointing at the revolver still in

Daryl's hand. "He's probably never even shot that before." I turned to Daryl. "Is it even loaded?"

"Nah, man." He tossed it and it bounced across the carpet, until if skidded to a stop against the far wall. "I didn't mean for none of this to happen, man. I just want to go. Dude's name is Larz Timm. That's like Tim, but with two M's. He's got a place downtown, the basement of a Chinese restaurant."

Jack dropped him and he collapsed in a heap. We turned to go and Daryl stopped me. "You got to be careful. Sounds crazy, but he ain't normal, man."

"Don't worry about us," I said. "Get out of town." I started out after Jack. "And when this is all over? Don't sell drugs," I said over my shoulder. "Drugs are bad."

* * *

The Red Pagoda was near the riverfront, not far from the civic center, nestled between a parking deck and an abandoned antique store. It appeared deserted. The late-afternoon sun was low in the sky and the buildings cast long shadows.

"You sure about this?" I asked.

He sighed. "The good Sister won't heal you without getting her sister back. Can't blame her for that."

"Maybe we should have demanded that she help me first?"

Jack looked at me and his face was cold and hard. "I'd have put a gun in her face and threatened to pull the trigger if I thought it would have helped. She's a strong woman and you can't force someone do the ceremony. They have to want to do it."

Something had been nagging at the back of my mind. "Jack? Why are you doing all this for me?"

He shrugged. "You're my responsibility. I never should have left Arcanum without checking if Silas was there. I'll never forgive myself for that." He got out and stuffed the sawed-off pump shotgun under his duster, then motioned toward the restaurant door. I took the Colt, checked the silver ammo, and put it in the waistband of my jeans.

"Let's do this," he said.

The Red Pagoda had seen better days. The windows were streaked with dust and the faded closed sign in the window was light orange and curled from age. I glanced at Jack. "You sure this is the place?" I looked around. The street was empty, with neither car nor pedestrian in sight.

"Can't you feel it?" Jack asked.

I closed my eyes and concentrated. I could hear the rumble of traffic on I74 just a few blocks away. To the south I heard sounds of the riverfront, the beat-beat of paddles from a paddle-boat leaving its slip, barges floating by on the river, and the occasional buzz of jet-skis in the distance.

I concentrated harder and it hit me, sending a shiver down my spine. Evil. There was a vampire nearby. It raked against my senses, like a physical vibration against my skin. "Yeah, I feel it." A thought occurred to me. "Can you bind it, the way you did those two at my house?"

He blinked. "No. I'd have to get someone to make the devices for me. Those were my last two. We're going to have to do this the hard way." He pulled a small device from his duster. It looked like a little gun, with a thin piece of metal protruding from one end. He inserted the metallic end into the lock of the restaurant door. "How are you feeling?"

I watched him pull the trigger on the gun and I realized he was picking the lock. "Well, a week ago I was fine. Now I'm watching a vampire hunter pick the lock of a restaurant so we can rescue a former nun from a vampire so I can be cleansed of vampire venom before I die and come back as an undead monster."

Jack shot me a long glance. "Sounds crazy."

I sighed. "I'm just going on adrenaline. If I stop to think about it, I might have a nervous breakdown. It's *all* crazy." I stopped. "Jack, what if it doesn't work? What if Sister Callie can't do the ceremony?"

The lock clicked open and Jack smiled at me. "Don't worry, Sam. We'll fix it."

"But what if we don't? Father Jameson said I'd have to make a choice. I don't want to be a monster. I just want my little girl back."

Jack put the lock-pick back in his duster. "What about Stacie? We haven't talked about it, but she's the one who bit you. She wants to turn you. There's no saving her. You know that, right?"

"There's nothing, Jack? In all your years, you haven't seen anything that can help?"

He shook his head. "She's under the influence of her maker. If I kill Silas, then she won't be his to control. But understand, even without Silas influencing her, she won't ever be the woman you loved. She's gone. The *thing* she is now needs blood, and she won't think twice about what she's got to do to get it. Maybe Silas is the one telling her to feed off your daughter." He paused. "Or maybe he isn't."

I brushed past him into the restaurant. "I can't believe that."

Jack followed me in. The smell was overpowering. The tables were still covered in plates and bowls, the food still on them rotted and blackened. It looked for all the world like people had stood and walked out, customers and staff alike. I turned to Jack. "This is weird."

"It's the vampire. When he moved in, it drove them out. They probably don't even know why they left."

"Vampires can do that?"

"They have an aura. It's what you sense. Normals? They can't tell you what they feel or why, but they know something is wrong." He pointed to the door in the corner, covered in so much paint it appeared to be holding the door together. "That leads to the basement." He pulled the shotgun from under his duster. "I don't like to just rush into things like this. We don't have any idea about who this vampire is, where he came from, or how old he is. But if we wait any longer, the sun will go down. He'll be a lot stronger."

"Yeah, and I'm going to die soon, right?"

He blinked. "Surely that is a fact." He slowly opened the door and we looked down at the wooden stairs. The descended a handful of feet, then made a ninety-degree turn. A single dim bulb hung from a bare wire. I flipped the switch, but it cast very little light. "Get ready," he said.

I nodded and pulled the Colt, following Jack down the stairs and into the basement. An overpowering stench made me gag. I could taste it in the back of my throat, the air thick with the putrid smell of old blood.

It was a large room, almost the width of the restaurant. The hard concrete floor had cracks that spread in all directions, and there were a few brick pillars supporting the upper floors. A dirty wooden door was set in a far brick wall. Jack pointed to it and crept forward. My heart hammered in my chest, but I followed close behind. We were almost to the door when it exploded open.

The vampire was upon us.

He moved faster than I could track, knocking the shotgun out of Jack's hands, sending it clattering into the darkness. I tried to aim the Colt but Jack was in the way.

The vampire hit me in the chest hard enough to send me flying back, tumbling across the hard concrete. I looked up in time to see the vampire's hand connect with Jack's head. Jack spun and fell to his knees. The vampire came up behind him and grabbed him by the neck, but Jack's elbow connected with the vampire's mouth and there was a sickening crunch. The vampire wailed, an unholy sound, then hammered Jack in the back of his head.

Jack went down to the concrete floor, unmoving.

I struggled to my knees and the vampire came at me. The face was twisted, muscles and tendons pulled tight. Its eyes were sunken and the pupils were red. They were focused on me the way an animal looks at its prey.

Its razor sharp claws slashed at me. I tried to bat them away, but I wasn't fast enough, and they tore great furrows across my already-wounded neck. I screamed at the sudden pain and felt the hot rush of blood where his claws opened the skin.

The vampire was going to kill me.

Its tongue stretched out and it licked at my neck like I was piece of candy. I shuddered as the coarse tongue worked through the bloody wound, then the vampire spat the blood out and recoiled.

"You've been given the gift," it croaked. "Someone has turned you." It rocked back, smiling wickedly. "Who was it, human? Who gave you the gift?"

I knelt on the floor, looking up at the monstrosity. "My wife."

The vampire's face lit up. "Your wife?" it hissed. "True love gone bad? Exquisite. I can't kill you now. You belong to her." His smile grew even bigger. "Of course, I could make you suffer until you turn. I *could* do that for you. When your heart beats its last beat, you'll see me standing over you. And when you wake, I'll be the first to greet you in your new life."

"That's not going to happen," I managed.

The vampire shrugged. "It is inevitable. You *will* become one of us."

"I'll take my own life before I allow that."

The vampire nodded. "I understand. Even more reason to keep you safe until you turn."

"Leave him alone," a voice spoke up.

A woman stood in the doorway. She was naked and looked closed to death's door, but under the blood, the sores, and the complete filth, I recognized the face.

It was the same as Sister Callie's face. We had found Sister Katie.

The vampire hesitated. "You shouldn't be standing. Go rest. You need your strength."

I used the distraction to put my hand over my neck-wounds, trying to compress the skin and slow the bleeding. "You're Katie," I said. "You're Callie's sister."

The woman nodded. "She sent you?"

The vampire turned to me, and raised an eyebrow. "You've been sent? To do what? Kill me?" He turned back to Jack, laying prone on the floor, and the realization dawned on him. "That's one-eyed Jack. Oh my, this is delicious. I've killed Jack Harlan."

"Callie sent you?" Katie asked.

I nodded. "She said you were taken. She sent us to rescue you."

The vampire laughed, a wheezing sound that grated against the nerves. "She's not going anywhere. I've never tasted sweeter. The blood of a fallen nun? There's nothing like it. She's *my* little meat treat." His tongue darted across his lips, snake-like. "No, she's not going anywhere. I *can't* let her go anywhere." His hand shot out and grabbed my bleeding neck. "I'll kill you before I let you take her."

The pain made my head spin. "I thought you couldn't kill me," I gasped. "I thought I've been given the gift."

The vampire glared at me. "It's rude to take another's young before they turn. Yes, quite gauche. But for my meat treat, I will make an exception." He lifted me up and his eyes found mine. "I'll never let her go. Not now, not ever. If you had tasted her, you would understand."

I saw the madness in his eyes and figured I only had one chance. With all my strength I kicked him in the balls, like I was kicking the longest field goal in history.

He managed an oomph and dropped me to the floor. His eyes got big and his face contorted and I knew that it wasn't enough to stop him.

As he reached for me, there was a deafening roar and his head exploded backwards.

I turned and saw Jack sitting, the giant pistol in his hand. He grinned, and I don't know which was more terrifying, Jack or Timm, then I felt the vampire's hands on me, clawing at my face.

Jack jumped to his feet and sprang across the room. I ducked and he hit the vampire, the two of them flying across the basement. There was a bone rattling crunch when they hit the old brick foundation and it cracked from floor to ceiling. The vampire pushed feebly back at Jack, who pulled a wooden stake from his duster and sank it into the vampire's chest.

That was the end for Larz Timm.

Timm screamed and his eyes widened as his body burned. He staggered across the basement floor to Sister Katie, his arms outstretched, but he only made it half way before he fell to the floor, consumed with fire. Soon he was nothing more than a greasy pile of ash.

I turned to the Sister. Her eyes were big. She nodded weakly, then spat upon the floor. "Fucking vampire," she said.

* * *

Jack dressed Sister Katie in some old clothes we found in Timm's temporary bedroom, and then we took her home.

It was less than a dozen blocks to the diocese, and I shook my head. "How did they not know a vampire was so close? Why didn't the church do something?" I held a handkerchief against my neck, staunching the blood flow.

I was woozy, but still upright. Sister Katie sat between us, her eyes closed. Jack glanced over at her, then at me. "You saw how old the priest is. You think he was out walking the streets at night, looking for vampires? He'd have to have been right at the door-front to have found Timm, and even then, he doesn't have the strength to take on something like that. He's just an old man, now." He grunted. "Just a tired old man."

I wondered if Jack was talking about Father Lewinheim or himself. He attacked Timm like a linebacker, and it was hard to believe that Jack was older than Lewinheim. We drove the rest of the way in silence, then helped Katie through the front door, past the old nun, and to Lewinheim's room.

The priest wasn't there, but Sister Callie was waiting. We filled her in on the details of Katie's rescue, and she glared at her sister. When we were done, she hugged Sister Katie fiercely, who winced at the touch.

"What were you thinking?" Sister Callie demanded. "I can't imagine what was going through your head."

"She's been through enough," Jack warned. "Leave her be. It's time for you to perform the ceremony."

"Jesus, Jack, let her at least get cleaned up first," I said. I smiled at Sister Katie. "You feeling okay?"

Katie shook her head. Her eyes were haunted, her face hollow. "I don't think I'll ever feel okay."

"Whatever possessed you?" Sister Callie asked. "You *knew* about vampires."

"It wasn't like that," Katie responded. "Not at first. It was the church. We never really got to experience the real world. We were shuttled off to America when we were children. Then, reading Father Lewinheim's journals. I couldn't believe it. What kind of God would allow such creatures to exist? Unless there was no God. I started with pot, to help me relax. To forget. Then Daryl got scared. He told me someone was asking about me. And then Larz came." She shuddered. "He said he'd never hurt me, that he wanted to keep me forever. But he kept feeding off me. It hurt, Callie."

Sister Callie hugged her again. "I'm sorry, Katie, you're right, I can't imagine what it was like."

"Every time he fed it was like dying. Every time." Katie looked at me and tears welled up in her eyes. "Thank you, both. I'll never forget what you did for me."

I smiled. "Just glad we could help."

"It wasn't for free," Jack said. "Sam's going to turn soon unless Callie can perform the ceremony."

Sister Callie nodded. "Of course. The chapel is ready and Father Lewinheim is waiting."

"I want to help," Katie said. "It's the least I can do."

"It's not safe," Sister Callie said. "You know that."

"I don't care. I want to be there."

Jack stepped forward. "Sister, maybe it will help if she's there."

Sister Callie debated, then hugged her sister again. "Fine, but you're only there to watch."

Katie nodded. "Just to watch."

* * *

The chapel on the first floor was empty except for Father Lewinheim, who sat in the first pew, head bowed. Sister Callie led the way, an old box under her arm, and Katie, Jack and I followed behind.

The chapel was well-used, the soft glow of lights above playing across the golden brown wooden paneling. I took a deep breath and smelled the age of the chapel, the years of services, the harshness of the stains and lacquers used to preserve the wood.

It looks like a decent place to die.

I put the thought out of my mind. The ceremony *had* to work. I walked down the carpeted aisle and stopped. A large crucifix hung behind the altar. I stared at the figure of Jesus, his pain evident, bloody spikes through his palms and a bleeding gash across his side.

His eyes were painted solid white, as if rolled back in agony. I could relate. I had never given religion much thought, but I was seriously considering the big questions.

Like, whether there was a God and what he thought of all this.

I agreed with Katie, I wasn't sure what kind of God would allow creatures like vampires to exist. Or maybe God just didn't care anymore. I nodded at the crucifix.

If you're listening, I need help.

Sister Callie waited at the front. The carpet had a light spot where the podium stood, but it was now pushed against the far wall. She appeared confident. I wished I was. My body felt like I'd gone ten rounds with a dump truck, the bloody wounds on my neck throbbed, and I was feeling tired. In fact, I was past exhausted. Jack's words kept playing in the back of my mind.

Surely, it was a fact. I was going to die.

Father Lewinheim lifted his head and I could tell that he hadn't been praying. He'd been sleeping. He nodded at me with red-rimmed eyes. When he turned his gaze upon Sister Callie, his face softened.

I could tell he cared for the young Sister. Then he switched his gaze to Katie and his face hardened.

On the other hand, forgiveness might not be Lewinheim's strong suit.

The Sister nodded at me. "Are you ready?"

Jack clapped me on the shoulder. "You'll be fine."

I took a deep breath. "What do I do?"

"Just lay down," the Sister said. She opened the box and took out two candles.

I sat on the carpet, then stretched out, staring up at the arched ceiling. My eyes burned and I rubbed at them, barely able to keep them open.

The Sister lit the candles and placed them in silver candlestick holders, one at my feet and one above my head.

"The candles are for purity," Father Lewinheim said. "Callie, are you sure you want to do this?"

"Yes," the Sister answered. "I know the words."

"It's not the words I'm worried about," the old priest said. "It's going to test you, Callie. Once you start, you must not stop. No matter what, you *must not stop*."

I saw Katie out of the corner of my eye, crossing herself. Apparently the rescue from Timm had reignited her faith.

Sister Callie bent over. "Relax, Samuel Fisher. Feel the power of the Lord flow through you."

I looked into her emerald green eyes and nodded. "Do it."

She pulled an old leather book from the box. I could smell the musty paper even from the floor. She began to read in a language I didn't understand, but it sounded like Latin. What I did understand was the growing look of concentration on her face, as beads of sweat rolled down her forehead. She absently wiped at them away and kept reading, the words becoming more of a chant.

Then it hit me.

Nothing in my life prepared me for the pain I felt. Every nerve in my body fired at once and it felt like I was being electrocuted. My heart was pounding as liquid fire boiled through me. Stacie's venom had infected me, and it had mingled with my blood. It was in every artery and every vein.

Now those arteries and veins were a scalding flame, consuming me from the inside.

I screamed so hard I gagged on my own tongue. I tried to gasp for air, but my lungs weren't working. I convulsed, arching up from the floor, my back completely off the carpet, the weight of my body carried by my heels and the back of my head, and I could feel the joints cracking and popping.

"That's it," Father Lewinheim shouted. "It's working!"

If this is working, I'd prefer death.

I collapsed back to the floor and was finally able to take a ragged breath before the wave of fire hit again. This time the scream didn't even make it past my throat. It went on for an eternity, but when I collapsed back, I turned and saw Jack, looking on with concern, and realized it must have been seconds.

Katie stood next to Jack, her face pale, her emerald eyes wide in shock. Father Lewinheim's face was aghast.

He had known all along the agony I would suffer. For a moment, I felt anger toward the old Priest, but then I remembered. I was dying. This was my only chance.

I tried to tell Sister Callie to continue, but only managed a weak croak. She continued anyway, the chanting picking up speed, and she turned her head skyward, tendons bulging in her neck, her hands clenched into fists.

Every heartbeat was like a cannon firing. I had an insane image of my heart exploding through my chest. The electric fire surged and I arched, muscles spasming, and I wondered if it was possible for a human being's muscles to lock into that position.

I had the absurd notion that they would hospitalize me, the doctors showing the effects of a vampire cleansing, the poor victim reduced to a sideshow freak from the aftermath.

Time lost all sense of meaning. All that was left was the endless string of words, until they receded, growing fainter, and then it was still.

I stood alone, in a room of pure white, and I knew that it was a construct of my imagination, a safe room I had created. I stood in that room and the pain gradually faded. The silence was absolute.

I'm dead.

No, that wasn't right. I wasn't dead. Just somewhere else.

I had never been deeply religious, but I thought maybe I was in Purgatory.

No, that's not right, either.

I heard a voice behind me. I turned and found a mirror, tall and wide, my image reflected in it. The man in the mirror was speaking.

"You're not dead, Sam," my image said. "Not yet. You have to choose."

"Choose what?" I asked.

"You know the answer. I'm you, Sam. The part that's been holding on for dear life. *Your* life was good, but your wife wasn't happy. You pretended not to see it."

I started to protest, but my image raised a hand. "Don't lie. Not to me. I'm the real you, the primal you. All I want to do is to eat and fuck and sleep, then do it all over again. I'm never truly satisfied. I think being a vampire is probably a lot like that. All just primal need. But, you have to choose. Are you going to give in? It's not all bad, you know. Think of all that happens because of primal need."

"And if I do?"

I smiled back at me. "If you do, then the ceremony fails and either Jack kills you, you kill yourself, or you turn into a vampire."

I considered that. "And if I don't?"

"Then you choose life. You fight that need. Be warned—it's insatiable. You'll never be the same."

I nodded at me. "I don't think I've been the same since the night Stacie was taken. I thought I knew the world. Turns out I was wrong about everything. I just wish I had my family back."

Mirror me nodded in agreement. "Good point. So, choose life and save your daughter." My image in the mirror dissolved, and was replaced by Stacie, her arms wrapped around Lilly. Lilly's smile was sweet and innocent, but Stacie's wasn't.

Stacie's smile was perverse, her eyes turned down to Lilly—not in a mother's love—but in a hunger that screamed to be sated.

"I'm dreaming," I said. "This is all a dream and I'll wake up back in Arcanum. Stacie will still be asleep next to me. Lilly will still be in her bed, down the hall."

Stacie licked her lips, pink tongue darting across them, but I heard my voice speak. "You really think that? You think this is just a dream? It's the vampire venom, that and the essence of that vampire you absorbed. You don't even know enough to be scared, Sam. It's sad. Are you prepared to do what you must to save your daughter? There's a cost. There's *always* a cost."

"What the hell does that mean?"

The voice laughed and the white room faced to black, then my eyes opened wide and I screamed in agony while Jack held me down.

Father Lewinheim knelt beside me. "Something is wrong," he shouted.

I stopped screaming long enough to manage a question. "What happened?"

"We don't know," Jack said.

Sister Callie was on the floor, shaking violently. She was still chanting and I heard each incomprehensible word ring like a bell in my head.

I felt a ripping from within and my head exploded with light. I opened my mouth and took the deepest breath of my life, and when I exhaled a dark cloud spewed forth, moving like a thing alive.

The cloud spun in the air, a whirling dervish of inky black, then slammed into Sister Callie. Her screams joined mine, forming one long cacophony of rage and fear and pain. She spoke the last word and there was something akin to shattering glass, then sudden silence.

Father Lewinheim raced to Callie's side, but she did not move. Katie watched in horror as the priest shook her. "Callie! Callie! Wake up, child. Wake up!"

It was no use. Sister Callie lay as unmoving as the dead.

Jack watched, mutely. He shook his head and blinked his good eye. I tried to sit up, but I didn't have the energy. I managed to sit and stare at the motionless form of Sister Callie.

Father Lewinheim turned to Jack, his face red. "What have you done?"

CHAPTER SEVEN

Sister Callie lay in Father Lewinheim's bed. Katie sat at her side, holding Callie's hand. Jack and Father Lewinheim stood near the door to Lewinheim's apartment, arguing.

I interrupted them. "Father, what's wrong with her?"

He shook his head. "If the ceremony was successful, she should be tired, but otherwise unharmed. Instead, she appears to be in a coma. This has never happened before."

"That *you* know of," Jack said. "You were listening. Did she say the correct words?"

"Yes," the priest said wearily. "She performed the ceremony exactly as written."

"Are you sure she's of the blood?" Jack asked.

"What does that mean?" I asked. "What does blood have to do with any of this?"

The priest sighed. "It was a long time ago. A thousand years, more or less. A dozen families united to fight the vampires in Britain. Some were English nomads, some Celtic warriors. They killed a vampire and took his blood and used it as the basis for a ritual. A vampire's body—its blood and its skin—has certain magical properties. These families found they could infuse themselves with the blood, with the vampires energy, and with that power and their faith in Jesus Christ, they could cleanse someone of vampire venom. In the years since, the families have devoted themselves to fighting the evil scourge. My own family comes from that line. Even through the centuries, even with all the intermarrying, the bloodline still continues. The girls are the same. The Calahane bloodline remains a strong member of the church, both in England and Ireland."

"At one time the families were numbered in the tens of thousands," Jack said. "But over the last century, the numbers have shrank."

"Yes," the priest agreed. "There are fewer of us now. Plus, as you know, once we give ourselves to the Lord, we are not allowed to have children."

I understood his point. Much like my dying hometown, they were a victim of a dwindling population. "The Calahanes were one of these families?"

The priest nodded. "A long time ago, yes."

A thousand years?

It sounded ridiculous, but Sister Callie lay motionless on the bed and I was alive. Even my neck wounds had finally scabbed over. "What happened to the Sister?" I asked. "Whatever she did, it worked."

The priest shook his head. "It doesn't make sense. Unless…."

"Unless what?" Jack asked.

The priest turned and eyed me critically. "You weren't just infected." His eyes widened in horror. "Had you killed a vampire?"

"Yeah," I said. "A guy named Munzinger, the night my wife was turned."

The priest's legs buckled. "Oh, no."

Jack caught the old man before he could collapse. "Edmund?"

"You don't understand," the priest said. "The ceremony must not be performed on someone who's been changed."

"I thought that was the point," I said. "To cleanse the infection."

The priest shook his head, face ashen. "Not the vampire's venom. When you killed the vampire, it changed you. The ceremony only works if the victim was bitten, not if they had a vampire's essence." He glared at Jack. "You should have told me. You don't know what you've done."

Jack looked startled. "I didn't know, Edmund, I swear I didn't. What can I do? How can I fix this?"

Tears welled up in the old man's eyes. "I don't know. There may be nothing. The poor girl may die."

"There's *got* to be something," Jack said. "Something we can try."

Katie had quietly joined us. "What's wrong, Father? What happened to Callie?"

The priest told her and Katie turned to Jack. "You've got to fix this! She can't die because of me!"

Jack shrank back from her fury, his face wooden. "How could I have known? With everything action I take…." He sat on the Father's recliner, hunched forward. He looked up at the priest in anguish. "Where is your God, Father? Why does He allow this to happen? Is He punishing us? Does He even care?"

He yanked his arm from the sling, snapping the fabric. He gripped the edges of the recliner and squeezed, muscles in his arms standing out like rope, his knuckles white. I heard the wood inside the arms crack and then splinter. "Tell me, Father, because I have no faith in Him. Do you understand? Not after all I've seen. You tell me! Why does He allow this?"

The old priest sagged, deflated. "I don't know. I've thought about it over the years, even prayed on it. I just don't have the answers."

"Can't you think of something," Katie implored. "Father?"

The old man spoke slowly. "Tell me, Jack, this Munzinger that Samuel killed. Who turned him?"

"Silas."

"And who turned this woman who bit Samuel?"

"Silas."

The old man nodded, thinking. "The interaction between Munzinger's essence and the woman's venom must have combined in some way to turn back on Callie. Because of her bloodline it's trapped within her. What do you know about Silas? Who turned him?"

"That vampire is dead," Jack said, voice heated. "A long time ago."

The priest started to ask a question but stopped when he saw the look on Jack's face. "If the bloodline stops with Silas then perhaps killing him will free Callie."

"What about killing the woman?" Katie asked softly.

"You're talking about killing my wife," I said.

Jack shook his head. "I told you, Sam. She's gone. She tried to turn you. She's feeding off your daughter. What do you want? Do you want Lilly back? You'll *have* to kill her. You need to make a choice. Kill your wife and save your child. Or, try and save your wife. That way will get only get Lilly killed, I guarantee it. And, not just your child. Sister Callie can't last long like this. Right, Father?"

The priest nodded. "She can't be turned by the venom and the vampire essence can't find a home in her. Her blood and her faith will sustain her, but yes, eventually she will die."

Katie nodded. "We can't let that happen."

I just stared at Jack. Something had been gnawing at me. Of all the crazy things I had seen over the last week, it finally hit me. Jack was old. He was much older than the Jameson. What terrible things had happened to him over the years? "Jack? Jameson told me you've killed more vampires than anyone. Is that true?"

His world-weary face gazed back. "That's a fact."

"And killing Silas might free Callie?"

"That's conjecture."

I continued. "You've been hunting Silas for a long time, haven't you?"

"Yes."

"Why haven't you killed him yet?"

Jack shrugged. "Because he's strong, Sam. You saw Timm."

Katie shuddered at his name and Father Lewinheim took her hand in his, squeezing gently.

"He was strong and it was still daylight," Jack continued. "Imagine how strong he would have been once the sun set."

"But we killed him," I said.

"It was close."

"That's because your arm is broken. Was broken." I pointed to it. "How could it heal so fast?"

Jack sighed. "I heal a lot quicker than I used to."

"It's the vampire essence," Father Lewinheim said quietly. "It's changed you."

Jack looked up. "It's still changing me, Edmund. You know it is."

The priest nodded. "I figured as much. You haven't aged in years, have you?"

Jack shook his head.

"Then surely *you* can kill Silas," I said. "How many vampires have you killed? How can Silas be so different?"

"Because he is," Jack spat out. "He's old and he's smart and he's strong. I've never been able to catch him in daylight. I've tried, Sam. You don't know. I've killed his younglings whenever I find them, dozens over the years, but he always escapes. He's dedicated his entire existence to tormenting me. Can you understand what that means? He doesn't care about anything or anyone. He just wants to make me suffer!" He stood, lightning quick, his good eye fixed on me. "He won't ever stop! Not ever! Vampires are the purest form of evil. You don't know what that means yet, and I pray you never will. You should *never* have been caught up in this!"

I felt my stomach sink. Everything Jack said rang of truth, but there was something else, something nagging at me. "Why did he come to my house?" I asked. "Why does that torment you?"

Jack turned away. "Don't ask me that."

I felt a churning in my gut. There was something there, something he was hiding. Katie and the priest watched the exchange silently. "Tell me, damn it! Why did he come to my house? Why did he turn my wife?"

The old priest took a step forward but stopped when Jack fixed him with a stare. "You *must* tell him," the priest said.

I turned from Jack to Lewinheim. "Tell me what?"

The priest started to speak, then shook his head. "It's not my secret."

I knew something was coming, I felt it in my bones. "What secret? Jack, what's he talking about? What *aren't* you telling me?"

Jack tuned his good eye back to me. "Silas came to your house because of me. Because of who I am to you."

Part of me didn't want to know. That part screamed to stop, but I was so close to finally learning the truth, I just had to know. "What are you to me?"

"Your kin."

* * *

I stared at Jack. "That's impossible."

Jack sat back in the Father's recliner. "Your mother, Sam. Karen was my great-great-granddaughter. You're my great-great-great-grandson."

I couldn't believe it. "That can't be. It's a mistake."

"There's no mistake. My son, William changed his name to Miller. William Miller. He had a boy David, and David had a girl, Linda. She married and had a girl of her own. Karen. Your mother."

I remembered back to what my father had said about my mom's side of the family. They all died before I was born. My mom died when I was only a child. I remembered something my father said, once, about my grandmother. Linda Weaver. It made sense. Karen Weaver to Linda Weaver, Linda Weaver to David Miller, David Miller to William Miller, William Miller to Jack.

Anger knifed through me. "Why didn't you tell me before? Why hide the truth?" The sickening realization dawned on me. "It's because of Silas, isn't it?"

Jack bowed his head. "Yes. He killed my wife, Mary. He told me I would never know peace, that he'd torment me the rest of my life. He's been true to his word. He killed my daughter and son, Clara and

Jacob. I took William and ran. We made it to Pittsburgh and changed William's name. I hunted vampires—killed them where I could—but Silas was always just outside my grasp. Somehow he found William, waited until William had children of his own, then killed him. When William's son David had children, he killed David's brother, Frank, and his sister, Emma. He's made it a tradition." He took a deep breath. "I've tried to save them, but he always escapes. I've watched my family die, generation after generation."

Horrified, I asked, "My mother?"

Jack looked at me and tears flowed from his good eye. "She didn't die in a car wreck, Sam. It was Silas."

I felt like I'd been punched in the gut. Father Lewinheim looked at me sadly and Katie's face was a mask of shock. I wanted to throw up. "Silas killed my mother? Why didn't you tell me? Wait, did my father know?" I felt panic rising. "Did Silas kill my father, too?"

Jack shook his head. "No, your dad died of a heart-attack. Silas had nothing to do with it."

A million questions raced through my mind, but I waited for him to continue.

"You have to understand," Jack said, "I've been watching over you your whole life. From afar. I was afraid if I met you, told you about who I was or what kind of threat Silas represented, that it might put you in more danger. Ever since Lilly was born I've been tracking Silas, trying to keep him tied up in Chicago or Indianapolis. He slipped by about four years ago, but I managed to kill one of his children. He let you be, until the diner. I'm sorry. It's all my fault."

"But why? Why does he hate you so much?"

Jack sank back in the father's chair, lost in memory. "Because I killed his maker. Sometimes when you kill their maker it frees them. Like the Father said, it can break the blood line. Other times it drives them mad. It drove Silas mad."

"You killed his maker?"

"Yes. She attacked us and we managed to drive her off, but when she came back, I killed her. I didn't know what she was. I didn't even know what I was doing. Silas swore revenge."

I felt the world crashing around me. I thought that learning about vampires was the biggest shock I would ever face.

Until now.

"Jack, I don't know what to say. The whole things is just—"

He shook his head. "Crazy? I know. It doesn't do any good to wallow in it. I tried. The only thing you can do is keep going, keep fighting. Because if we stop, the Sister dies. And Lilly, too."

* * *

I paced the Father's room. It was near midnight and the Father was asleep in his recliner. The day's events had taken its toll, until he was barely able to keep his eyes open while talking with Jack.

Jack sat on the floor, his back against the wall, and I was shocked at how tired he looked. He had removed his leather trench-coat and his faded blue denim shirt hung loose on him. He opened his good eye and caught me staring. "I'm not sleeping," he said. "Just resting my eye."

I laughed at the absurdity of it. Jack was my great-great-great grandfather and he was over one hundred and forty years old. Then I remembered what was at stake, and my smile faltered. "What are we going to do?"

Jack closed his eye. "I've got an idea. Silas turned a man about eighty years ago, name of Barlow. Silas let him go, just turned him right out. He's never done that, before or since. Barlow lives in Indianapolis, keeps a low profile. I know where he lives."

I stared at him. "Then why haven't you killed him?"

Jack opened his eye and squinted, the silence long and uncomfortable.

"Because you thought you might need him," I concluded. "What about Barlow's victims? Aren't you responsible for them?"

Jack exhaled slowly. "I can't save everyone, boy. I haven't even been able to save my own family. Don't judge me. You haven't got the years or seen the tragedies. I hoped for better for you. I hoped for better for *all* of you. To see what Silas has done? The worst thing that can happen is outliving your children. To outlive your grandchildren? Silas knew I would give my own life to save them. That's why he hasn't killed me yet. It makes me suffer."

He was right. I couldn't begin to understand what he had seen through the years. "It's not your fault, Jack. Should I call you Jack?"

Jack frowned. "Keep calling me Jack. You call me great anything and I'll kick your ass."

The door creaked open as Stacie returned to the Father's room with sandwiches from the building's kitchen. I wolfed down a turkey club, and then another. Sister Callie may have saved my life, but my hunger was back.

Jack opened his eye and accepted the sandwich Katie offered, then closed it, eating mechanically.

Katie nibbled at hers and I caught her watching me.

"What?"

She took a deep breath. "I want to come with you."

Jack didn't even open his eye. "Out of the question."

"Hear me out," she said, voice rising.

"No need," Jack said. "There's no way this conversation ends with you in my truck." He finished his sandwich and wiped his hands on his shirt. "You'll get killed or get Sam killed. I won't have your death on my hands." He opened his eye and nodded at Callie stretched out on the Father's bed. "Bad enough the Sister got involved."

"That's why I have to go," she pleaded. "It's my fault. She would never have agreed to help if it wasn't for me. It's my fault," she repeated, tears running down her cheeks.

Jack opened his eye, regarded her for a moment, then shook his head. "She wouldn't have helped if Sam hadn't been bitten. That's *my* fault. It's *all* on me."

She scowled. "Why do you blame yourself for the actions of that monster?"

"Because, girl. If I had done my job, Silas would be dead. I wouldn't have spent my life killing vampires, and my kin would have lived and prospered."

"You're just one man," I said. "You can't hold yourself responsible. Katie's right."

"It's not an argument. She's not going. I don't want to hear another word."

Katie bit her lip and I knew the issue was far from over. She was eager to place the blame upon herself, just like Jack.

She was also stubborn, just like Jack.

"Get some sleep," Jack said. "I'm wore out and I know you must be, too. We'll leave in the morning."

Katie shook her head and looked to me for support. I shrugged, helplessly, and she rolled her eyes. I stretched out on the floor and lay my head on the tiny pillow Katie had scrounged. The rug provided scant comfort, and even though my body was relaxing, my mind was racing.

I turned my head and watched Katie crawl into bed, next to her sister, and turn off the light.

Jack was right. I *was* tired. I was also jittery. And, afraid. Even so, I was the tiniest bit happy. I wasn't alone in the world.

Jack said it best. I was kin.

I watched the shadows in the room, the light peeking from under the hallway door providing little illumination, and my brain played tricks as every shadow became Silas, or one of his younglings, coming to kill me. Given all I had been through, I knew it would be a long time before I felt comfortable in a dark room.

My brain replayed the fight against Timm, then Stacie dead on the kitchen floor. Lilly shrieked as Silas swept her out the back door and into the night.

I reached behind the pillow and found the Colt. I wrapped my hand around the cool grips, then pulled it close to me, reassured by its heavy weight.

A long time before I feel comfortable.

My eyes closed and I was surprised as my mind finally slowed, and then blissful sleep claimed me.

* * *

I jerked awake, the creaking of floorboards sending me into a panic. The room was dark and I had no idea how long I had slept, but as the Colt came up, I realized the dark form in front of me was Katie.

She was on her hands and knees, leaning into me, her eyes watching mine. My heart slowed and I stopped shaking, the gun barrel dropping.

Katie didn't say a word as she came close, then hesitatingly snuggled next to me, her eyes still on mine.

It was the simplest of human needs. The need to hold and be held, the intimate act of skin touching skin. I felt her body heat, radiating against me. I hadn't noticed, but now that she had cleaned up, she was actually quite beautiful, with dark red hair and emerald green eyes, a light dusting of freckles across her nose.

She was close enough that I smelled the lingering mint of her toothpaste. Her skin smelled fresh and clean, a result of the scrubbing she had given herself when we got her home.

It wasn't sexual. Not exactly. More like two broken people connecting in the dark. She held me and I held her and I felt tears on my cheek, a reaction to the stress and horror. I felt a hot wetness against my neck, running down over the scabby wound to my neck, and I knew that she was shedding her own tears for Callie, for what she had put Callie through, and for what Larz Timm had done to her.

We held each other in the dark and I felt the connection, different than what I had felt with Stacie or any other woman. We had something, a deep and primitive connection. We had survived.

There was a sudden intake of breath from Jack, then a wheezing snore. Moments after, Father Lewinheim joined in, the raggedy noise alternating between the two.

Katie squeezed me tight and I heard the slightest giggle from her. I joined in with my own quiet laugh and, like that, the moment was broken. I felt her relax, and then a slight jerk from her body, a twitch as she gave herself to sleep, then another. Soon her breathing was deep and slow. I sighed, then felt my body relax until I joined her.

* * *

Saturday

The sound of boots thumping across the floor woke me. Sunlight streamed through the thin curtains over the window, and I knew morning had come. Katie was gone.

Jack stood in her place. He smiled. "Ready?"

I groaned and managed, "I was born ready."

He reached down and yanked me upright. "Next time, try a little more sincerity."

I nodded, and felt my neck crack and pop. I vaguely remembered Katie taking my pillow in the middle of the night, leaving me to rest my head on the worn carpet. I stretched my head from side to side until the cracking and popping finally subsided.

Jack prodded Father Lewinheim awake, who looked at us with crusty tired eyes, rubbing them with his fingers. "Where's Katie?" Lewinheim asked.

Jack shrugged. "Getting breakfast, if she's smart. Sam and I have to go. We think we have a way to find Silas."

The old priest glanced back at Sister Callie, who was still in the priest's bed. "Good luck, Jack. God bless you."

Jack bowed his head. "Thank you, Edmund. I promise we'll do all we can for her."

I shook the old man's hand. "Thank you, Father. For everything. We'll find a way. Jack won't let you down."

I barely noticed Jack's sidelong glance. As we were walking down the hallway to the stairs, Jack spoke. "Nice moves in there with Katie."

I turned to him. "It wasn't like that."

"Sure it wasn't," he said, mouth quirked up in a rare grin. "It only makes sense. You helped rescue her from a monster. Your wife tried to kill you. Two ships in the night, is all I'm saying. I get it. It makes sense."

"You've got it all wrong," I protested. "We were just...comforting each other."

"I'm not judging, boy. If there's one thing I've learned, you take comfort where you can get it. Just remember what she's been through. And, what you've been through. We don't have time for distractions."

We took the stairs down to the lobby. The old nun was still there, listening to her Walkman, eyeballing us as we headed for the front door. Jack gave her a toothy smile and she dipped her head in a silent salute. I wondered if she knew what had happened the day before, or if she knew who and what we were.

From the steel in her eyes, I believe she did.

We walked the half-block to the parking lot, the crisp September morning a nice contrast to the oppressive heat we had been experiencing. The thin strip of grass surrounding the parking lot was wet with morning dew and the sun cast a red baleful eye through purple clouds to the east. I blinked up at the great ball of fire in the sky and realized how glad I was to still be alive to see it.

It's funny how you take little things for granted and it's funny how you notice them once you've been close to death. Coffee, for instance. In the diner, coffee was the lifeblood. It was cheap, drew in the crowd, and glued the community together.

Katie waited in Jack's truck, a paper tray with three large cups of steaming coffee in her lap. Jack's face hardened as he opened the driver's door, but Katie's face was a rigid mask.

She spoke first. "I'm going." She thrust one of the coffees into his hand.

He looked at me and chewed his lip. "Who am I to argue with a lady?" He slid in next to her and cast a forlorn eye at me through the cracked passenger window. I sighed and yanked on the crumpled passenger door until it opened with a screech.

Katie smiled as she handed me the coffee. "It's from the Huck's down the street. I didn't get creamer, just sugar. If you want some."

She handed me a handful of sugar packets and I took them with a weary shrug, then slammed the passenger door shut. "Welcome to team Jack," I said.

CHAPTER EIGHT

We pulled into Indianapolis during the mid-morning rush, the Interstate exchanges snarled with traffic thanks to the massive construction project that seemed determined to ruin many people's mornings. Jack navigated slowly through the mess, then continued to downtown, until we found ourselves parked across from what appeared to be an abandoned two-story brick warehouse. The tall buildings were plainly visible in the skyline, and I squinted at it skeptically. "You sure this is the place?"

"I'm sure." He opened the door and Katie started to follow, but Jack put a hand on her shoulder. "Absolutely not."

"I'm going with you," she said stubbornly. She reached under her shirt and pulled out a silver crucifix. It dangled from her hand by a large chain. "I have my faith."

Jack eyed me, then her. "The faith you gave up so quickly? The faith that led you to drugs? The faith that led you to a vampire? You know what vampires can do," he said surprisingly gentle. "I can't protect both of you."

"I also have my blood," Katie said, defiantly. "The blood of a Calahane."

Jack paused, then nodded as he came to a decision. "I don't think Barlow is a threat, but just in case, stay behind me. Better yet, stay behind Sam and keep that crucifix ready."

I mouthed a quick thank you to Jack and we followed him across the deserted street to the front of the warehouse. Jack carried his spare shotgun under his duster and I carried the Colt, firmly holstered on my hip. Katie clutched the crucifix, holding it over her chest.

I wondered if we looked as ridiculous as I thought, then I remembered what we were facing and the humor evaporated.

As we approached the door I felt the electric surge against the back of my teeth, a profound sense of wrong. I glanced at Jack who glanced at me quizzically.

"There's definitely a vampire near," I whispered to Katie.

Her face paled, but she held the crucifix as if her life depended on it. "I'm ready."

The door was wood, with a frosted glass top. It had thick coats of rippling red paint and Jack opened it slowly, then stepped carefully inside. I followed, Katie bringing up the rear. We were in another dark hallway, a matching red door at the end barely visible in the dim light. Jack held up his hand and I stopped. Katie bumped into me and grunted.

The door creaked shut behind us and Jack turned his eye on Katie, who looked both terrified and apologetic. I strained, listening for movement, but it was silent. Jack pulled the shotgun from under his duster and took a step forward, then another. We crept like that down the hallway, our feet stirring the thick coat of dust, always listening, ready to fight for our lives.

The stillness was absolute.

We reached the end of the hallway and Jack put his hand on the door, then yanked it back. He shook his hand like he had been shocked, then inspected the dented brass doorknob.

"What?" I whispered.

"I don't like this," he answered.

"Why?"

"Something's wrong. Can't you feel it?"

I turned to Katie. The hallway stretched out behind her, the darkness broken only by the light that entered through the frosted glass panel in the top of the door. Katie held her crucifix in a death grip and I smiled, reassuringly, but I knew Jack was correct. Something was not right.

Jack turned the doorknob and pressed against the door. He took a deep breath, then swung the door wide.

We were staring down another dim hallway, identical to the one in which we stood.

Jack kicked the door with his boot, knocking it completely off its hinges. "Sonuvabitch!"

"What? What is it?"

Jack ran down the hallway and opened the next door. Another hallway stretched out beyond. He turned to look at me and I saw anger in his face, and something else. He was afraid.

My heart sank as he yelled, "Go back," running to us.

I turned and found Katie already halfway back to the street-front door. She yanked it open, but instead of the street, another hallway stretched beyond, a red wooden door with a frosted glass panel at the end, the frosted glass panel glowing faintly with daylight.

I turned to Jack. "What the hell? How could there be another hallway? We *just* came from the street."

Jack went running past us, all the way to the door. He raised the shotgun and pulled the trigger, the blast echoing in a deafening roar down the hallway. The frosted glass exploded outward and I could barely discern another red door in the distance.

He walked back, the gun hanging low, scowling. "We're trapped."

* * *

"How can we be trapped?" I asked. "Why are there so many hallways? What happened to the street?" Katie pressed close against me, and I felt her trembling.

Jack shook his head. "Magic," he said. "It's magic."

"Magic?" I sputtered. "This is where I draw the line. I can accept vampires, but magic?"

Jack pointed down the hall. "Accept it quick, because we're stuck in it. We can walk in either direction, but we'll never get out."

I heard Katie whisper, "A magical trap. Lord, please help us."

A booming voice echoed through the hallway. "The Lord won't be helping you out of this, I'm afraid." The voice suggested a man of middle age, and had a lilt to it, a way of speaking that reminded me of Jack's.

Jack sniffed the air, the way a dog picks up a scent. "Barlow? I know it's you."

"Jack Harlan. Come to visit or to kill? Mr. Harlan, what *are* your intentions."

Jack snarled. "Let us out of this trap or you're going to find out."

There was a soft mirthless laugh. "That's exactly why I *won't* release you. Better you stay there until you speak politely. Or, die of thirst. It's a distinct possibility, you know. A human can only go three days without water. I'd give you five, Mr. Harlan."

I put my hand on Jack's shoulder. "Maybe we should try talking to him."

Jack glared at me. "He's a vampire. You don't listen to evil. You kill it."

"I can *hear* you, Mr. Harlan. How can I seriously consider your request for freedom when you make it abundantly clear you plan on killing me?"

I shrugged at Jack. "He has a point."

"He's a monster. Don't ever forget that," Jack said, turning his glare down the hallway. "What do you want?"

"What do I want?" The voice went from polite amusement to a dull roar. "Why did you come to my house? Why are you threatening me?"

"We came for information," I said, grabbing Jack's arm before he could answer. "We need to know about Silas."

The silence lingered. Finally, "Jack? Can I call you Jack? You were here, in 1962, if I remember correctly. You knew I was near, but you left. Odd behavior for a vampire hunter. Why?"

"You weren't killing anymore," Jack muttered. "I watched you for weeks. You overcame your hunger."

The door at the end of the hallway opened and a dumpy little man with a receding hairline stepped out. He was dressed in a plain black shirt and sweat pants, and his beady eyes and doughy face were pasty white, but when he smiled, his face lit up. "Yes, I did. Thank you for noticing." He held out his arms. "Please, I mean you know harm."

"You're a vampire," Jack said. "All you *mean* is harm."

I heard Katie gasp and I turned as the silver crucifix she held glowed, the blinding light blazing, casting long shadows down the hall.

Barlow held his hand over his eyes, shrinking back against the wall. "Please put that away, young lady," he said. "It hurts. If I meant to kill you, I would simply leave you here."

Katie turned to Jack, who nodded slowly. She put the crucifix under her shirt and we all turned back to the vampire who waited patiently at the end of the hallway.

He regarded us with interest. "Why do you look for Silas?"

"If we kill him," I said, "we save this woman's sister. Also, he's got my daughter." I paused. "Well, he turned my wife and *she's* got my daughter."

Barlow watched us, waiting for the others to speak, but Jack and Katie just nodded in agreement. "If you promise to refrain from foolishness," he finally said, "I will grant you an invite to my home."

We nodded and the vampire turned and motioned for us to follow.

The hallway opened to the main floor of the warehouse, the bare wooden floor covered in dirt and grime. "Sorry about the sad state of affairs. We don't entertain visitors."

I turned to Jack. "We?" I mouthed.

He shrugged and put the shotgun under his duster.

We trudged up a long flight of stairs to the second floor, the wooden steps creaking under our weight, then through a door and into a formal living room.

A formal living room as it might have appeared in the thirties.

Peeling gray wallpaper covered the walls, gaps exposing plaster and lath. The floors held tattered rugs, and a doorway led to what appeared to be a kitchen. An ancient sofa stood against one wall where a woman lay on the couch, her body shrunken, her hair thin and white. I was tempted to dismiss her as catatonic until I saw her eyes turn to us. They were bright and sharp and full of anger.

A cold wind blew around us, and I felt the air pressure drop, like it was being sucked from the room. My ears popped.

Barlow approached the woman and took her skeletal hand in his. "Eva, please. They are guests."

The woman's eyes narrowed, but the wind slowed and finally came to a stop.

Barlow bowed his head. "You have to forgive my wife. She doesn't like strangers. Especially strangers who want to kill me."

I reeled in shock. I had just seen magic. Jack shocked me even more by bowing back. "Beg your pardon, Ma'am. No offense intended. I promise that no harm shall come from me or mine."

The old woman's breath rattled deep in her chest. She harumphed, but her eyes softened and she nodded her ancient head.

Jack turned to Barlow. "She's a witch."

"She's the one who built my hallway. A few other things, as well."

Jack raised an eyebrow. "For me?"

Barlow nodded. "For you. For others like you, should it come to that, though hardly anyone knows I exist. I have taken pains to remain hidden these many years."

Jack eyed him critically. "How did you do it?"

Barlow smiled. "You came for Silas and that's your first question? The answer is simple. It just happened."

"Silas turned you," I asked. "When was that?"

Barlow regarded me thoughtfully. "And you are?"

"He's Sam," Jack said quickly. "Just Sam."

Barlow's gaze shifted from Jack to me. "Well, just Sam, it was July, 1932. A terrible time for me. The stock market reached its lowest point, the great depression was raging, and Silas found me walking home on a hot summer night. I think he meant to feed, but something tickled his fancy. Perhaps he thought it comical, making a man such as me a vampire." Barlow spun around slowly, displaying his diminutive height and ample girth. "I'm sure a young man such as yourself can't imagine what it is like to be plain and ordinary. So underwhelming. Instead of feeding, he gave me the gift. I died the next night."

"And you fed," Jack said.

"Of course," Barlow said, shrugging. "I fed as an animal, to sustain myself, to quench my thirst. I had never known such hunger, but Silas was there to help me. To guide me." Barlow smiled bitterly. "What Silas did *not* know was that my wife was a witch. She knew I had been bitten. She knew I would turn." He smiled fondly at his wife. She blinked slowly at him, then nodded her head.

"I was unaware of the true nature of the world," he continued. "I was unaware of my wife's power. But, as I lay dying, she told me about her world, the world she had kept so carefully hidden from me. She also read my fate. She held my hand as I passed." He turned back to us and his eyes held the same angry depth that I had seen in the other vampires. "She was gone before I awoke, fled from our house. She knew what I would become. I tried to make sense of what had happened, but the hunger consumed me. Silas was waiting. He guided me and helped me feed, taught me about my vampire nature. The bond between a vampire and maker is very...*strong*. Very *intense*. *Intimate*. We roamed the city until he tired of me. Then he found Pearl and gave her the gift, and Cassandra soon after. We traveled the countryside as a pack. Oh, how we fed. Times were different then. The Depression weighed on the country. We killed when we wanted. The misery of the nation made it easy to roam the night...." Barlow trailed off. "But Silas was never happy."

"Because of me," Jack said.

Barlow nodded. "Because of you. He was obsessed. Your grandson, David, had a child that year. The first of three, if memory serves. Silas was delighted. He saw each of them as an opportunity."

I felt a chill run down my spine. "He would kill them to punish Jack."

"Rightly so," Barlow acknowledged. "So the years did pass, our merry pack of vampires feasting, Silas raging, the rest of us following. Then one day I found I could stave off the hunger. I wasn't free. Not yet. Silas felt his control slacking. The harder he pushed the more concerned he grew. I slipped away, searching, until I finally found my dear Eva. She told me I could test his will, but there was danger there. Silas could easily kill me, especially with the help of Pearl and Cassandra. It took another five years, but I finally slaked my thirst. I could control it. Like the sheriff." He squinted at Jack. "I believe you know of whom I speak?"

Jack nodded.

"Rumor has it that it took the sheriff seven hundred years to control his hunger. With the help of my wife, I managed it in six. Silas pushed harder and harder to control me, and I resisted his orders, never completely rising against him. In 1938 he finally released me. I was finally free to be with Eva."

The old woman on the couch growled in her throat and it raised the hairs on the back of my arms. Katie instinctively drew closer to me and I saw Jack's eye widen.

"You're not truly free," Jack said softly. "You can't be."

Barlow smiled wryly. "Silas released me from his pack, but only his death will break the bond between us. I can feel it, a buzzing in the back of my head. He could call at any time. I could resist, but ultimately I would *have* to obey. No matter how hard I push against him, I can only make it difficult." He stamped his foot against the thick rug on the floor. "I want my freedom." He went to the couch and stroked what remained of his wife's cotton-white hair. She looked up at him and smiled, her eyes glistening.

"She's dying," I said. I didn't know how I knew, but it had the ring of truth.

Barlow face turned up and bloody tears trickled from his eyes. "Yes. Her power has kept her mind sharp, but her body fails. She doesn't want to pass before I've secured my freedom."

The old woman stared up at her husband, then turned to us, eyes shining bright. Her lips parted and the faintest of words came out. "Help him," she whispered. "Kill Silas and save him. And, yourselves."

* * *

93

We argued outside Barlow's warehouse-turned-home.

"We can't trust him," Jack said, pacing up and down the sidewalk, his boots clomping against the cracked concrete.

Katie stood a few feet away, her fingers still clutching her crucifix, giving us ample room to talk.

"I don't see that we have much choice," I countered.

"There's always a choice. He's a vampire. No matter how reasonable he seems—no matter how much he claims he controls his hunger—he's *still* a vampire. You can't trust vampires."

"What about his wife? Can we trust her?"

Jack's eye narrowed. "Hard to say. Witches aren't my specialty. They're usually shrewd and fair, otherwise they go mad with power and become warlocks. She's not a warlock."

I shook my head. *Warlocks.* "How can you tell?"

"You can tell. You'll be able to smell it on them."

"How's that?"

He shrugged. "Same thing you get from killing a vampire. It makes you sensitive."

"You've killed a warlock?" I don't know why I was shocked, not after what I had learned. "Anything *else* you'd like to tell me?"

He squinted, then grinned. "Not particularly." He turned to Katie. "What do you think?"

Katie frowned. "We have to kill Silas. To save Callie, and to save Lilly. How are we going to do that if we don't even know where he is?"

Jack leaned his back against the dirty brick wall. "It's always something. First we had to save you. Now we have to save Barlow. Did it ever occur to you two that we might not be able to kill Silas? He's fast and strong and he's probably got a nest full of younglings ready to kill us. Least of all, don't forget that he's got a back-door into Barlow's head. If he calls, no matter what Barlow intends, he *will* respond."

Barlow stepped out of the faded red door as Jack finished. "That's what I'm counting on," he said. He locked the door, then turned to Jack. "I'll help as much as I dare. I *am* a seventy-year-old vampire. I can take the younglings."

"A few, maybe," Jack said, doubtfully. "But what if there's dozens? And what about Pearl? Or Cassandra? There's at least three or four more who aren't younglings. That's just the ones *I* know of."

"Please, Jack, I've watched from afar. He has many younglings, but only a handful of adults. We will sweep through them and when he realizes I am there, he will try to reassert his control. When I resist, he will be forced to push harder. That will allow you a moment where his grasp over the others will fade. I believe they will flee. In that moment, before he fully gains control, you will have your opportunity to kill him." He turned to Katie. "I will be free and your sister will be saved."

"What if your plan doesn't work?" Katie asked.

"Then we must kill the woman," Barlow said. "At least some good may come of this—"

"My *wife*," I interrupted. "You're talking about my wife."

Barlow turned to me, his face sad. "Decide now, young man. Decide if you are willing to do what must be done."

"What if killing Silas saves Callie and frees my wife?" I asked. "Maybe she can tame her hunger like you did? Isn't that possible?"

Barlow shook his head. "I wish that were true. I was an exception. Even if your wife could quickly learn control, you would still have years to wait. I'm afraid your little girl doesn't have time. She's feeding on her, yes?"

I nodded.

"You'd be risking her life. I wish it were another way, I truly do, but if you want to save your daughter, you *must* kill your wife."

* * *

Barlow ushered me through the door of the sports bar, not far from downtown Indianapolis. The bar was mostly empty, the few customers nursing their beers and sodas. Nobody looked up as we entered.

"Are you sure this woman will help?" I asked.

"She has no love for Silas."

I would have felt a lot safer with Jack and Katie accompanying us, but Barlow insisted that Jack's presence would terrify her. We traipsed through the bar, making our way through the remains of the lunch crowd, and I felt a sudden longing for my diner.

I missed it and the Arcanum town-folk. There was a sense of family there, where people cared for their neighbors. My quiet life with Stacie and Lilly seemed so far away. The diner had comforted me, tuning out the problems of the world. The constant cleaning, the coffee, frying eggs and bacon and burgers. My biggest concern was splashing myself from the hot oil in the deep-fryer. I almost laughed at my naiveté.

Almost.

Barlow led us to the back room where a plain-faced man greeted us. "Mr. Barlow."

Barlow tipped his head at the tall man. "Reginald. Thank you for accommodating us on such short notice."

"Please, take your time," Reginald said, handing Barlow the keys. "Lock up on your way out."

We made our way through the back of the kitchen. Barlow used the keys to unlock a metal door set in the wall. We walked down a shallow flight of stairs to the basement below, and, in the corner, Barlow unlocked another door and picked up a lantern, then ushered me through.

It was cold and damp in the brick tunnel, a pleasant change from the heat outside, but the air was stale and moldy. "What is this place?"

"The catacombs," Barlow answered. "They stored perishables below the city before the advent of refrigeration. When the city built over it, most forgot they existed. They wind through downtown Indianapolis, but this section is cut off from the rest. She makes her home here, in the forgotten dark."

The light from the lantern played against the walls, and I couldn't help but feel a spark of fear. Confronting a vampire in her lair seemed like a bad idea, but Barlow promised we would be safe.

I only wished I believed him.

There was a grating, the sharp scrape of brick on brick, and we turned to see a section of the wall swing inward.

I was shocked to see a brass bed in the tiny alcove, yellowed lace sheets pushed back. The woman who stood glaring at us was another matter.

Her hair was black, shot through with gray, and tied up in a bun. Her eyes were too large for her face, and she was husky. She looked like a grandmother. She wore clothes that were at least thirty years out of date, but still neat and clean. The eyes had that weight behind them and when she opened her mouth, I saw fangs inside.

"What are you doing here, Milford?" she asked, voice cold and rough, like she hadn't spoken in a long time.

Barlow bowed. "Gloria, this is Sam. He would like a word with you."

She moved quicker than I could follow, and suddenly she was standing in front of me, like magic. She was so close I could smell her, a clean, antiseptic heaviness that almost masked the odor underneath, the one that was earthy and primitive and smelled like death. Her body was close to mine, but she hadn't touched me. Still, I wasn't taking chances, and I almost tripped trying to take a step back.

"You would like a word?" she hissed.

I felt Barlow's hand on my arm, his fingers biting into my skin, holding me steady. "Please, Gloria."

Her face was devoid of emotion, but she hesitated. "Why?"

"Silas."

She jerked, eyes widening. "Really? Why should I help? He will just lead Silas here."

Barlow nodded in my direction. "He's with Jack."

The woman's mouth dropped in astonishment, exposing her fangs. "The vampire hunter? Are you insane? How did you escape?"

"We have an agreement. He will leave me in peace if I agree to help him find and kill Silas."

She glared at Barlow, then turned her attention back to me. "Let me guess. You don't know where he is."

"I'm sure *you* know his location," Barlow said. "You hear everything in your little burrow."

She threw her head back and laughed, then stopped, her face frozen. "The homeless know many things, but *that* is a very valuable piece of information."

I cleared my throat. "Please. I'll do anything."

The vampire stared at me and I felt myself wilt under her gaze. "What could you possibly offer? I'm safe *in my little burrow.*"

I shook my head. "Maybe for now, but things change. Times change. How long have you been hiding down here? A hundred years?"

The corner of her eyes tightened. She started to speak, but then her mouth quirked up. "Since 1962, young man. How old do you think I am?

"My mistake," I said hastily. "I know better than to discuss a lady's age. It's impolite."

Her dead eyes regarded me thoughtfully, and then she smiled. It warmed her face, making her seem almost human. "I was a nurse at Methodist Hospital when I was given the gift. I was sixty-one. When I woke, the vampire was gone and I had changed. My hunger was strong, but I held it back while I made my clean and precise kills. I took those already dying, those who suffered greatly. Death was a release from their misery, and was the very least I could offer them. When I first encountered Silas, he wanted me to join him, to become one of his flock. I refused. He threatened to kill me. I fled. I found this place and I've been hiding ever since. Risking that would be foolish."

I nodded. "You'll let him scare you into hiding forever?"

She nodded. "Spoken like the living. When the years start passing like a casual moment in the sun, you will feel different."

"I don't..."

She raised her hand. "Yes, I know about Jack, the one-eyed vampire hunter. If you are with him—if you become a hunter—the years will roll off your back until you become a man out of time, like him. He's hardly human himself, I've heard."

I didn't have a response because I had begun to suspect the same thing. I wanted my daughter back and I wanted Sister Callie whole again. I wanted Silas dead so that I might survive. I had no desire to become a hunter, not after I recovered Lilly and made sure she was safe.

Jack might have other plans.

I let the thought fade away. Doubts and fears weren't going to help me with Gloria. "Ma'am, you seem like a decent person..."

She raised an eyebrow. "For a vampire?"

I smiled and nodded. "Why is it someone like Silas, a complete monster, should thrive? Who made him king of Indianapolis?"

Her mouth opened and closed, then her brown eyes narrowed. "That's a very good point, young man. What do you do? Your occupation? You don't seem like a killer."

"I own a diner. Owned a diner. Before Silas turned my wife and stole my daughter away."

She considered that. Finally, "Say I know where Silas makes his nest. You really think Jack will kill him? I've heard he's tried before."

I nodded. "Yes. It is time for Silas to finally be put down." Then it dawned on me. "Why do you fear him?"

"Because he's a monster," she said, as if it was obvious. "You are correct. Why should *he* be allowed to live? He knows no decency. Even after all these years, he's never overcome the trauma of his death. Remember that when you face him, young man. When you think of vampires, when you think of the evil that we do, you're thinking of him. We are not all alike."

"I'll remember," I said. I meant it. Neither Milford nor Gloria were like I expected. They weren't like Larz Timm, or any of Silas's crew. Or even Stacie.

Milford and Gloria were more like my high-school science teachers. Oh, they would bleed me if they were hungry, but they weren't overtly evil. Not like Silas.

I shuddered at the memory of my house in Arcanum, how I could practically feel the malice rising from Silas.

Gloria smiled again, a real smile that made it to her eyes, her anger gone. "I'll write the address for you. It's where he last made his nest. He may not be there, but if he is, kill him. You will be doing the city a service."

She took pen and paper from the nightstand next to the bed, scribbled something on it, then folded it and handed to me. "Promise me that you will never disclose my location to Jack. I have no desire to meet him. Never come here again."

I took the paper. Before I could move, she grabbed my wrist. Her eyes changed, growing dark. "I can smell you."

I tried to pull back, but Milford held me in place. "I smell?"

She nodded, her face slack. Her demeanor changed. She wasn't the polite older woman. There was lust in her eyes, but it wasn't sex that she wanted. "I don't usually entertain humans. It's been years since I've had a healthy young man down here."

"Gloria." Milford's voice was calm. "Show some restraint."

She turned to him, hesitant. "I…I'm sorry, but it's been so long. So long."

"Gloria," Barlow said patiently, "he's not food."

She nodded, her jaw hanging open. "I know, but I can't help it. I can smell the blood in him, right below the surface. It's so hard to feed from the homeless. I only take those who are already dying. I ease their transition from this world to the next. I don't feed from the young and healthy. The homeless sustain me, but it's not the same. It doesn't fill me up, fill me to my toes." She pulled, but Barlow held me fast. "I control it, it doesn't control me. I *control* it."

"Ma'am?" I said, as softly as I had ever spoken. "If that's true, why are you pulling on me?"

She looked down at her hand, as if seeing it for the first time. "Oh, my." She let go and I jerked back. Barlow caught me before I could slip.

Gloria shrank back against her bed. "That was terrible of me, young man. I've not lost control in years." Her eyes returned to normal and they looked everywhere but into mine. "You should go. Go and find Silas. Try not to get yourself killed. It would be a shame to waste all that fresh blood."

The way she said it, the heat still in her voice, I realized just how close I came to being food. I nodded. "I'll do my best."

She turned back to her bed as we left. On the way back up the stairs I turned to Milford. "Could you have saved me?"

His face told me all I needed to know. "I could have held my own, but if she had lost control, she would surely have killed you. I'm sorry about that. I didn't expect her to be so close to the edge. The hunger drives us all. Never forget that."

I remembered the look in her eye. No, I don't think I *could* forget.

CHAPTER NINE

It was late in the afternoon, the sun sinking in the west. The house spread out over several acres on a small hill on the outskirts of Indianapolis. The fresh-cut rolling grass and well-groomed trees were picture-perfect. The brick on the Tudor-style home was a rich brown and the white paint sparkling clean.

Appearances were deceiving. I could sense the vampires, even from the street, a foul sensation in my head, like a rumbling truck or a faraway chainsaw grating against my nerves.

Jack eased his truck to the side of the road. It looked wildly out of place in the opulent surroundings and I turned to him. "Silas has lived here for the past fifty years? How did you never find this place?"

Jack eyed the house. "It's a big city. Why would I ever think to look here?" He glanced at Katie. "This is your chance, girl. Sam and I have an edge. All you've got is that crucifix and your bloodline." She started to speak, but Jack interrupted her. "I'm not going to try and stop you, I just want you to know that we might not make it through this. Even if Barlow's plan works, we might still die. I'm good with that. Sam has lost everything. But you? You still have a long life ahead of you. You don't have to do this."

Katie glared at him. "You think I'd leave my sister to die? I don't want to go in there, but what choice do I have? How could I do that, after all she risked for me?"

Jack tipped his head. "I didn't think that you could. Just wanted to make sure you had the chance." He took his hand from the steering wheel and roughly patted her hand. "You've been through a lot, girl. It speaks well that you're still in the fight. I'm willing to give my life for yours, Katie." He turned his gaze to me. "You too, Sam." He shook his head. "This isn't a fairy tale. Good doesn't always win, and even if it does, it can demand a terrible price. I'm living proof of that. So, we go in, we fight the good fight. If we kill Silas, we can save the Sister. If not, we kill Stacie."

"What about Lilly?" I asked softly.

"She may not be here. But if she is, you get her and get the hell out. Don't look back." He paused. "If I don't make it out, I have a will. It's in a lock-box at the State Bank of Toledo. The key is in my desk and your name is listed at the bank. The house and everything I own goes to you. I've managed to put some money aside. Take it and start a new life. There's enough there to buy a new diner. Start over."

I started to protest but Jack cut me off.

"Damn it, boy. I know we haven't had a chance to know each other. I'm sorry for that. You're a good kid. You deserved better." He turned back to Katie. "You both did."

His good eye glistened and for the first time I saw through his gruff exterior to the man within, a man who had seen generation after generation of his family born and die, all at the hands of one creature. Silas.

"I just realized," I said, "I hadn't thanked you for saving my life."

Tears streamed down Katie's face. "Me, too. My faith lapsed and I acted like a child. Larz almost killed me because of it. Thanks for saving me, Mr. Harlan." She took my hand in hers. "You too, Sam."

Barlow pulled up behind us in his Edsel and we got out and joined him. Jack opened the toolbox in the back of his truck and clipped four shiny balls the size of peaches to his leather belt.

"Are those grenades?" I asked, startled.

"Cast from silver with silver spikes and wire. If it comes to that, hit the floor," Jack said. He took a short gun with a drum magazine from the tool chest, pulled the bolt back, and inserted the drum.

Barlow joined us and arched an eyebrow. "A Thompson?"

Jack smiled grimly and jerked his thumb to his chest. "Original owner."

Barlow rolled his eyes and Jack took two spare drums and put one in each of the front pockets of his duster. I checked my own Colt and nodded to Jack.

We started for the mansion and Katie stopped us. "If you don't mind, I'd like to say a prayer."

Jack hesitated, then shrugged. Barlow gave Katie an inscrutable look and shrugged as well. I nodded and Katie bowed her head.

"Lord, give us the strength to strike down this evil. Let us stop this plague of vampires and save the lives of our loved ones." She hesitated. "I'm sorry for losing my way. Please bless us and protect us. In Christ's name we pray. Amen."

We nodded, even Barlow, who looked genuinely touched. Katie grabbed her crucifix and shot us a fierce smile.

Praying time was over. It was time for killing.

* * *

Jack turned to smile at us as he rapped his weathered knuckles politely on the front door. "Always time for proprieties."

Barlow shook his head and Katie actually managed a grin.

The door opened and we found ourselves face to face with a black man in his mid-twenties, dressed in a red pin-striped track suit and bushy hair, all twenty years out of date. His eyes widened in fear and then Jack kicked him in the chest. He flew back and slammed into the wall ten feet behind. There was a bone-crunching impact when the vampire hit, plaster exploding in a spider web of cracks, and then the vampire was came at us with a ferocious snarl.

Jack lifted the Tommy gun and cut loose. It was like thunder from the heavens.

The vampire's chest exploded as the silver bullets stitched across him, and then we were moving past, Jack tossing me a wooden stake with his left hand.

I slammed the stake into the smoking remains of the vampire's chest, and he screamed as he burst into flames, thrashing across the floor in a greasy mess of soot. I yanked the stake back and tossed it into my left hand and pulled my Colt with my right, following Jack as he turned left and headed deeper down the hallway.

Time slowed for a moment, and I marveled at the paintings on the wall. The house dripped wealth, outfitted tastefully from a bygone time. For a crazy moment I wanted to stop and stare, then we ran down the short hallway and turned right into what must have once been the mansion's great room.

A dozen vampires were standing around in shock and I saw the nearest one, a chunky woman in her early thirties, do a double take, her mouth dropping open. "It's Jack," she screamed before Jack unloaded the Tommy gun into her.

The results were intense. The bullets pounded into her chest, over her heart, and the silver alone was enough to send her into a fireball.

That broke the spell and the rest of the vampires attacked en masse.

A Chinese woman lunged at Barlow, but he stepped forward and grabbed the woman's head and yanked, ripping it from her body in a gory spray of blood. Chunks of meaty flesh hung from the head, and I saw parts of the spinal column, a yellowy-white that stood in contrast to the red blood spraying from her torso. Her eyes went wide, intelligence still in them and Barlow chucked the head into the face of another vampire, a well-dressed man in black slacks and skin-tight black shirt. The head became a flaming ball that hit the vampire in the chest, who recoiled in horror. Jack unleashed the Tommy gun on him and the man jerked from the impact and started to run, trying to find cover from the hail of silver bullets spraying across the room.

I saw a bright light flash behind me—pure and hot—wash across the room, like lightning, and I heard Katie screaming the Lord's name. Another vampire was rushing at me from my right and I fired the Colt right through the man's eye. He dropped to the floor and then sprang back onto his feet with a cat-like grace. He caught me in the chest, one hand shielding his face from Katie's crucifix, and his talons raked against me, shredding the leather duster, then Barlow was on him.

I tossed Barlow a wooden stake and he slammed it into the man's chest. He moved on to the next, a beautiful young blonde. She hissed and Barlow slashed across her neck, his talons spraying a gout of blood. Muscle and skin flew in great pieces against the floor and wall.

The Tommy gun continued to thunder and I saw Jack mowing through the remaining vampires, some dropping and spasming in pain, some on the floor in flames. The Tommy gun ran empty and Jack dropped the drum magazine and was loading a new one, his face drawn back in a grim smile.

We had almost cleared the room when Silas appeared.

One second he wasn't there, the next second he was. His lips pulled back in snarl and he moved in a blur, streaking across the wood floor through puddles of blood and piles of ash. He yanked the Tommy gun from Jack and threw it sideways. The gun flew across the room and embedded itself in the far plaster wall.

Barlow jumped at Silas, screaming incoherently. Silas registered this with surprise, then struck Barlow sideways, hurling him across the room and into me. The impact hammered me to the ground and Barlow and I went down in a heap.

I heard the wham-wham of Jack's .45 and turned to see Silas skipping around the line of fire.

Barlow turned to me, eyes wide, screaming over the gunfire. "It's time, Sam!"

I threw him up and off with all my strength. The tubby vampire flew up, spinning, then his feet caught the ground and he rushed Silas, grabbing him by the back of the neck. Jack had emptied his .45 and used the butt-end to bludgeon Silas's temple.

Blood sprayed from the impact, arcing out across the floor, but Silas laughed. "Milford, you wormy little bastard, you finally decided to make your move?"

Barlow struggled to hold Silas. "Nothing personal."

Jack struck him in the temple again and Silas glared at Barlow, then at Jack. "It's always personal. Isn't it, Jack?"

Jack grunted, reached into his duster, and pulled a wooden stake. "End of the line, boy."

Silas laughed again. "I *doubt* that. Milford, you answer to me. *I am your master.*"

Barlow jerked like he'd been shocked, then shook his head. "You do *not* control me."

I struggled to stand, ready to help Jack kill Silas, when the light from Katie's crucifix dimmed. I turned to see a large man approach her, a twisted smile on his face. Katie's eyes widened, her hands shaking, the silver crucifix bobbing on its chain. I aimed my Colt at the man, but he slid behind her, putting her between us, making the shot impossible.

Katie recoiled as the man advanced. "He's going to kill me," she screamed.

It was Larz Timm all over again. I could literally see the light from the crucifix dim as her faith faltered. She was scared and panicked, and if her faith failed, the vampire would have her.

"Pray, Katie," I shouted. "Pray as hard as you can!"

I saw the woman, Pearl, out of the corner of my eye as she scrambled across the room and tackled Jack, knocking him to the floor. She struck him again and again, desperate to draw blood. He managed to block her blows to his head, but she kicked him hard in the chest

Katie was screaming and shaking, trying to avoid the man. I aimed carefully, squeezed the trigger, and the Colt roared. The bullet hit the man in the arm. He staggered back with a smoking hole in his bicep, and his smile evaporated as he lunged at Katie, hissing like a cat.

I felt a hand on my shoulder. Before I could react, I was yanked to my feet and spun around.

I looked into the eyes of my attacker, the pale blue eyes I knew so well, the fine nose and delicate cheekbones, the golden skin. I was looking into my wife's face.

"Stacie," I pleaded. "For god's sake, help me. We can kill Silas and save Lilly."

She glared at me, eyes cold and hard. "Why on *earth* would I want to do that?"

"Sam," Jack yelled. "Shoot her!"

I saw Barlow struggling with Silas, and Silas appeared to be winning. Jack was crouched down on his hands and knees. When Pearl kicked him in the side, I heard his ribs crack. He stabbed at her with a wooden stake, but she easily knocked it from his hand and sent it clattering across the floor.

I had the Colt at the ready. I knew I should pull the trigger and put the silver bullet through Stacie. I knew it was the right thing to do. But, she was my *wife*. She had Lilly. If I shot and killed her, I may never see Lilly again. I tried one last time. "Damn it, Stacie. This *isn't* you. Help us and we'll get out of here."

Her fingers dug into my arms, holding me tight. She laughed, but her eyes showed no amusement. "I'm right where I'm supposed to be, honey." Her knee came forward and struck me in the crotch. I choked on my own scream, hitting the floor and vomiting.

Katie's screams slowed, then stopped. I struggled to turn my head, to see what was happening, but Stacie dropped to her knees, slamming me to the floor.

It happened so fast, I didn't have time to brace myself. I hit the dark wood floor so hard I heard it splinter and everything went black as the shock of the impact knocked me senseless. I blinked, gasping for air, and Stacie spun me on my side. Through the tears streaming from my eyes, I saw the man holding Katie, his face buried in her neck.

Katie whimpered like a frightened puppy. It filled me with a maddening rage, even through the pain, and I tried to roll away from Stacie's grip.

She picked me up and slammed me into the floor again, only this time, it took me several moments before I could open my eyes. When I did, I knew we were in trouble.

Pearl had Jack pinned to the floor with her foot. She ground it into his side and he gasped as his eyes rolled back. I could tell he was in excruciating pain.

I tried to stand, but Stacie held me down, effortlessly. I watched, helpless, as Barlow released Silas and then dropped to his knees.

Silas stood over Barlow. "So, this was your plan?" he asked. He spat at Jack, a big bloody globule that struck Jack in the face. He turned back to Barlow and squinted. "After all this time, Milford? Really? This is how you repay me for your *freedom*, you little wretch?"

Barlow looked up at Silas, then turned his gaze upon Pearl. "You don't understand freedom. Either of you. It's not really freedom when you can still call."

"You used to be one of us," Pearl snarled. "Now you side with them?" She ground her foot into Jack's side.

He coughed and swung uselessly at her leg, but she kicked him in the head. He rolled back, stunned.

It was futile. We were beaten.

Silas turned and regarded the room, the blood and ash and bullet holes. A pair of vampires were still alive, convulsing in the swatch of destruction, older vampires that hadn't died in the hail of silver bullets from Jack's Tommy-gun. "It was a nice try, Jack, I'll give you that. Using Milford to distract me? You almost had me. After all these years you were finally ready to do it."

Jack glared up at him. "Your time has come and gone, boy. The things you've done. What you've become."

Silas whirled, mouth split wide in a wicked grin. "The thing I've become, he says. What do you think of that, Sam? Do you think I'm some kind of monster? Stacie told me all about you, about her life before I gave her the gift. Do you blame Jack?" His smile grew wider. "Have you seen enough? Do you *know* enough?"

Before I could answer, he turned his attention to Katie. "Little girl, you were somebody's property not long ago. You were someone's meat treat. I can *smell* it on you. Do you blame Jack for bringing you here? It's *his* fault."

Jack spun out from under Pearl's foot and kicked her in the knee with his boot. There was a sickening pop and she howled in pain and fell to the ground.

But, before he could get to his feet, Silas was on him. Silas appeared inhuman, his face drawn back and his fangs out. He punched Jack in the face and Jack's head snapped sideways. Silas hauled him up by his duster and punched him again and again, each blow landing with inhuman strength.

Jack looked to me, his good eye swollen, and he was crying, tears rolling down his face.

"Jesus," I said. "Stop. You're *killing* him."

Silas turned to me and the grin on his face vanished. "What's that? You want to *save* him? After all he's done? *He's* responsible. Don't you see?" His eyes had turned a solid black, the whites completely gone, and he moved across the room with inhuman speed and grace, until he dropped to his knees and grabbed me by the throat.

His sharp talons drew blood from my neck, reopening the same scabbed wounds from Timm's attack just days before. "You still don't understand. You still don't know the truth."

"What truth?" I asked. If I kept him talking, Jack might think of something to save us. "Jack's my kin. He told me."

That stopped him. He eyed me critically. "Did he," he mused. "He told you *that* secret? What else did the old man tell you?"

"He told me you're a sick bastard who killed his children. You've been killing his family for a hundred years," I said. "You get off on torturing him."

Silas pulled my face close to his and the foul stench of his breath made me gag. He peered at me and I felt that weighty feeling, like I might sink into his eyes. "I could glamour you, Sam. I could reach inside your mind and twist and turn until you would do my bidding. You're not strong enough to resist. Not yet. I could make you put that gun in Jack's mouth and pull the trigger. I won't. That won't cause him enough pain. In fact, I'm done with this charade."

He released me and Stacie yanked back on my arms, pulling up the slack. I grunted in pain, but that just made her yank harder.

She giggled, and I felt her breath on my shoulder. She used her strength and leverage to position me so that I could watch Silas.

"No," Silas continued, "the time for games is past." He grabbed Jack by the duster and yanked him to his feet. "It's time, father. I'm going to give you the gift."

* * *

I couldn't have heard him correctly. "Jack, what is he talking about?"

Jack turned to me and I read it in his face. Anger. Disgust. Shame. "I'm sorry, Sam. It's all my fault."

Silas turned to me with his toothy shark's grin. "He never told you? Jack's not a father or a husband. He's a killer." He turned back to Jack and slapped him across the face. It echoed like a gunshot in the open room, even over the ringing in my ears from Jack's Tommy gun. "Isn't that right, Jack? You weren't much of a man. Just a killer." He backhanded Jack again, then dropped him.

Jack slumped to the floor, dazed. Katie whimpered loudly behind me. I felt sick to my stomach.

"He's not like that," I said. "Right, Jack?"

Jack looked up and his face spoke volumes. "It's not like he says. I did my best."

Silas spun around. "Your best?" he seethed. "You killed your own wife, then left me to die!"

I shook my head. It couldn't be true. Silas had to be a lying. "It's not true, is it, Jack?"

Jack looked to me, then turned to Silas, who paced the room. "Let them go. Please. I'm begging. Sam's nothing to you. The girl, neither."

Silas glared at me, then back to Jack. "I'm not going to kill them. Not yet. I promised Stacie she could give Sam the gift." He glanced around at the remains of his nest. "It's a shame you killed so many of my younglings. It will take months to rebuild. In the meantime, Sam will be hungry. The pretty girl will make a tasty treat. Milford, though...."

He scowled at Barlow, who stood rooted in place. "Milford is a special case. I might have to make an example out of him." He reached down and grabbed Jack by the face, claws digging into skin, rivulets of blood dripping scarlet sheets down the old man's face. "Don't worry, Jack. You'll watch it all. I'm going to give you the gift and you'll be reborn as one of us."

* * *

Silas grabbed Jack's ponytail and yanked, snapping his head back, baring the old man's throat.

I screamed for him to stop but it was no use.

As Silas neared Jack's throat, there was a pressure behind my eyes, like the first time I had sensed a vampire. It was a massive weight inside my head, and it threatened to overwhelm me. I was acutely aware of the hairs on my body standing up.

All of them.

My stomach tightened as dread washed over me. My skin turned slick with sweat, and it pooled down my back, soaking through my shirt.

Katie's whimpers quieted and I knew she felt it, too, even through the pain of the vampire's feeding. I managed to turn my head and glance her way. Her eyes widened, unsure of what fresh horror we were about to face.

Silas must have sensed our reaction because he stopped and whirled around.

The man stood at the edge of the room, still as stone. He was over six feet tall and broad shouldered, with shaggy brown hair and large brown eyes set deep behind his prominent nose. There were hard lines across his face, the kind that hinted at great laughter or great sorrow. His button-up shirt stretched across his massive chest, his denim jeans, tan jacket, and cowboy boots making it hard to tell what era he stepped out of.

A yard-long sword hung loosely from his left hand, shining like quicksilver.

He stood, watching us, his face bland, like he stumbled across us by accident.

Jack's face lit up in recognition, then his good eye went wide in disbelief.

Silas turned his attention to the man and started to speak, then stopped. Finally he managed, "Hello, friend. I'm afraid I haven't made your acquaintance."

The big man coolly regarded Silas. "Name's Henry Hastings. I'm the sheriff of Hot Springs, Wyoming."

"I've heard of you," Silas said, glancing around. "You're well known among us. Unfortunately, I'm busy with a family matter. I'm afraid the rules of hospitality will have to wait until I've concluded my business."

Henry eyed Silas impassively, then his gaze swept the room and finally settled upon the old man. "Hello, Jack."

Jack managed to cough up some blood and spat on the floor next to Pearl's cream designer shoes. "Hello, Henry. What brings you so far from Thermopolis?"

"You've got yourself in a situation."

"Excuse me," Silas interrupted, "this is a personal matter. I don't see what your interest is, Mr. Hastings."

Henry raised his hand and pointed to Jack. "He's my business. You're going to turn him. I'm afraid I can't let that happen."

Silas looked at the man and I could see the anger welling up as Silas lost patience. "Sorry, friend, but this is *my* family. I don't know why you're here, but Jack is not your concern. Beat your feet."

"I'm not just the sheriff of Hot Springs. I'm also the Sheriff."

For a brief moment, Silas's mask dropped and I saw confusion, anger, and something akin to fear. "Bullshit," Silas said. "There's no such thing." He turned to Jack. "He's lying."

Jack continued to stare at Henry. "I figured it was like that."

Pearl turned her head from Jack to Silas. "What's he talking about?"

Barlow stood slowly as Silas's fragile control slipped. His eyes were riveted on Henry. "The Sheriff works for the Ancients, the oldest vampires in the world. Twelve of them, correct?"

Henry nodded. "That's right. They have concerns about Jack. He's a special case. No one has racked up that number of vampire kills. He's changing. He's close to turning, even without receiving the gift. Isn't that right?

Everyone turned to look at Jack, who stared at Henry. "How could you tell?"

"When you came to me for help, what, twenty years ago? You had a hard time sensing the younglings. The closer you get to turning, the harder it is to feel them. You're not human anymore. You're not quite a vampire, but you're closer than anyone has ever come."

"This changes *nothing*," Silas growled. "I'm going to give him the gift and he will belong to *me*."

"No," Henry said, "he won't. If he turns now, there's no telling what might happen. The amount of vampire essence that he's absorbed? It would make him a power to rival the Ancients. They won't allow it."

Silas took a step toward Henry—who made no obvious movement—but Silas stopped and narrowed his eyes. "I've waited many a long year for this and I will *not* be denied my prize."

Henry ignored him and addressed Jack. "I'm sorry about this, Jack, I truly am, but you know it's for the best. I'll take the boy and girl away from here. I *can* do that for you."

Stacie yanked back hard on my arms and I howled in pain as my shoulders burned with fire.

"He's mine," Stacie said. "You *can't* have him."

Henry turned to us and Stacie flinched. "You don't have a say in this, little youngling. The boy lives." He turned his attention to Katie, her eyes rolling back in her head. The vampire feeding from her stroked her hair softly. Katie's face had gone from terror to sheer bliss as the vampire drained her. "The girl goes as well."

The vampire holding Katie shook his head and stopped feeding long enough to speak. "We can't let her go. She's delicious." He ran his fingernail down the side of her neck and caught a drop of blood, delicately rolled the drop of crimson onto the end of his finger, and flicked his tongue out. As the blood hit his tongue, his eyes relaxed, his face slack.

"Clearly we have a disagreement here," Silas said reasonably. "Surely we can come to an understanding."

As Silas was speaking, one of the few younglings left alive managed to stand and approach Henry from behind. The youngling moved, shakily but steadily, and was almost close enough to strike when Henry spun, the sword swishing, a flash of silver fire almost impossible to see.

The effects were not. The youngling's head went spinning through the air and the body burst into flames.

That got everyone's attention. Henry stood holding the sword, relaxed, as the body and head burned to ash. Silas watched the big man carefully, the fear now evident on his face. Pearl continued to hold Jack down, but she looked back and forth between Silas and Henry, uncertain.

Henry sighed heavily. "I mean you no harm. Well, except for Jack, and that isn't personal. I know he's your father, Silas, and I know you hate him, but I have a job to do. I'll make it quick and painless, Jack, because I like you. You don't want to become what you're going to become, and the Ancients don't trust what you *might* become." He flicked the sword and a line of blood misted across the floor in a delicate pattern of fine red lines. His gaze became hard and steely, voice deeper, losing his western accent. "What say you, Silas? Will you give up the man, Jack Harlan? Will you submit to my will, or prefer you to suffer the wrath of the Ancients?"

Silas started to protest, but his gaze fell, his face sullen. Apparently, he could recognize when he was beaten. He nodded.

In that moment, when I thought our fight had been for nothing, Jack kicked Pearl in the crotch.

Hypothetically I knew that kicking a woman in the crotch had the same effect as kicking a man in the crotch. I just hadn't seen it done. Apparently, it also held true for vampires.

The statuesque woman screamed and fell. Jack sat up and opened his coat. I knew what he was going to do and I shook my head, trying to will him to stop, but Jack yanked the shiny grenades from his belt and tossed one at Henry and one at Silas.

The room exploded into motion. Silas, Pearl and Henry fled the room, their movements a blur, the rush of wind the only sign of their departure. Stacie tried to yank me with her, but Barlow, his bond with Silas broken, appeared beside her.

He struck her in the chest, knocking her backwards and through the wall behind us. The vampire holding Katie stared stupidly at the grenades spinning across the floor and Barlow tossed me aside as he ran toward the man. He yanked Katie free of the vampire's grip and tackled her to the floor, using his body as cover.

I saw Jack turn to me and scream. "Get down!" He rolled away from the grenades, spinning through the blood and ash. I pressed myself against the wooden floor, the blood now cold and sticky against my face.

The grenades went off in a blinding whump that reverberated through my body. My side lit up with a stinging shock of hot fire, and I knew I had taken a piece silver.

I turned to the vampire that had been holding Katie. He stared at me fearfully, and I looked down as the multiple holes across his body began to smoke from the silver shrapnel. He threw his head back and screamed as his body began combusting.

I shook my head, trying to clear the dizziness. I didn't know if it was from the shock of what I had seen, the detonation of the grenades, or from the ringing in my ears, but I knew we had been given a second chance. Katie rolled out from under Barlow and I yelled at her, "Are you okay?"

She looked at me, uncomprehending, and I knew her ears must be ringing like mine. Barlow stood, shakily, trying to reach behind him, frantically looking to see if he was hit by silver. Miraculously, he was unharmed.

The same could not be said for Jack. I watched as he stood, faltering, and I saw several holes through his duster. They were smoking, just like the vampires. He grimaced in pain and then gathered his .45, looking around. The room was clear, and he stumbled to the wall and yanked his Tommy gun from the plaster, cycled the chamber, then fit in a new drum magazine. Satisfied that the other vampires had momentarily fled, he turned and yelled something to me.

"What?" I yelled back.

He mouthed the word and this time I understood. We had to go. I grabbed my Colt. With Barlow's help, we made our way out the front door before the other vampires could return.

Jack staggered backwards while we retreated, the Tommy gun trained on the house. I heard him say, muffled, "There's no way they will risk coming after us in full daylight. I'd blast them to hell. Even Henry."

We made it to the truck and Jack turned to Barlow. "Will we be safe at your place?"

Barlow's face fell. "I'm sorry, but I can't put my wife in danger. She's warded the place from the likes of Silas, but the Sheriff? No, you won't be safe there." He pulled a card from his pocket. "You can reach me at this number."

Jack took it. "I'm sorry, Barlow, I really am."

Barlow shook his head. "Not as sorry as I am. I wondered why Silas hated you. Now I know."

Jack looked at the house and shook his head. "We're going to hide until I can heal up, come up with a plan. We still have to kill Silas. It's the only way to save you all." He stopped and worked his jaw. "Before I change," he muttered through clenched teeth.

CHAPTER TEN

We were headed southwest, out of the city. Jack pushed the truck to the speed limit, but not over, constantly looking in the rear-view mirror. He pulled his cellphone out of his duster and squeezed it until it cracked. He kept squeezing and I heard the grinding of plastic on plastic, then he cranked down his window, stuck his hand out, and let the pieces scatter to the wind.

He glanced over to us. Katie's head was in my lap, her eyes glassy. He reached behind the seat and handed me a paper bag full of beef jerky. "Give her this. She needs the protein and the iron."

I tore open the package and took one of the dried pieces of jerky and gently placed it in her mouth.

She looked up, then started to chew. "Ugh. Salty."

I smiled. "You're going to be okay. She's going to be okay, isn't she?"

Jack nodded. "She lost a lot of blood, but she'll be fine. There's a bottle of Ensure in the bag, give her that, too."

I reached around in the bottom of the bag and found the bottle, twisted off the cap, and held her head up so she could drink. She took a small sip and coughed, but managed to keep it down. I gave her another piece of jerky and she wolfed it down. She held her lips to the bottle and slurped at the contents. Some of the color come back to her face, either from the food or because she realized we had made it out of Silas's house alive.

For now.

I watched Jack as he drove. Wisps of smoke steamed from holes in his arm and side. He appeared not to notice. I felt a burning in my own side, and took the opportunity to lift Katie's head and raise my shirt. Small amounts of blood trailed down to my pants. It didn't appear life-threatening, but it hurt like a million bee stings.

Jack drove, constantly shifting his attention between the road and the mirror. We soon found ourselves on a highway, driving through the soybean and corn fields of rural Indiana, heading into the setting sun. The crops were almost ready for harvest, but the farmers were not in the field yet, and the smell of drying corn was sweet and rich. Jack kept driving, face grim.

He caught me watching him. "What?"

"We have to talk."

"We *need* to get somewhere safe. I doubt Silas knows enough to trace a license plate, but I damn well know Henry does. He's a cop. He knows how to work the system. We've got to get holed up, get the plates changed."

I kept staring at him.

"Fine," he said. "You want to talk? Talk."

"You've lied to me from the start," I said.

"I never lied. I just didn't tell you the whole truth."

"That's a form of lying," I said. "That's not something family does to each other."

Jack laughed glumly. "That's all families do, Sam. We all lie, to each other and to ourselves."

"That's not true, families—"

"Bullshit," Jack interrupted. "Sometimes the lies we tell are harmless and sometimes they hurt. Sometimes we do it because we are looking out for each other and sometimes we do it because we can't face the truth. What do you want me to say? You want me to say I'm sorry? I am. You have no idea how sorry I am. I never asked for any of this. I've lost everything that ever meant anything. You know what the measure of a man is? It's not doing the right thing when *everybody's* watching. It's doing the right thing when *nobody's* watching."

I struggled to find the right words. "You say all that, but it's pretty simple. You didn't tell me the truth. You *should* have."

He watched me out of the corner of his good eye. "You want the truth? Let's get holed up first. I've got a place not far from here."

The fields passed and Jack wound the truck through the countryside until we reached his hidey-hole, an abandoned motel set back from the road. The place had seen better days, probably decades before, and the tan bungalows spread across several acres looked ready to fall apart. He drove up the weed-filled driveway and around to the backside of the farthest bungalow, parking the truck between it and the tree line that separated the property from the neighboring corn fields.

Katie had fallen asleep, from exhaustion or from shock, I wasn't sure. I shook her awake. "We're here."

She opened her eyes and sat up too quickly, tumbling forward. I caught her and she grabbed my hand to steady herself. "I still feel woozy," she said, her hand trembling.

Jack got out and shut the door quietly, then grabbed the Tommy gun laying on the floorboards. I saw how he moved. Clearly he was in a lot of pain, and I wondered how bad the silver shrapnel was hurting him. My own wound still stung and I worried about it getting infected. Hopefully Jack would have some idea how to treat it.

I helped Katie from the truck. We came around the back and Jack opened the tailgate and rummaged around in the giant toolbox in the back. He slammed the tailgate shut and motioned us to the bungalow.

Katie and I followed him as he led us through the knee-high grass to the door. The building looked abandoned and covered in moss, but the lock on the door was shiny and new. He opened the lock with a key from his key-chain, then opened the door and motioned for us to go inside.

We entered the musty room. The interior was pitch dark, the windows covered in aluminum foil. Jack fumbled around, then clicked a portable lamp, and I could finally see. There was an old wooden table, a plain brown couch, and a small kitchenette. A stack of cardboard boxes lined one wall. Everything was surprisingly clean.

"The bathroom is in there," Jack said, pointing. "It's on a septic. We've got water from a well, no power though." He turned on another portable lamp, this one on the table. "We've got plenty of batteries," he said, pointing to a cardboard box on the floor. "The bedroom is in there, but only one bed."

He shrugged off his duster and I saw smoke still rising from his body. He dumped the shoulder holster on the floor and sat the Tommy gun next to the lamp on the table. "Sam, I'm going to need your help. Katie, too, if she's feeling up to it."

He kicked off his boots and then proceeded to strip down to his white briefs.

Katie looked on in horror. "Oh. My. Lord."

Jack's body was a jigsaw of scars. There were faded ones and giant hard masses that snaked across his chest, down his arms, and across his legs. He glanced down, as if realizing for the first time just how bad the scars looked. "Don't worry, they only hurt when I laugh," he said. He pointed to a case of bottled water sitting on the kitchenette counter. "Katie, can you get a couple bottles and a roll of paper towels?"

She nodded and brought him the bottles of water and a brand new roll of white paper towels while he handed me a set of long locking forceps and a scalpel from the medical kit. He placed several tubes of superglue on the table next to his Tommy gun, then sat down gingerly on the wooden chair. He pointed to a smoking hole in his arm. "Use the scalpel to cut it open, then use those to dig around and pull out the shrapnel. When it's out, wash it out with the water and superglue it closed."

"I've never done anything like this before," I said. "How will I see it?"

"You won't see it. You'll hear the forceps clicking against the shrapnel. You can do this, Sam." He pulled the leather belt from his pants and unhooked the remaining two grenades and put them on the table as well, then took the leather belt and stuffed a length of it between his teeth.

He nodded and I sucked in my breath, gritted my teeth, then used the scalpel to make a long incision across the hole in his arm. He grunted and I put the scalpel down and picked up the forceps. Katie winced as I jammed the forceps into the hole.

Jack grunted again, biting down on the leather belt. I moved the forceps around until I heard a clicking. I locked on to it and pulled out the piece of silver metal. As I did, blood gushed from the wound.

The shrapnel was a piece of razor-sharp wire no bigger than a pencil eraser, smoking and glowing a dull red. Jack nodded and I dropped it on the table, then washed out the hole with water from the bottle. When I had it cleaned as best as I could, I sopped up the bloody mess with the paper towels, then squirted superglue in the wound and pinched the skin shut. There was a small puff of smoke as the glue set and Jack flinched, stomping his foot as the wound sealed shut.

My hands were shaking, but we were only getting started. Jack eyed me, then nodded again. I turned my attention to the smoking hole in his side, the slick and wet entry the size of a dime. I used the scalpel to open the wound up and rooted around with the forceps as Jack grunted. It took over a minute until I felt the sharp clicking again. I pulled the shrapnel out, but it got stuck against his ribs. He groaned as I yanked hard, pulling it free.

We repeated this again and again until all the shrapnel was removed. I would like to say it got easier, but that would be a lie. Several times Katie helped steady me, even though she could barely stand.

Jack's face had gone pale. He spat out the leather belt and motioned for me to take off my shirt. It was stuck to the bloody hole in my side, right below the rib cage, having dried against the skin. I tugged the shirt loose, opening the wound again, the blood flowing freely.

We exchanged places and Jack offered me the leather belt. I bit down on it and found it soft and bitter between my teeth. Katie held my hand while Jack used the forceps to dig around in my side, looking for the silver.

I struggled to hold still as Jack moved the forceps, and I bit down on the belt, my teeth mashing against the leather. I groaned and willed myself still, but my body disobeyed. The harder I tried to remain calm, the more I squirmed.

"Damn it, quit moving," Jack said. "I think I've found it. Just hold still."

I glared at him. The pain was so intense it was making me light-headed. I nodded and he grabbed my other arm to steady me and yanked out the piece of metal.

He held it up so that I could see. "It was barely under the skin," Jack said.

I spat out the leather belt. "Barely under the skin?"

"It was a long way from your heart," Jack said. "You'll live." He washed out the wound and glued it shut. The heat from the superglue burned anew, and I fell back in my chair, but it quickly set and the pain finally receded.

Jack nodded, satisfied. "You'll heal up in a week or so."

I looked at Jack and all the wounds we had just cleaned. "How long will yours take?"

"A few days," he said. "Maybe less."

He rummaged through one of the boxes and withdrew a handful of crudely made devices. Katie and I watched as he pinned it to the floor next to the door and strung steel wire from it to the door, pulling it tight.

"Trip wire," Jack said. "The C4 and silver shot will give any vampire a hell of a shock. Hopefully kill him. Maybe only stun him. Either way, it's an advantage."

119

He grabbed plastic bags and placed them on the table. "MRE's. Eat one. You too, Katie. There's a heater in the bag. Fill it with water and put the meal next to it."

He rummaged through another box until he found a bottle of Jack Daniels. He motioned for me and Katie to sit on the couch and he took my place on the wooden chair, facing us.

He broke the seal on the bottle and took a long slug.

"It's time," I said.

He took another long slug. "Yes. It's time."

* * *

"We're not that far from where it began. Tangier, Indiana, 1909. July 7th. A Wednesday. It was hot that summer. I was forty-one years old and I was happy. Mary and I were blessed with four children. William was a good and honest boy of twenty four. Silas was twenty-two then, and a hard worker. Clara was sixteen, a pretty thing who loved her mother and spent her time tending house. Jacob was just fifteen. He was a quiet boy who thought before he spoke.

You have to understand. You're young, both of you, you've never seen farm life. Not like it was then, anyway. We had a hundred and twenty acres, and it was a lot of land for just one family.

William was married to a girl named Ruth. She was kind and smelled like flowers and never spoke a word against anyone. I promised that if he helped for one more year, I would help get him his own place. His own farm. A place for his own family. I would give him twenty acres and help him buy twenty more, to get him started.

Silas was courting a girl named Hazel who lived not far from us, and I told him that the year after William left I would do the same for him. Silas was patient, more patient than William, but they were both ready to start their own families.

But that's not what you're wanting to hear, I expect. You want to hear how things went so very wrong.

Mary was a church-goer. Every Sunday we would dress in our finest and take the wagon into town. Tangier was small, but we had a fine church. The pastor's name was Clayton. I thought he put on airs, but he was smart and he had a love of the Lord. I never fancied church much, always thought it was between a person and the Lord. I only went to please Mary, because I loved her.

There was never a sweeter woman than my Mary. I loved that woman. I've lain with women since then—I'm no saint. But, Mary? I've never loved another, not in all my years.

We would attend Sunday service and Mary would pray and the children would sing hymns. Clayton preached about evil, but I took it to mean evil in the larger sense.

I hadn't seen evil yet.

It was hot that Wednesday. We worked hard to get the last of the hay in for the summer. It was good. The boys laughed, even though it was hard work pitching the hay up in the haymow. When we finally finished, the sun was low. The women had a good supper waiting for us.

We sat on the porch after the heat died down. The boys told stories while I smoked my pipe. We didn't have conditioned air, the only thing to break the heat was the breeze across the front stoop. It was a good time. A quiet time.

We turned in after sunset.

We had only slept for a short spell before the dogs commenced their barking. It wasn't unusual to have a raccoon or opossum wander in from the field and get the dogs stirred up. A fox was rare, but it happened.

The chickens joined the dogs, making a god-awful racket. I rolled over, trying to sleep in the stifling heat, but then the cows and horses joined in.

The horses concerned me. They usually didn't respond to wild game. Mary put her hand on my shoulder. 'What's wrong?'

'Probably nothing,' I said. I figured that was the case, but I wanted to go check, just to be safe.

I lit my lantern and grabbed my shotgun. William and Silas were already awake, William with his shotgun and Silas with his hunting rifle. We went out into the dark to investigate.

You can't imagine how dark the night was back then. No lights from cities polluted the sky. The darkness was like a living thing. Our lanterns cast enough light for us to see where we stepped and nothing more.

The dogs barked but we couldn't see what disturbed them.

William and Silas shushed them.

'You think it's a coyote?' Silas asked.

'Not likely,' William said.

'Let's check the barn,' I said.

We made our way to the barn and found the horses in their stalls, which was unusual for the summer. They were skittish, whinnying in fear. The cows were pressed against the barn, trying to enter, but there wasn't enough room for them all.

I tried to inspect the pasture, but the lantern cast little light. William and Silas opened the gate and walked through the pasture. They found nothing.

The horses calmed down, and I figured that whatever spooked them had left. I nodded to the boys and we headed back to the house.

As soon as I stepped through the door I knew something was wrong. There was a...stillness in the air. That's the only way I can describe it. I hollered for Mary, but there was no response. The three of us went to my bedroom. My bed was empty, no sign of Mary. The quiet was disturbing, and it made me uneasy.

I tried to tell myself I was spooked for no reason, but a little voice was whispering in my head, telling me that something had happened while we were outside. It was telling me to run, to get away, but I was a man and not given to being spooked like an animal.

We headed up the stairs, but found a body at the top. I held my lantern high and saw that it was Ruth, William's wife, dead on the floor, naked and covered in blood. There was so much of it....

William shrieked and grabbed for her, dropping to his knees, holding her. She had released her bowels. It covered her. I looked on, trying to make sense of it.

Silas stood in shock. His lantern swayed, casting a dancing light over her body.

Death is not noble. It is an inglorious end. As the years pass, I have come to despise the dead, at the unfairness of it, as if it is their fault that something yanked away their essence.

William spoke to her. I don't remember the words. I can remember the smells, the darkness, but not what he said to his wife.

Funny how the mind plays tricks. Maybe I don't want to remember. Maybe it hurts too much to remember my first-born crying and begging for his wife to come back.

I stood there, dumbstruck, until I realized no one had joined us. I turned and headed for the other bedroom, but the door was closed. I nudged it open with my foot, my lantern in one hand and my shotgun in the other. Jacob was on the floor, his eyes wide in shock, and he was breathing fast and shallow, like a wounded animal.

'Jacob. Get up,' I whispered.

His eyes caught mind and I saw terror, and something else. He collapsed and that's when I saw the ragged hole in his stomach. It was wide and bloody and terrible.

'Oh, Jacob. Oh, please no!'

Jacob's eyes went glassy and still, the way a slaughtered animal's will. 'No, no no,' I begged. I rushed to his side, trying not to drop my lantern, still holding the shotgun in case whatever hurt my family came back.

'Who did this to you? Jacob?'

His eyes focused, and he tried to speak, but he couldn't manage any words.

I didn't know what to do. I dropped the shotgun and put the lantern on the floor, then tried to cover the hole in his belly.

I'd never seen blood like that. It was slick and warm and it smelled thick and coppery. He began to shiver, then his body relaxed and he stared off at nothing.

I pulled him to my chest. I was crying and couldn't stop.

I heard a noise behind me and turned to find Silas at the door. He stood, eyes wide in disbelief.

'What happened?' he asked.

I shook my head. It made no sense. We had only been away from the house for minutes. What could have done such a thing?

I stood and grabbed my shotgun. 'Where's Clara?'

There was a cold pit in my stomach. Silas turned to leave, but I grabbed him and held him behind me while I went into the hall.

William still held Ruth—in his grief, he was unaware of anything around him.

I opened the door to Clara's bedroom, holding my lantern high. Clara lay in her bed. 'Clara!' I whispered. 'Clara!'

She didn't move. I stepped closer and Silas followed. He was so close I felt his body heat against my back. I banged my knee against Clara's bed, but she didn't move. I turned and handed Silas my shotgun, then gently shook her shoulder.

She was limp. I rolled her over and that's when I saw the blood. It ran down her neck and covered the bed sheets, turning them a hot and sticky mess.

'Clara?' I asked. I put my finger to her neck. There was no pulse. My sweet little girl was dead.

I refused to believe it. I thought I was in a nightmare, that I was living a horrible dream. I shook my head and felt the tears down my face.

It was not a dream.

I turned to Silas. He was as scared as I'd ever seen.

'They're all dead,' he said, his face white as a sheet. 'What could have done this?'

I had no answers. I sat on the bed, stroking Clara's hair. The room was spinning and I felt I was losing my mind. In less than ten minutes, my son, daughter, and daughter-in-law had been killed, and my wife was missing from our bed.

I heard a noise and turned to the door.

William stood, watching us in shock. 'Dad? What happened here?'

I wanted to sag into the bed and hold my precious Clara, but I knew the boys expected me to have answers. To act.

'Gather Ruth and Jacob. Bring them here.'

William nodded and he returned with Ruth's body soon after. He laid her next to Clara. They looked peaceful, except for the blood. There was so very much of it. It stained the white cotton sheets a scarlet red that appeared almost black in the glow of our lanterns.

William returned with Jacob's body, maneuvering around Silas, who was still in shock. William's knees shook as he placed my son next to my daughter and Ruth. The three of them crowded the bed, and I wished their dead bodies were a bad dream, but the stark reality couldn't be denied.

I turned to the boys. 'We have to get to town. Bring your guns and lanterns. We'll get the horses hitched to the buggy. Let's do it quietly and get moving, quick as we can.'

The boys nodded. We headed down the stairs, watching for movement. I eased the side door open and motioned for the boys to follow. We made it out and to the barn and as the boys bridled the horses and hitched them to the buggy, I kept watch on the darkness, waiting for something to try and kill us.

As they prepared the horses, my mind spun. Where was Mary? What killed my children? How could it happen so fast? I wanted to run screaming through the night, looking for Mary, but I was afraid that whatever had killed the children had also taken her.

No, something was wrong. I felt it against the back of my neck, prickly against the skin. Something was out there watching us.

We made the four miles to town as fast as we could. The roads then were barely more than dirt lanes, but there'd been no rain for a week, so the road was dry and passable. We hung lanterns from the buggy and they provided a little light, but the night was a fearsome dark.

Reverend Clayton's house was a small two-room clapboard shack house next to the church and his was the door I knocked on.

There was noise inside as the Reverend woke. He opened the door holding his kerosene lamp and stared, his flat face wrinkled and wary, his gray hair slick with sweat and plastered against his head. 'Jack Harlan?'

I nodded. 'Reverend. We need your help.'

'What's wrong, Jack? What brings you out at this time of night?'

'Can we come in, Reverend? Best we talk inside.'

'Please, come in, by all means,' he said.

We entered the house and sat at his table, next to the cast-iron stove. I explained to the Reverend what happened, how we found the bodies, how Mary was missing. He listened in disbelief, but I noticed his eyes shifting from us to the door.

As I reached the part about my children, his face paled.

'Reverend? I'm telling you the truth. It sounds crazy....'

'I believe you,' Clayton said. He stood and pulled an old Bible from a wooden trunk in the corner and opened it, holding his lantern close enough to read aloud. I couldn't understand the words. He read for several minutes, his voice rising, until he was practically shouting near the end. When he stopped, I thought I heard a bell ringing, then I felt the hackles on the back of my neck relax.

He looked wrung out. 'We should be safe now,' he said, slumping into his chair, struggling to keep his eyes open.

'Safe from what?' William asked. 'What killed my wife?'

The Reverend sighed heavily. 'You've been scourged.'

'Scourged?' I asked. 'What the hell does that mean?'

Clayton winced at my curse. 'I'm going to tell you a secret, one that I learned in seminary. There are things in this world that aren't talked about. This is one of them. You've been attacked by a creature of great evil.'

'A creature?' Silas asked. 'Like a fairy tale? Something real attacked us, and it wasn't make believe.'

Clayton shook his head sadly. 'I can assure you it is *absolutely* real. You've been attacked by a vampire.'

'A vampire?' I asked.

'Yes. Nobody knows where they came from. They've been around for thousands of years. They feed on blood. They kill for amusement. They're fantastically strong, unbelievably fast, but they *do* have weaknesses. They lose their vitality when the sun is up. They burn when touched by silver. Enough silver will kill them. So will a wooden stake to the heart.'

Clayton sounded like a raving madman, but something *had* attacked us.

'Why?' I asked. 'Why come after *my* family?'

'I'm sorry, Jack, but it is just bad luck. It probably picked your farm at random.'

I wanted to argue with him, but his demeanor was deadly serious. 'What about Mary?'

'Vampires reproduce by infecting and turning their victims,' Clayton said with a pained face. 'The victim dies, but they come back. They lose all sense of morality. They become a being of pure hunger, without God's love or grace. An unholy evil. If the vampire took Mary, it wasn't to feed. It was to make her one of them.'

William looked ill. 'It has our Mother. There must be some way to get her back.'

'I'm afraid it's too late for that,' Clayton said. 'If the vampire has her, she's probably turned.'

I shook my head. 'I can't believe that.'

Clayton leaned forward, frowning. 'You have to accept this. The thing that killed your family and took your wife is more powerful than you can imagine. It's a killer. That's what it does. It's a stain against God.' He reached for my hand, but I pulled away.

Silas had quietly watched us, but now he spoke. 'How do you know all this, Reverend? How do you know about these things?'

Clayton leaned back and shook his head. 'The Catholic church has fought these creatures for thousands of years. During seminary, I was taken aside and told of them. It sounded like madness, but they were adamant. They have tried to exterminate them, but the vampires keep coming back.' He gingerly picked up the Bible. 'There are people who devote their lives to killing vampires. They are called hunters.'

'Have you met one?' I asked.

'No. The church maintains a loose affiliation with them. So does the Odd Fellows and the Masons.'

'What can we do?' I asked. I looked at my boys, the fear in their eyes, and knew I had to try something. 'You have to help us, Reverend. I don't know what else to do.'

The Reverend took my hand and this time I didn't resist. 'I'm afraid it's too late. The best thing to do is run. Get out of the county. Start over somewhere else.'

'What about the vampire?' I asked. 'What if it takes another family? We can't let that happen.'

'The Catholic Church in Indianapolis is the best hope,' Clayton said. 'They *could* contact a hunter. It will take days, maybe weeks, before help arrives.'

That was all I needed to hear. At least it was something, some kind of hope. 'We have to try, Reverend. We can't let this creature escape. We can't let it kill again.'

Clayton nodded, his face determined. 'Of course. If we leave in the morning, we can reach Rockville by the afternoon. There's a man there who belongs to the church. He has an automobile. He can make the trip to Indianapolis in a day. We can go and beg the church for help.'

I shook my head. 'Sorry, Reverend, you'll be making the trip alone. I'm taking the boys back to the farm. We'll stay there and if that thing comes back, we'll kill it.'

Clayton's eyes widened. 'You can't be serious. It *will* kill you, and if Mary has turned, she'll be with it. She won't be a good Christian woman.'

I stood and the boys followed suit. 'We'll take our chances, won't we, boys?'

Silas and William stood and nodded, even though they both looked scared as could be.

The Reverend stuck out his hand. 'Good luck, Jack. Remember, they're weaker during the day and silver will hurt them. If you can cut them or stab them with enough silver, it might kill them. If not, a wooden stake to the heart. Don't take any chances. Watch out for your boys. I'll pray for you.'

Until that moment, I'd never considered prayer to be necessary. Now, I felt it was a requirement if we hoped to make it until help arrived. 'I'll pray for you too, Reverend. Hurry back.'

We left. It was still dark, and as we made our way back to the farm, every bounce and jolt of the buggy wore at our nerves. I watched the darkness, waiting for an unholy creature to jump out, but our trip was uneventful. By the time we arrived, the sun peeked over the horizon, the sky turning a light shade of purple, and I felt a sense of relief.

They were weaker in the daylight, Clayton said. I prayed he was right.

We entered the house and found it just as we left it. I checked my bedroom, but it was still empty. I followed William and Silas up the stairs. The bodies were still in Clara's bedroom, the smell of death heavy in the air.

I'd killed and dressed most anything that walked, crawled or flied, but I'd never smelled human blood like that before.

I put my hand on William's shoulder. He had tears in his eyes. Silas was crying, too, but both boys nodded as I pointed to the door. I led them to the kitchen.

'Get the loading supplies,' I said.

Back then, shotgun shells were solid brass. We loaded them ourselves. I headed for the barn and took the metal nippers from my harrier's tool kit, then used a five-pound sledge to hammer out a stack of silver Morgan dollars into thin flat discs on my anvil. My arms stung with the impact of the sledge and the sweat ran from me in sheets, but I had enough that when I held them tight and cut them into little pieces with the nippers, I held a handful of silver shrapnel, small as bird shot.

I joined the boys in the kitchen and we loaded a dozen shells with silver and crimped them closed. I handed each of the boys four shells. 'Load your shotguns with these. If that thing comes back, we'll see what silver does to it.'

They nodded, took the shells, and loaded their shotguns. I did the same. 'Come with me.'

They followed me back to the barn where I selected a dozen sticks as big as my thumb. I held them in the shaving horse and used my drawknife to clean the bark. When I was finished, I whittled the tips into sharp spikes.

'Remember what the Reverend said,' I reminded them. 'A stake to the heart. If he's right, that thing won't be back during the day. We should be safe until tonight.'

We returned to the house and waited, the sun rising high in the sky. The heat bore down and the house got hot. It began to reek of the foul stench of the dead.

Silas watched through the windows, William joining him now and then, but there was no movement. The cows were getting restless, having missed their morning milking, but I refused to risk any of us to do the job.

I wanted to reassure the boys that everything would be fine, but after what we had seen, I couldn't bring myself to lie. I watched them looking through the curtains and finally realized just how scared they were.

I was, too.

We sat through the day, only leaving to get water and use the outhouse. We moved as a pack, watching all directions, waiting for the creature to return.

It was the longest day of my life. Time had no place there. We held our guns and stakes in that house full of dead, and I thought hard about Clayton's words.

Late in the afternoon I finally prayed to God to allow my boys to survive.

The sun was low on the horizon, the sky a hazy purple. I could feel twilight coming. It was like a physical thing, waiting to pounce. We lit our lanterns, eager to have some protection against the dark, and soon the sweet scent of kerosene mixed with the smell of the dead, the house now hot as a stove.

I stood and moved the curtain aside and watched through the window as the sun disappeared. Night was upon us.

She came, then. So sudden.

There was a squeak from the porch, the faintest jiggling at the door. Before we could react, there stood Mary, my beautiful wife. Only, it wasn't her. Not anymore.

I saw it in her eyes. They were cold and hard and there was something else, something I had never seen, but would come to know well.

She was hungry.

She was still dressed in her white housecoat, but it was covered in dirt and hay, her feet bare.

She stood so very still.

'Jack?' she asked so softly I could barely hear. 'What happened?'

The boys glanced at each other and raised their guns.

I swallowed. 'Something attacked you. Where have you been?'

She glanced at the boys and her face changed, just for an instant. I saw a longing there, and something else. It was the face she made when we were loving each other.

She blinked. 'I don't know. I was waiting for you to come back from the barn and then I woke in the field under a pile of hay. Someone covered me up, I think.' She took a tentative step forward and the boys started to lower their guns.

'Mary,' I said. 'Stop. Do you remember anything else? Anything at all?'

She turned those eyes to me and her lips parted. Her tongue flicked out like a snake. 'I think—I think someone bit me. I think….' She hesitated. 'I died?'

There was a noise from the back and the boys tried to raise their guns, but it was too late. The door to the kitchen exploded in splinters. I squeezed the trigger and my first blast went wide. The thing turned to me and I saw it for what it was. A man, no older than my boys, dressed in homespun clothes and dirtier than my wife's housecoat. He had long black hair, colored ebony, a heavy beard, and his eyes were black as coal.

His eyes widened and his mouth drew back in a delighted grin. I saw the fangs, and I knew Clayton was right. This was no man. This was a beast.

He flung something at the boys and it hit William, knocking the gun from his hand. Silas staggered back and fired his shotgun, narrowly missing Mary, who easily stepped aside. The flung object bounced from William and rolled across the floor and with a dawning horror I recognized it.

It was Clayton's head.

I fired my other shotgun barrel at the vampire. It sidestepped the blast and came at me. It was like watching a lightning bolt. Its speed was unbelievable. I tried to club it with my shotgun, but it ripped it from my hands and slapped me across the face.

It was like a kick from a mule. Everything went black and I saw little points of light. When I came to my senses, I realized I was on the floor. I rolled my head to the side and focused my eyes and saw Mary on top of Silas, slashing at his neck, then her mouth latched onto his skin like a wicked kiss. I saw her throat working and realized she was gulping down his blood.

The vampire held William like a rag doll, William's boots dangling above the floor. The vampire laughed, and it was a soul-grating noise from hell. 'You have such a wonderful family, Harlan. I've been watching you. It was hard. I was *so* hungry. I knew it would be worth the wait. Now I have your wife, and soon I'll have your sons. Don't worry, you won't be alive to see it.'

I saw Clayton's face, his mouth open in a scream, eyes empty. It was worse than a nightmare. The vampire had ripped the Reverend's head from his body, and bits of skin and muscle were still attached.

Sudden understanding washed over me. The vampire followed us to the church, then killed Clayton after we left. Clayton never made it to Rockville. He never got word to the church.

As my mind raced, I knew I had once chance to save my boys. I grabbed the stake that lay on the floor next to me and struggled to sit, keeping the stake behind me, out of sight.

I spat at the thing's feet. 'Clayton said you're a vampire. A creature of pure evil. He was right.'

The vampire turned his gaze upon me, still holding William without effort. He was calm. We were less than nothing to him, this monstrosity from a different time. 'That's what the holy man said? Well, mayhap he was right. But a man has to eat, doesn't he? A man gets lonely and looks for company. There's nothing evil about *that*. It's the way of the world.'

His words filled me with a rage like I had never known. 'You killed Clara and Jacob and Ruth. You're evil and you're going to hell. I'm the one who will put you there.'

Mary turned to me, and I have no words for the look on her face. The only thing that comes close is...sexual. Silas slumped back, eyes wide, Mary astride him. She snickered and then guffawed. A squirt of bright red blood dribbled from her nose. 'Jack. You can't kill him. You're just a *man*. He's a *god*.'

The vampire released William. My son collapsed, his face blue, and gasped for air. 'I'm going to drain you slowly,' the thing said to me. 'I will savor every drop of you. It will *not* be an easy death.'

I looked the thing in the eye. 'I'm going to kill you.'

Its eyes went wide and like that, it moved, coming to kill me. But, I was ready. It was directly over me when I kicked out at his ankles. My feet caught him, and his bare feet slipped back.

I thought it would be enough to cause even a vampire to fall, and fall it did. I pulled the stake out and braced it against the floor. With his feet slid back, the vampire came crashing down on me, but I rolled and the vampire landed chest-first on the stake.

Its eyes widened and it started to speak, but couldn't manage a word. It gasped, lips moving, then its chest exploded in a shower of light and fire, body flopping on the floor.

I felt the essence of him enter me, a white-hot knife plunging into my body. I screamed until my throat was raw, but somehow I managed to absorb it. It was the change. My first kill. I struggled to get the burning vampire off me, kicking and shoving until I managed to knock it away.

As soon as I was free, Mary was on top of me. I beat at her with my fists, but it was like hitting stone. Her hand darted out and I felt her nails at my face, like an animal's claws, and there was a horrible pain, worse even than the change, as she ripped my eye out. I screamed again and she flung her head back, shrieking like a banshee.

There was a powerful blast and she went spinning off me. I turned, and with my remaining eye, saw William holding his shotgun, his eyes wide, horrified.

Mary stood on unsteady legs and tried to run for the door, but I kicked out, tripping her. She struggled to stand, but so did I. I grabbed my shotgun, opened it, and replaced the two shells with two fresh ones loaded with silver shot.

By the time I had reloaded, Mary was out the door and into the night. I followed, leaving William with the burning pile of greasy ash. Mary limped across the grass, toward the barn, and I followed close behind. I could barely stand. The pain in my head made me lightheaded and slipped in the grass. The sky was dark, but the starlight was enough to follow her to the barn.

She was staggering, obviously in great pain. The silver had taken her in the leg, but it wasn't enough to set her burning.

She turned to me. 'Jack, please.'

I held up the gun to the woman I loved. She was beautiful, even then. 'I'm sorry, Mary. May God forgive me.'

She backed against the barn, pressing herself it, her eyes wide. I saw the whites, even in the dark, and that image haunts me to this day, those white eyes in the starlight.

I pulled the triggers and put both barrels through her chest, before I lost my nerve.

She jerked and a geyser of flame erupted from her chest. I slumped forward and watched her burn, the shotgun propped under my arm as a crutch. She glared, her mouth clenched tight, but she never screamed as the fire consumed her.

She just glared at me with eyes full of hate.

I felt it again, the agony of fire rip through me, and I almost fell to the ground, but the shotgun held me steady. Soon enough, there was nothing but a little fire that I managed to stamp out before wearily heading back to the house.

I found William standing over Silas. 'I think he's hurt bad,' he said.

I looked at Clayton's head, then at the burnt greasy spot that had been the godforsaken creature. The smell was overwhelming.

On the floor, Silas was dying. I knelt beside him.

He looked up, uncertain. 'Did we do it?' His voice was weak, his face pale, his eyes unfocused.

'We did,' I said. I looked over to William who stared at me. The shock of losing my eye was starting to hit, and I wasn't sure how much longer I could go on.

Silas frowned. 'Am I going to die?' he asked.

I wanted to lie, but nodded my head.

'I'm not afraid,' he said. 'Don't be sad. I'll be home soon.' His eyes rolled back and he started breathing heavy, long drawn out rasps that tapered off as his life drained away.

William and I held him, together, as he went limp, his eyes empty, his face slack.

It's a crime against nature, outliving your offspring. There's a time for living and a time for dying. The old make way for the young so the young can have their time. I believe that. Watching Silas die was the hardest thing I have ever done. Harder than finding the bodies of my children. Harder, even, than killing what used to be my wife.

When his breathing stopped, I turned to William. 'We have to leave.'

William was crying, and he shook his head in disbelief. 'Why?'

I staggered up, managed to upright a chair, and slumped into it. 'Look around, son. If the sheriff finds this, he won't believe us. We have to go.' I stood and stumbled into our bedroom. I tore apart a cotton shirt and made a crude bandage to wrap around my head, covering my eye. I stuffed an extra pair of coveralls and a few shirts and socks in a bag.

The wooden chest at the end of the bed held my wife's possessions, the things she had hoped to leave to Clara. Under her old wedding dress there was a small wooden box. We had prospered, and it contained our extra money, in cash and silver and gold coins. I stuffed them in the bag, then went to find William.

He was in Clara's room, lantern held high, staring at the bodies. 'We can't just leave them,' he said. 'We need to give them a proper burial.'

'There's no time,' I said. 'Get some extra clothes. I'll get some food and prepare the horses.'

He stood, unmoving.

'*William*. We *have* to go.' I put my hand on his shoulder. 'There's nothing for us here.'

He nodded, reluctantly, and left to pack his things. I stood, looking at the remains of my family. Everything I knew about the world had changed. I felt exhaustion, grief, and a lingering terror. My knees turned rubbery and I wanted nothing more than to sink to the floor, but William needed me.

He was all I had left.

I checked and found him in his room tossing clothes in a burlap gunny sack. I nodded and made my way out of the house, through the dark, to the smokehouse. I took another gunny sack and put two hams in it and tied it off. But, as I did, I felt a hunger so deep and...vast...that the vision in my remaining eye blurred.

We smoked our own hams, back then, after the fall butchering. Once smoked and cured with salt, they would last until the next fall. Most of the hams were gone, but a few still dangled among the empty hooks. The smoking and curing process didn't cook the ham, just removed the moisture and kept them from spoiling.

I didn't care.

I took one down from its hook and cut a big piece off with my pocket-knife. I scraped the salt from the side and popped it in my mouth. It was salty and hard and dry, and just about the best thing I'd ever tasted. I chewed on it the way a dog chews on a bone, my spit working to soften the meat, then swallowed. I cut another piece, and then another, until I staggered out to the wellhouse. I primed the pump and worked the lever, pumping cold water into the bucket on the wooden platform below. I dunked the remaining ham in the bucket, then used my knife to scrape off as much salt as I could. I took the ham out and poured out the salty water, then repeated the process. When I'd removed much of the salt, I tore into the ham with my bare teeth.

A fire grew in my belly and I felt the exhaustion return, but this time my aching body felt better. I was gnawing on the hambone when

William found me in the wellhouse. He watched me chew, his eyes big as saucers.

'I'm fine,' I said, but even as I spoke I knew it wasn't true. Something happened to me when I killed that creature, when I killed my wife. I didn't know it yet, but the change was coursing through me, making me into something else. A hunter.

We gathered our horses, and I bridled a third to carry the gunny sacks of clothes and food.

William turned to me in the starlight. 'Where do we go?'

'East,' I said. 'We go far from here and we never look back.'"

* * *

The sky outside was dark when Jack finished his story. He'd been talking for hours. The whiskey bottle was long since empty and Jack's voice was ragged. His face was pained as he told the story, and I could tell reliving events so far in the past still hurt.

Something occurred to me. "Did you know?" I asked. "Did you know Silas turned?"

Jack turned his good eye to me. "It took years. The more I learned about them, the more I replayed the events back in my mind. The attack, the vampire, Mary, how we left...." His eye got bright and shiny, and I saw tears welling up. "If I had known, I would have staked his body." He shook his head. "I've asked myself ever since. Could I have done it differently?"

"What happened?" Katie asked. "How did you find out?"

"William changed his last name to Miller, met a good girl named Margaret and had three children. Frank, Emma, and David. They were just children when Silas attacked. He killed Frank and David. Slaughtered them, like you would an animal. Silas left Margaret alive and gave her a message. William was to contact me. I was in South Carolina when I got the telegram, and I hurried back. Silas was waiting."

"He blamed you, didn't he?" I asked.

"Yes, he did," Jack said bitterly. "I was a hunter by then, but I didn't expect him. He caught me, told me he would kill everyone I ever loved, that he would follow me until the end of my days. He's kept that promise."

"And you really haven't been able to kill him? With all your experience?" I asked. "Tell me the truth, Jack. He was a youngling. How could you not stake him?"

Jack glanced away. "I learned a lot about vampires over the years and I've pieced some together on my own." He turned his gaze to Katie. "Tell me, girl. You've read the church's records on vampires. What gives them their power?"

Katie shrugged. "It's a function of their age, isn't it? The older they are, the more powerful they become?"

Jack nodded. "That's what they say, but there's more to it. A vampire's power comes not just from their age, but from who they were before they turned. Take Henry. He was a prince—an honest to goodness prince—before he was turned. That carried over. Even as a youngling, he probably had better control than a vampire with a hundred years. It's the same with Silas. He was a youngling, but he was strong and fast and completely in control, and he wanted to punish me for what happened."

"It doesn't make any sense," I said. "He *knows* it wasn't your fault."

"He knows," Jack agreed, "but vampires don't always think straight. They become obsessed. That's what happened to him. Or, it could be because I killed his maker before he turned. That might have something to do with it."

"Was Henry telling the truth?" Katie asked. "About the Ancients?"

Jack shrugged. "Probably so. That's something I realized over the years. I killed vampires that were hundreds of years old, but I never come across a truly old vampire—except for Henry. I always wondered what happened to them. Where did they go? There were rumors of the Ancients. Twelve of the oldest vampires, thousands of years old. They don't like change, and they don't want to be exposed. There's just so many more humans...."

He continued, "In ancient times, humans would cower in fear for only so long before they would rising up and massacring the vampires. The Ancients understood this. So, they appointed one vampire as Sheriff. He would track and kill any vampire over a certain age. No one has actually ever met the Sheriff. Until today, I wouldn't have believed it myself. Now, it makes sense. Henry is a man from a different time. He might not tell you the whole truth, but he won't lie to your face. No, the Ancients are real."

"And the part about you changing?" I asked softly.

Jack turned away, his face weary and drawn. "It was years ago. I felt a change, something…different. Maybe it's because I was a farmer before a hunter, but it's like the seasons are changing. My life has rushed by, the spring, summer and fall. Now I'm heading to winter, the time of dying. All the vampire kills? I'm becoming one of them. I don't know when it's going to happen, but it will happen soon, and when that time comes, I think Henry might be right. There's no telling what I could become."

Katie put her hand on his. "Tell me you have some kind of plan. Tell me that there's some way out of this."

Jack patted her hand. "More like the start of an idea."

* * *

I sat in the chair with my .45 in my lap, staring at the door. My watch said it was midnight, the time my dad called the witching hour, and the events of the day replayed in my mind. In just a few days, my life had become one of horrors and monsters and things that went bump in the night. I smiled bitterly. I wanted to wake from the nightmare, but I was not asleep. This was now my life.

I turned back to Jack, fast asleep in a sleeping bag on the floor. We decided it best that we all sleep in the same room. He was motionless, and for a brief moment I wondered if he was already dead, but then his chest rose, ever so slowly. His arm was flung out on the floor, only inches from the Tommy gun he insisted on keeping close.

The man was my kin, and I tried to imagine what it would be like, to lose my family, to have my son turned, to watch as he killed generation after generation of my descendants just to torment me. Then I remembered that my own wife was now with Silas and that my own daughter was out there, somewhere, with the monsters. Or, perhaps she was dead. I shook my head. No, Lilly had to be alive. I couldn't consider a world without her.

Katie tossed in her sleeping bag, the nylon swishing against itself, then she opened her eyes. She held my gaze, then unzipped her bag and motioned for me to join her.

The temperature outside had dropped and the cabin was edging toward cold, but when I snuggled in next to her, I felt the heat of her body against mine.

As nice as it was, it also made me feel guilty. I had always been faithful to my wife, and here I was, in a sleeping bag, with a beautiful woman.

She stared deeply into my eyes, then spoke softly. "I have to say something and I'm afraid you're not going to like it."

"After what we've been through, I think you've earned the right to say anything."

She hesitated, and her hand sought out mine. She intertwined her fingers with mine. "You hesitated today, with Stacie. She would have turned you or killed you. You're not going to save your daughter that way."

"I couldn't just shoot her, not without giving her a chance to help Lilly."

Katie bit her bottom lip, then slowly shook her head. "You're going to get us killed, Sam. You know what you have to do. If you really want to save your daughter, you're going to have to kill her."

"I know what I have to do," I said stubbornly. "I understand what's at stake."

"Do you?" she asked. "I'm not just along for the ride. I'm trying to save Callie's life. I want to help you, I want to help you find Lilly, but I have to help my sister. You promised me. Remember?"

I wanted to argue. I wanted to hate her for what she said. I couldn't. "I'll do what I have to. It's just not easy. I keep forgetting what she's become. I want to remember her as she was."

Katie leaned in and put her face close to my neck, her hands wrapping around me. "You loved your wife, Sam, you truly loved her like a man should. I'm sorry, but that woman is gone. The next time you see her, you have to understand what she is now. She's not human. Not anymore."

I felt her against me, so much like my wife's warm body, the way we used to hold each other. "How did this happen? My life was normal. Everything was...*normal*."

"Life is anything but normal," she said, "and if you keep denying that, we're all dead."

I pulled her close. "A week ago my biggest problem was whether I should raise the price on the meatloaf special by a dollar. Now I'm hiding in a cabin with a woman I just met, my daughter is missing, and I'm preparing to kill my undead wife." As I spoke, I realized why I was having such a hard time coping. My life before was so...irrelevant. "Fine, I know what's at stake. I'll do it. I'll kill her. I'll save your sister, but I have to find Lilly. I can't give up on her."

"I know you can't, and I'll do everything I can to help save your daughter. But, what about Jack? What if he manages to kill Silas? What if he turns?"

I tilted my head until I could look her in the eyes. "We know what happened to Silas after he turned. What would Jack become? In all the books you read, all the records from Father Lewinheim and the church, did you ever read anything about a hunter turning?"

She shook her head. "It's terrifying, Sam. He's stronger than any hunter in the records. There's not many who survive long enough to acquire that kind of power. He could be unstoppable. That's probably why the Ancients are so worried."

I thought about that, then shuddered. I agreed with her assessment. "What else do you know about the Ancients?"

"There were very few references in the church documents. A snippet here and there. They were the first vampires to conquer their hunger, and they realized that wealth and power could insulate them from humanity. Empires rose and fell, but they endured. No one knows who they are and no one has ever met them. They have only one long-term goal that unites them and that's to survive."

"If that's true," I mused, "then they've got the money and the means to find us, eventually."

She eyed me carefully. "They're not interested in us, Sam. We're less than nothing to them. Why would a giant care about an ant? They only care about Jack."

I sighed. "Then let's hope that Jack's plan works better than his last one."

CHAPTER ELEVEN

Sunday

My dreams were feverish, barely more than flashes of memories. Stacie and Lilly playing in the diner while I cleaned, Stacie kissing me and Lilly hugging me in our living room, then Stacie holding my arms, twisting them as Silas spoke.

Everything shifted and I was running through my house, Stacie close behind me. She was screeching, a high and chitinous scraping, like a bug's body when squished. Katie stood in front of us, beautiful, her skin glowing, luminous in the twilight.

The landscape shifted again, from my house in Arcanum to an empty field, dark shapes chasing me. I tried to see what hunted me, but it was dark and I only glimpsed shadows. I kept running, never any closer to Katie, never catching site of Lilly.

Stacie's fingers wrapped around my neck and I jerked awake to find Jack, bent over, gently shaking my arm.

"Jesus," I said. "You scared the hell out of me." I was pressed against Katie, spooning her. She moaned softly, then went still.

Jack's mouth quirked up, almost managing a smile. "Time to get up, boy."

A soft light glowed between the window sill and the aluminum foil. "What time is it?"

Jack took a seat at the table. He poured instant coffee from an MRE packet into a bottle of water, shook it, then gulped down the brown concoction. "The sun is barely up. Maybe six or six thirty. We have to talk."

I extricated myself from the sleeping bag, careful not to disturb Katie. I winced at the pain in my side, but it hurt less than the night before. I joined Jack at the table, and he offered me a bottle of water which I gladly took and gulped down. It was flat and plasticy, but it was wet and took the edge off my thirst. My stomach churned, the change still driving my hunger. There were several MRE's on the table and I opened one, using the long plastic spoon to wolf down the green-colored eggs. The flavor was horrible, but I was so hungry it didn't matter.

Jack watched me eat, then spoke softly. "Silas has killed all my descendants, Sam, but you're not the only one left alive. There is another. Silas thought he killed him, but I managed to hide him away, gave him the opportunity to live out his life. If Silas knew he was alive, he'd come for him."

My mind reeled at the news of another living relative. "Who?"

"Your great-uncle Warren. Your grandmother's brother."

"You're proposing we use him as bait?" A shiver ran down my spine. "Isn't that kind of cold?"

Jack shook his head. "We're out of options. Warren will help, I'm sure of it. It's my only chance to put Silas in the ground and for you to stake your wife. If we do that, you'll be safe and Callie will wake from her coma. Then we can track down Lilly and you'll have a chance at living a normal life."

I dropped the empty MRE pouch on the table. "What about Henry? What about the Ancients?"

Jack shrugged. "We have to hold him off until we finish our business."

"And after?"

"I'm not going to lie to you," Jack said. "I can't be allowed to turn. If we pull this off, Henry needs to do his job. I can't become one of them." His good eye was haunted. "Come what may, don't wait for Henry. You understand? If I turn, put me down. Empty your gun in my chest, then stake me, just to be safe. No hesitation. No foolishness. Do the job and do it right."

His eye was deep and dark and I felt myself sinking. I nodded. "I understand."

Jack leaned back in his chair. "I've seen people, before and after. They'll do things in death they never would have considered in life. You're young. You've had a rough patch, but you don't know how bad things can get. I hope you never learn what they're capable of, because as bad as Silas is, I've seen much worse." He reached out and took my hand, his grip still strong, and his eye bore into mine with that heavy weight. "They're monsters, boy, and don't you forget it. You do what you have to do to get your daughter back, you do what is necessary to save Katie's sister, but you make sure I'm in the ground. I won't let this all be for nothing. I won't become one of *them*."

My mouth went dry, because in that moment, I felt something toward Jack I had never felt. Not in my house in Arcanum, not in St. Louis or Peoria, or even in Indianapolis.

He scared me.

I swallowed hard, then nodded.

* * *

Katie rolled over, the sleeping bag swish-swishing. I smiled at her and handed her a water bottle of warm coffee.

Her eyes widened. "How in the world did you manage this?"

I watched her sit up and take a sip, her emerald eyes blinking in the dim morning light. "Instant coffee from the MRE's. I used the MRE heater to warm it up. I was a cook in a diner, remember? It's my only useful skill, you know, from before."

She smiled as she sipped more coffee. "It's not hot and it's certainly not good, but thanks. Where's Jack?"

I pointed to the door, half ajar. "Prepaid cell phone. He's trying to reach the church, see if they can help."

As I finished, Jack came inside, slamming the door behind him. Katie looked from me to him. "Did you speak to the Father?"

Jack nodded. "Sister Callie is still in a coma." He took a seat across from me at the small table, slumping in his chair. "The church can't help. There's just not enough people. It's age, pure and simple. The older generation died off, and the younger members of the church don't have the will to keep fighting. There's a few exceptions, like Father Jameson, maybe a handful of others across the country, but it would take weeks to organize them."

"What about other hunters?" I asked. "Surely there's *someone* who can help."

"There's not many," Katie said, shaking her head sadly. "I know that much from the records. There are only a handful left in North America, and they are pretty territorial. They're not active like they were fifty or a hundred years ago, isn't that right?"

Jack focused on her with his good eye. "I work solo. Less people get killed that way. I've had little dealings with them. I guess I didn't realize how many had died."

"There's been no one to train them or replace them," Katie murmured. "It's not your fault, Jack. You can't be everywhere. You've kept the Midwest under control for the past hundred years."

Jack leaned forward and held his face in his hands. "I could have kept in touch with Garski in New York, or Platt in Dallas. Even Butcher in Los Angeles would be a help, but they're all dead and in the ground. I thought the church would be more help. Guess I wasn't paying much attention to them, either."

"What are we going to do?" I asked. "It's just us."

Jack lifted his head. "We're going to see your great-uncle."

* * *

We were heading west on US36, south of Dana, mile after mile of corn and bean fields passing by as the truck roared through the morning dew, when I asked Jack the question. "How did you save him?"

Jack never took his eyes from the road. "It was 1945. I was just back from the war. Silas grew bored with killing my heirs. He decided to turn Warren."

"Wait," I said. "You were in the war?"

He nodded. "The concentration camps made a perfect hiding place for vampires. Millions went in and very few survived until the liberation. The whole world had heard the rumors of the camps, but it seemed unbelievable. Madness. Not to me, though. I figured it was the perfect opportunity for them. The camps were thick with vampires. The country was sick of war, and the church put a lot of effort into convincing Eisenhower that the liberation of the camps would be strategic to reviving the nation's outrage. They helped get a few hunters inserted into the troops and we cleaned out the camps as best we could, among the aftermath." His voice had grown gravelly while he talked, and he slurped heavily from the cup of coffee he had purchased at the Casey's gas station in Rockville.

We drove in silence. I caught Katie, out of the corner of my eye, watching Jack in awe. Neither of us could bring ourselves to break the silence.

Jack finally continued, "The Russians had it worse, I found out later. The Red Army had their own hunters. Apparently Stalin knew about vampires and wanted them exterminated." He turned his good eye to us. "They represented a threat to socialism, in old Uncle Joe's mind. He managed to kill every vampire living in the Soviet Union."

I took a deep breath. Jack had *lived* through the twentieth century. He was like a history book. "What happened when you got back?"

"William's boy, David, had three kids. Warren, Bob and your grandmother, Linda. Warren was thirteen years old in 1945. They lived in Chicago, and I had a house a block away. David knew who I was, of course. He also knew about Silas. Nothing prepared him for what happened. Silas and Pearl took Warren in the middle of the night. David came to me, knocking on my apartment door, begging for help. I tracked them to Wisconsin, to an abandoned movie theater. Silas had already infected Warren, giving him the gift." Jack's hand tightened on the wheel and his knuckles went white. "I found them, shot up Pearl real good, but couldn't kill her. Killed another one of his younglings, a greasy little bastard named Ralph. Nasty piece of work, that boy was. When I saw Silas next, he had a bit of fun with me. Taunting me. Asked how I liked staking my great-grandson."

"You didn't kill him, did you?" Katie asked. "You saved him."

There was a long pause as Jack worked his jaw. "How could I kill the boy? I had to try something. I knew a priest. Lewinheim. After Reverend Clayton, I made a few contacts in the church, especially the Catholics. Edmund was a young man, but he knew more about vampires than any other priest in the Midwest. So, I threw Warren in the back of my car and drove like hell to Peoria. I begged Edmund to help. Told him that if he couldn't help Warren, I'd have to stake him. Turns out, Edmund *could* help. He performed the ritual. We saved Warren's life, but then what? I couldn't take him home. Silas was watching. He'd just turn him or kill him. I couldn't take him with *me*. I was too busy hunting. He would have been dead within the week. So, Edmund helped me find a home for him, a young couple who couldn't have kids. They raised him as their own. We gave Warren the chance to live a normal life, far from Silas. Far from vampires."

* * *

Jack pulled the truck up the steep drive, through the woods, next to Lake Decatur. The house was older, a dark wooden contemporary with small windows, the trees so dense and close that the leaves a dark canopy obscuring the sun.

The three of us got out and walked through the carpet of damp leaves that covered the sidewalk, the smell of years of decay heavy in the air. There was another smell, like the grease from my fry-bin mixed with rotten corn.

Katie sniffed. "What is that?"

Jack turned to us. "They say it's the smell of money. Archer Daniels Midland is just a mile that way." He pointed across the brackish green lake next to the road.

I shook my head. "Wonderful."

We reached the front and Jack rapped loudly. It was several minutes before it finally opened.

The man who stood there was old, back stooped, his hair thin and gray. There was an uncanny resemblance to Jack, but where Jack's dark eye carried weight, the man's eyes sparkled with intelligence. We stood looking at each other, until the man tilted his head. "Jack."

"Warren."

"I thought I told you not to come."

Jack shrugged. "You did. We need your help."

My great-uncle Warren turned to me. He stared, appraising, and I stood steady under his gaze, then he turned his attention to Katie, before finally returning to Jack. "Not my problem."

Jack took a step forward. "He's family."

"And her?"

Katie started to speak, but Jack shushed her. "A Calahane."

Warren's eyes widened, then shook his head. "Doesn't matter."

"Damn it, Warren."

"Tell me why I should care?"

"Because he's family," Jack said, raising his voice. "*Your* time has come and gone. Give *him* the same chance."

Warren's face went red. "That's what this is? Calling in the favor?"

Jack's face was cold. "Yes."

Warren opened his mouth and started to speak, then stopped. He sagged against the door-frame. "You're a real son of a bitch," he managed at last. "How do you live with yourself?"

"I'll do anything for family," Jack said, finally breaking into a grin. "You know that."

CHAPTER TWELVE

Warren looked at us as if we were crazy. "You want *me* to be bait?"

Jack nodded. "He'll go batshit crazy when he realizes you're still alive."

I glanced between them, sitting across from each other at Warren's kitchen table. "How will that help us? We almost died in Indianapolis."

Jack smiled. "Warren's studied for years, isn't that right?"

Warren sighed heavily, nodding at me. "How much does he know?"

"About what?" I asked.

"Magic," Warren said.

"You're a magician?" Katie asked.

Jack turned his eye on me. "Everyone has the ability to perform magic. You, me, anyone. It just takes a long time to develop. Well, that and a hell of a lot of practice. When Edmund helped cleanse Warren all those years ago, it heightened his abilities."

Warren nodded. "It's like a muscle. Everyone is born with it. Some are gifted with a stronger one, some weaker. If you work at it, it grows bigger, and if you let it go, it withers. After Silas attacked, everything was fuzzy. I was dying. When I woke up in the church, the light was shining bright and I felt something. It's hard to explain, but I could sense that muscle was suddenly bigger and stronger."

"The couple who took him in as their own called me a couple of years later," Jack said. "Strange things were happening. I came straight away, thought maybe Silas had found him. Turns out it wasn't Silas. Warren didn't even know he was doing it."

"Decatur is a strange place," Warren said with hooded eyes. "There's something about the land here. It's the most haunted places in Illinois. If you go just east of here, there's an old family cemetery, the most discomforting spot in North America. There are ghosts here, real spirits that wander the earth, not puffs of mist that glow in

147

the dark. Other things as well. Vampires can't stand it here. Jack didn't know it at the time, he just knew I'd be loved and safe. And, I was. Until I started seeing things."

"I didn't know," Jack said softly. "How could I?"

Warren shook his head. "Of course you didn't. One thing about age, it gives you perspective." He turned to me, his face sad. "The last time I saw your grandmother, she was seven years old. She had a little doll she used to carry. Bob and I loved watching her play with that doll. She would talk to it and hold it and hug it, just like a baby. I never saw her again, not after Jack saved me."

"Bob?" I asked. I had a vague memory of the name, but couldn't place it.

"My little brother," Warren said. "I never saw him, either. He died in Korea, isn't that right, Jack?"

Jack nodded slowly. "It was a bad bit of luck. Even if he'd made it out of the war, Silas would have found him."

Warren eyed Jack carefully. "Most likely. Like I said, Jack, age has given me perspective. Do you appreciate that you saved my life, gave me the opportunity to start my own family, away from Silas, yet Rita was unable to have children?"

Jack's face reddened and he sunk lower in his chair, deflated. "I'm sorry I missed her funeral."

Warren shrugged. "Not your fault."

Jack stood. "I need a drink."

"Sorry, no alcohol in the house," Warren said.

"I think I have a bottle in the truck." Jack left to get the bottle.

It was several minutes before Warren turned to us. "My wife died of breast cancer. Nothing I could do to help her. Nothing medicine could do to help her. I placed her in hospice. I held her hand as she approached the threshold of death. I watched her life force steal away from this reality. I could have summoned it, called her back. She would have returned as a spirit. What kind of man would do that to his wife? To someone he loved? Watching her die was bad enough. That's when I began to understand what it might have been like for Jack."

"We can't ask you to help us," Katie said.

Warren smiled, but it never made it to his eyes. "You didn't ask me to help, girl. Jack did. He's right, family *is* important. I've tried to forget them, but after all these years, when I close my eyes, I remember them the way they were. Before Silas."

Jack finally returned. He twisted the top off the Jack Daniels' bottle and handed it to Warren. "You deserve the first belt."

Warren took the bottle and knocked back a deep slug, then coughed as the whiskey went down. "So, you have a plan?"

Jack nodded. "How's your fire?"

* * *

Jack had finished moving the furniture and Katie and I rolled up the oriental rugs and placed them in the corner. The large room was now bare, our voices echoing between the hardwood floor and the wood-paneled walls. Jack nodded his head, satisfied, and we waited for Warren to begin.

He pulled a piece of chalk from a box and within minutes drew a pentagram, at least ten feet across, on the floor. He stood up, holding his back. "When you're younger, they never tell you how your back will hurt when you get old," he said with a frown.

"A pentagram?" I asked. "That's your plan?"

Warren chuckled. "It's a focus. The five points of the pentagram represent earth, air, fire, water, and spirit. The circle binds it all together. The symbology is as old as the hills, I know, but it works for me. Helps focus my energy."

I glanced around, doubtful. "Now what?"

He left and returned quickly with a dagger and a golden cup. Looking closer, I decided it was too ornate for a cup. It was a golden chalice. He slashed the dagger across his hand and held it over the chalice, his blood splattering in the bowl. We watched as the blood flowed, filling the bottom of the cup, until he nodded, satisfied, and wrapped his hand with gauze and tape to stop the blood flow.

"Powerful magicians can manipulate pure energy," he said. "I'm not that powerful. But what I can do is bind my life force, my blood, to the circle. It will power the spell." He knelt slowly, his knees creaking and popping, until he sat cross-legged. "Now I need to concentrate. No distractions, please."

He closed his eyes, his body going still, his breathing deep and rhythmic. His eyes danced behind his eyelids and he mouthed words to himself, guttural sounds like nothing I had ever heard before. As he went completely silent, his eyes finally came to a stop. There was an anticipation in the air, like a storm cloud about to erupt, then he waved his palm over the chalice and a thrumming that I hadn't even noticed ended in a bell-like gong.

I looked to Katie and her eyes were wide. She had heard it, too. I turned to Jack. but his eye was on the chalice, a peculiar expression on his face.

Warren stood, even more slowly, and flung the blood from the chalice into the circle, which flared to life in a blinding flash. When my eyes could see again, the circle appeared normal, and Warren staggered forward.

Jack caught him and held him steady. "It's ready?"

Warren nodded wearily. "Yes."

"You have enough power left to summon him?"

"You have something?"

Jack rummaged in his pants pocket and produced a few fine hairs. "I pulled these from his head in Indianapolis."

"Thinking ahead, were you?" Warren pinched the hairs between his thumb and index finger. "This will do."

Curious, I asked, "You can talk to him with that?"

"In a manner of speaking," Warren said. "I'll project directly into his mind, let him know that I'm alive and well, and leave the spell open. It will be as if I poked him right in his mind. It will madden him. He'll be able to follow the spell back to us."

"Won't he know it's a trap?" Katie asked. "Why would he come?"

Jack snorted. "Have you been paying attention? It's *who* he is. He won't be able to help himself. He'll come for Warren, and he'll come for me, even knowing it's a trap."

"Now all we have to do is manage to kill him before he slaughters Warren, turns you, and does who knows what with me and Katie."

Jack turned his eye on me. "That's a fact."

"Ready?" Warren asked.

Jack glanced at us and nodded. "Do it."

Warren held a small silver bowl in his left hand. He took the pinched hairs and murmured some words, then dropped the hairs into the silver bowl. There was a bright flash of light as the hairs burst into flame, then a cool breeze blew through the room.

"I can sense him," Warren mumbled. He sat the bowl on the kitchen counter and held out his hands. Jack and Katie held my hands, me in the center, then they each took one of Warren's, forming a loop.

An electric shock tingled through my body and I felt it, a voice far in the distance, soft and whispering.

Blood. So hungry.

"Silas," Warren said. "Silas!"

What?

"You failed to kill me, Silas. You failed in 1945. Jack saved me."

Who is this?

"Warren Miller, great uncle. You remember, don't you? You infected me with your vampire filth and left Jack to kill me. I survived. I had a long life. I had tragedies and triumphs. Unlike you, Silas, I *lived.*"

Through the connection, I felt a murderous rage, white hot and all-consuming. *I'll kill you. I'll rip the life from you. I'll tear your flesh from your body.*

"You couldn't do it then. What makes you think you can do it now?"

Kill you! I'll kill you!

"You will do no such thing," Warren scoffed. "You're a failure, Silas. You've done nothing but struggle to ruin my family, and you've failed."

The rage burned brighter and I felt something else, the hunger, a deep chasm of never ending want and need, stoking the anger into an intense wildfire.

I'm coming for you.

Warren yanked his hands away and the connection ended. I could still feel a lingering sense of hunger, and knew the connection wasn't completely broken. He turned to Jack, equal parts sad and triumphant. "He's on his way."

Jack took a deep breath. "Did you have to taunt him so much?"

"You wanted to make sure he came for me. Well, now he'll come."

* * *

I stood in the front room, watching Jack and Warren through the window. The waiting was driving us mad, and Jack and Warren had gone outside to stretch their legs. Seeing them side by side was a reminder of what Jack had sacrificed. They were both old men now, standing against the hill, the afternoon light shining down through the trees, the leaves not yet completely fallen. They stood facing west.

Jack would occasionally turn to Warren and speak, then Warren would nod and shrug.

Katie leaned next to me. "What do you think they're talking about?"

"Probably catching up. Jack's the kind to keep his thoughts to himself. He probably never told Warren why he saved him or how much it hurt to watch as Silas murdered his family. I'm sure Warren thought Jack abandoned him."

"That was years ago. Surely by now Warren knows that Jack kept his distance to keep him safe."

I nodded. "He probably knows in his head, but his heart? I think he's spent so much time hating Silas that he hates Jack, as well. I think his feelings are confused, that what he feels in his heart doesn't make sense to him."

I felt her hand touch my arm. "Are we talking about Warren?"

I turned to her and smiled. "Yes and no. My feelings are a mess. I know none of this is my fault, but I still feel guilty. I feel like my heart's been ripped out, that until I get Lilly back, the world doesn't make any sense. I want my world back. I was happy there."

She started to speak, but I stopped her. "I know Stacie is gone. I know it's not my fault. I know it's not Jack's fault. In a strange way, Silas isn't really to blame, either. He didn't ask to be turned. You have faith, Katie. Where is God? Why does he allow this? I mean, I was never deeply religious, but if vampires respond to faith, then God is real, isn't he? If he's real, why doesn't he do something? Why does he allow us to suffer?"

Katie bit her lip and her green eyes filled with a reflection of my pain. "I don't know, Sam. I want to say something to make it better, but I just don't know. I wondered if he would allow Timm to kill me, then you showed up. At first, I thought you were sent by God, but now I suspect it just…happened. I wish I could see God's will in it, but I don't. Maybe it's because we sinned. I used to tell people that when bad things happened, it was part of God's plan, but after Callie went into a coma, I don't know if I believe that anymore."

I watched her face. The light had left. She appeared deflated, shrunken, and her skin was dull and waxy. I realized her faith had propped her up and kept her going through all the insanity. Now that I was voicing my doubts, it echoed her own.

I took her hand and, before I could stop myself, kissed it. "None of that matters anymore. One thing I've learned in the last week is that I lived my life asleep, walking through day and night, with no rhyme or reason. I worked at the diner because it was my Dad's and I felt like I was supposed to work there. I didn't know what I wanted to do. Not really. Now I do."

She looked to me, her lip quivering. "What's that?"

"I *want* to kill Silas, to finally free Jack from suffering. I *want* to kill Stacie and save your sister. And, I *want* my daughter back."

I saw the fire seep into her eyes, her fine lashes blinking slowly, and I felt something then, a warmth, radiating from her, so loving and pure, like a hot wind against me.

She smiled and it made me feel good all the way to my core. "We're going to do it, Sam. We *will* save them all."

CHAPTER THIRTEEN

The late afternoon sun bled through the windows, still warm enough in September to heat the room to an uncomfortable degree. A trickle of sweat rolled down my back and I shifted my Colt from hand to hand as I wiped my palms against my jeans. Jack sat at the kitchen counter, shotgun cradled in his lap. Katie stood next to him, clutching her crucifix, her eyes closed and her lips moving in silent prayer. Warren knelt on the floor in front of the pentagram, eyes closed, arms extended.

I glanced nervously outside. If Jack's estimates were true, it was well past time for Silas to have located us. I tried to reach out, to sense any disturbance, to that oily feeling in the pit of my stomach, the evil I felt when a vampire was near, but there was only a jumbled sense of anxiety, like nails on a chalkboard.

Through the window, I saw an old man walking down the road in front of Warren's house. Only the man wasn't a man. It was thin and vapory, the whisper of a man, hunched over, holding a cane, wearing clothes that hadn't been fashionable since the Great Depression. I noticed that the cane wasn't touching the ground, nor was the man's feet. A small sound escaped my lips.

"I told you," Warren said, without opening his eyes, "Decatur is a haunted place."

The old man turned to me, his face distorted, then tilted his head and dissolved, the sunlight burning away his afterimage.

"That was a ghost," I managed. "A real ghost."

Warren snorted. "You've seen vampires and magic, but you didn't believe in ghosts? Don't worry, they can't harm you, they just give you the willies."

I nodded.

Me? Worried? No, not me.

Jack watched me with a sour expression. He caught my eye and gave a slight nod. I smiled and nodded back. The anticipation of the coming fight had us all on edge, none so much as Jack. His face was hard as rock, his good eye watched everything with a hard gaze, and I could almost feel the pain and anger and frustration that drove him. I shuddered. Jack had reached his breaking point, I was sure of it.

"Vampires," Warren whispered.

I jerked my head around, looking back out the window. Nothing moved in the September sun. The house was deathly quiet. I reached out again, and this time I felt it, the sickness in my stomach that indicated vampires.

Before I could blink, the door crashed in, sheared from its hinges. It flew across the room, past the pentagram, then skidded to a stop against the far wall. The big vampire that held Stacie in Indianapolis came through and Jack blasted him in the chest with the shotgun. The vampire rocked back and his shirt shredded as Jack hit him, shell after shell, but the vampire held his own and I saw the bulge under his shirt.

"He's wearing a vest," I yelled. My Colt came up, without conscious thought, and I squeezed the trigger. The vampire moved and the silver bullet caught him in the side of the face, tearing a smoking gouge from his cheek. My second shot missed the vampire and I heard Katie shout as her crucifix flared to life, the light blindingly pure in the early dusk. The vampire was down and burning, but the front door remained empty. I realized, too late, what was happening, and when I turned, I saw that Pearl and Silas had entered through the back door.

Jack dropped his shotgun and was bringing his monstrous .45 to bear when Silas ripped it away and smashed it against Jack's face. I aimed for Silas's head and was about to pull the trigger when Silas flung Jack's .45 at me.

It streaked across the room, striking me in the temple. I yelped in pain and when the tears in my eyes cleared, I saw that Pearl held Katie, the crucifix on the floor, the light gone, and Katie dangling from her grasp.

Warren was backed against the wall. "Jack!"

Jack and Silas were grappling, iron hard blows trading back and forth, arms swinging in blurs. Impossibly, Jack was holding his own.

They moved too fast for me to track Silas with the Colt. "Get him in the circle!"

Jack nodded and then he grabbed Silas and spun him across the room, into the center of the circle.

Time slowed as I saw Warren prepare to cast the spell. I had time to wonder why Stacie hadn't joined the fray. Had Silas left her in Indiana?

For a fraction of a second I thought the only thing missing from our complete victory was Stacie's death. I thought that right up until Henry Hastings entered through the front door, past the burning vampire still on his knees in the doorway.

I thought I'd seen vampires move fast, but nothing prepared me for Henry Hastings. His sword cleaved the kneeling vampire in two, and before the vampire's face could even register shock, Henry was through and across the room, his massive sword a silver blur.

He slammed into Jack and Silas in the middle of the circle just as Warren spoke the word to trigger the trap.

Silas flung himself back, carrying Jack with him, and for a fraction of a second Henry was alone in the center of the circle.

Warren finished his words and the spell activated.

There was an electric flash and Henry tried to move, but his feet were rooted to the wooden floor. I saw the look on his face, a resigned dismay, and the fire erupted. Everyone in the room turned to stare as Henry struggled in the flames, his body awash in yellow and white, the flames licking skyward, a solid wall of heat that blazed like the sun. His clothes turned to ash as he roared in pain, and then his skin melted like plastic in long stringy rivulets.

I saw Pearl move and I screamed, but Katie was too busy watching Henry burn. While Pearl's right hand held Katie by the throat, she plunged her left hand into Katie's stomach, then horribly, through it, and out her back.

Jack turned at the sound of my voice and Silas caught him across the face with an elbow that sent Jack reeling back. Silas turned to me, his lips pulled tight, his fangs bone white in the reflected blaze, and then he moved so impossibly fast, across the room to Warren.

Silas grabbed Warren's head. I squeezed the trigger on the Colt again and again, but it was too late. Silas twisted Warren's head from his shoulders in a fountain of blood. I watched in horror as Warren tried to gasp for air, his eyes wide in shock, then my silver bullet slammed into Silas, tearing a hole through the side of his right arm and stomach. Silas shrieked in rage and turned to me, the holes in his arm and stomach burning with a fearsome light. I waited for him to combust, but the chunk of flesh missing from his arm cast a ruddy glow and smoked as he advanced toward me.

Henry's bellowing went silent, his skin gone in a cloud of ash, and I could see the muscle below the skin. It was a terrible thing, like a skinned animal, but the fire began to consume the muscles as well.

Katie coughed and retched blood from her mouth. It hit the floor with a squelch. Pearl reared her head back and laughed like a lunatic.

"No," I said, before Katie hit the floor, her body going slack. "No!"

Silas turned to Pearl and smiled, delighting in the carnage.

Behind him, Jack was staring at Warren's body in shock. He staggered over and grabbed the headless corpse.

Silas turned to Jack, and then to me. "I'm going to give you the gift, Sam, because I made a promise to your wife. You can feast on the girl here," he said, pointing to Katie, "then I'll give Jack the gift. When he turns, we'll be one big happy family."

I shook my head. "I'd rather die first." I held the Colt to my head. "Take one more step and I'll blow my brains out."

Silas turned to Pearl and grinned wider. "The kid's hilarious." He turned back to me. "Suit yourself. Go ahead, do it. If you've got the guts."

I glanced at Katie, but she hadn't moved, the pool of blood growing larger around her. Henry was on the floor in the circle, his body awash in flames that cast a flickering light against the walls in the evening dusk. Jack held Warren's body, and Warren's head lay against the kitchen counter, the eyes sightless as they stared accusingly across the room.

It had all gone so wrong.

It's not supposed to end like this.

I wanted to pull the trigger, to end my life before Silas could turn me into another of his younglings, but the barrel faltered against my head. I wanted out of this nightmare, but I lacked the courage. I wanted to empty the Colt into Silas, but I knew the last four shots were worthless. He was simply faster than me.

And, the bastard knew it.

I looked into his eyes and felt the heavy weight of them, pushing against my skull, his face split in a delighted grin.

Jack shrieked and the sound was terrifying, part wounded animal, part curse from hell.

Silas paused.

It was too late. The fangs erupted from Jack's mouth as the change washed over him. An icy-cold wave swept across the room as

Jack ripped Warren's body in two, the blood and gore soaking his hair and clothes.

Silas and Pearl turned, shocked, then took a step back. Jack faced them, the look on his face terrifying and not even remotely human. He peeled away the eye patch and shook his head, as if waking from a long sleep. I was expecting a hollow dead space, but there was an eye, fresh and white and new.

Jack's eyes found Silas and Pearl, who stood still as statues.

"All these years," Jack said. "You've haunted me all these years. You should have *died* that night."

"But, I did," Silas whispered. "You *left* me to die."

Jack closed the distance between them so quickly it was like magic. He smacked Silas across the face and there was a crack, like a tree snapping, and Silas fell to the ground, his neck broken and his head lolling. Pearl blinked and tried to run, but Jack grabbed her and held her as easily as she held Katie just moments before.

Jack addressed Silas. "It's going to take a few minutes for your spine to heal," he said calmly. "For now, you're completely helpless. Pearl is one of your favorites. The bond is strong between you. I want you to watch."

Pearl hissed and slammed fist after fist against Jack's face without effect. Jack pulled his hand back and talons burst through the skin of his fingers. He put his hand over her heart and twisted. She thrashed about, but Jack pushed, slow and steady. Pearl shrieked, but it was too late. Jack's hand was completely through her chest. She convulsed as Jack ripped her heart from her chest, then tossed her body aside.

It promptly burst into a greasy flame.

Silas watched this, eyes wide, lips moving, trying to speak, but his broken neck kept his lungs from working. All he could do was watch as Pearl died.

Jack grabbed him by the neck and tossed him over his shoulder.

"Jack, don't do this," I pleaded.

Jack turned to me, his eyes catching mine, and I felt him in my head, like the voice of an angry god. "Goodbye, Sam."

With that, Jack left.

* * *

I rushed to Katie's side and felt along her neck. Her pulse was faint and thready. "Katie? Jesus, Katie?"

She didn't move. I gently rolled her over. Her body was limp and her arms flopped against the floor. "Wake up!"

The coppery scent of blood was thick in the air, but there was another smell, a foul odor from the wound in her stomach, and I knew that Pearl had torn into her intestines, maybe even her colon.

I knew enough about anatomy to know that even with prompt medical treatment, it would be a crap shoot. She would go into shock, then sepsis, then an agonizing death as her internal organs shut down, and that was the best-case scenario.

"Katie, can you hear me? Stay with me. Please, just stay with me."

She opened her eyes and stared, uncomprehending. Her lips opened and she tried to speak.

I didn't know what to do. Everything had gone so wrong. Pearl's body was nothing more than ash, the other vampire from Indianapolis a pile of ash in the front door.

There was only one option.

I turned to the circle. Henry was almost an almost unrecognizable corpse, nothing more than a skeleton covered in charred muscle. I dipped my hand in Katie's blood and smeared it over the edge of the chalk on the floor. There was a sound like glass shattering in my mind as the circle collapsed.

Henry—or what was left of him—scrabbled toward us across the hard wood floor. Everywhere he touched he left an ashy smear. I tried to pull Katie back, but he wasn't going for Katie. He looked up at me with squishy eyeballs, then his burnt and blackened tongue licked the blood from the floor.

The stench was overwhelming. The burnt skin and flesh had a nausea-inducing wrongness, and it mixed with the smell of blood and death in the room. I gagged and tasted bile in the back of my throat and barely managed to keep from retching. He licked the floor, chasing around the pool of blood with his tongue. I watched as the tongue swelled, plumping up.

His scalp was nothing but fat and bone, his brown hair long gone, but I could see the tissue start to regenerate. He held up his hands and they, too, were filling back out.

He looked at me and licked his lips, the blood a scarlet smear against the puckered pink skin. "Sam?"

I glanced down at Katie. "You have to help her. You have to save her."

He turned his gaze to her. "Can't," his voice crackled, like crumpled paper. "She wouldn't want it."

"I just saved your life," I said. "You *owe* me."

"You don't understand. I promised to…." He coughed and took a deep breath, then coughed up a mouth full of ash and blood. He gagged, then spat it out and fell back, exhausted. "Promised I wouldn't," he finished. "Never again."

"But she'll *die*," I said.

He shook his head. "Sorry. I can't."

I believed him. Whatever promise Henry made, it meant something to him.

He dropped to his belly and licked up more blood while I gently set Katie down and then kicked him as hard as I could.

He woofed and went sliding through the blood and ash, until hitting the wall next to the kitchen. His chest rose and fell, and I could see that he had more energy than just minutes before, but he still couldn't stand.

I grabbed his sword from the floor and stood over him. The sword was heavy and the tip quivered in my hands, but I didn't care. "You turn her, *right now*. Save her life!"

His eyes never left mine. "She won't be alive, Sam. Just a dead thing, like me. She doesn't want to live like that. You don't *want* her to live like that."

"She's *going* to die," I said.

He nodded his head. "Yes."

"It's not fair! We were going to kill Silas. We were going to save her sister. We were going to find my daughter." I threw the sword across the room, cursing in frustration. Henry watched but said nothing.

I returned to Katie. Her eyes stared off, sightless, and I felt for the pulse that was no longer there.

"It wasn't supposed to end like this," I said to no one in particular. "Not like *this*."

* * *

Henry's Chevy Suburban was parked down the road from Warren's house. Jack's Chevy was gone. There was still a glow to the west, the last few minutes of dusk disappearing. The remaining light glowed against the storm-clouds rolling in over the horizon. I could sense the storm coming as the clouds gathered, and I knew it would soon be upon us.

I moved like a sleepwalker, my feet stumbling over the grass and tree roots, slipping on the damp leaves. I opened the back door of the Suburban and found the blue Igloo cooler right where Henry said it would be.

I quickly carried it back to the house, where the dead waited, but stopped at the door. My mind was numb and I felt empty. Not only had I lost my wife and child, but I had lost Jack and Katie. I had lost everything that kept me sane since Arcanum. With them gone, what was my purpose? To find Lilly? How could I do that without them?

The *bad* thing, worse than Jack's transformation, worse, even, than Katie's death, was how I kept on going. There should have been sad music. The heavens should have opened. Something meaningful or significant should be washing over me. At the very least, I should have died from shock or sadness.

Instead, my heart kept beating, the seconds kept passing, and my mind kept churning.

I felt the tears on my cheeks and realized I was crying. I dropped the cooler on the sidewalk in front of the door and looked down at my hands, now stained with blood and ash.

It wasn't fair. None of it.

Please. God, or Jesus, or somebody, if you're listening, please help!

The seconds ticked by. Finally, I wiped my hands on my shirtsleeve, then carried the cooler inside.

Henry sprawled across the floor, eyes closed. His body was one giant scab, the muscle and fat and skin knitting itself back together.

"Here's the blood," I said.

He opened his eyes and croaked out, "Hand me one?"

I opened the cooler and took out a blood bag. It was barcoded and labeled AB Positive. The other bags were a mismatch of types. Apparently, Henry wasn't picky.

I fumbled with the bag. "Do you need a tube hooked to it or something?"

He shook his head and I handed him the bag. He looked up at me, then his fangs sprouted and he put the bag to his lips sank them in, sucking hard, emptying the bag in seconds. He coughed and his body was wracked with spasms.

I felt like I should offer help. "Are you okay? Does it hurt?"

He glared and his body stopped spasming. "Of course it hurts," he rasped. "I *almost* died."

"You mean died, again."

"Don't be an ass. I've been hurt before, but not like this. I've been tortured for weeks and felt less pain."

I thought about that, about what a man might see over a thousand years. The fact was, he was a vampire who needed blood to heal. I picked up a bag of A Positive. "Better have another."

He grabbed it from my hands and drained it as quickly as the first. The skin on his body pulsed and oozed yellow and clear fluids. "Another," he asked, his voice stronger.

I fed him bag after bag. It gave me something to do and it kept my mind from Katie's body, only feet from us.

Every few seconds my eyes would drift to Warren's head, laying on the other side of the room. I would notice his eyes, so empty, and then try and put it out of my mind while I fed Henry the blood he needed to regain his strength.

The bladder and sphincter opened after death, all control of bowels lost. It was death's final indignity. The smell in the house was nauseating.

My eyes flickered to Katie's body, her pants wet from blood and urine. I wanted to scream at the world. It was so unfair that death should reduce her from a vibrant young woman to a smelly and dirty piece of meat.

I caught Henry staring. "What?"

"I *am* sorry, Sam," he said, his voice almost back to normal. "I tried to warn Jack. He knew it was coming."

I shrugged. "It just doesn't seem right." My voice cracked and I winced, embarrassed. It took everything I had not to cry again.

Henry nodded. "I've seen a lot of things in my life, boy. I know you're hurting. I know you feel lost. It gets better. The pain may never leave, but it *will* fade. We have to focus on Jack."

"You still want to kill him?"

"I must," Henry said. "It's my job. He's become something else. He's not just a vampire. He's...more powerful. The Ancients can't allow that. It's probably not a good thing for humans, either."

I turned my head. Warren's severed head stared back, his mouth open in an O. "Jack asked me to kill him, if he was going to turn."

"That might give us an advantage," Henry said. "If he hesitates, we might have time."

I whirled around. "*We?* You're over a thousand years old. Can't you kill him yourself?"

He shook his head. "I'll be ready to travel soon, but it will be days before I'm back to full strength."

"Can't you wait?"

"No. I think I know where he's going. Besides, I put a GPS tracker on his truck. Sooner or later he'll find it, and then I'll have to track him again. There's no telling how many he might kill before I catch him."

"Why do you care? I mean, I get some old vampires want him dead, I guess, but why do you care if he kills humans?"

"I may be a monster, but I still feel like a human. It took years to conquer the bloodlust, and when I did, I felt the same as I did before. One thing I hated in my former life was watching innocents suffer. Innocents like you. Because that's what you were before Silas pulled you into this—innocent."

I scowled. "That life belonged to someone else."

He stood, feet unsteady, and stuck out his hand. "I'm making you a promise. If we kill Jack, I'll help stake your wife and find your daughter. It's the *least* I can do."

I squinted at the old dead thing, considering whether the word of a vampire had any meaning, then took his squishy and scabby hand. "Deal."

* * *

I sped through the night in Henry's SUV, the Suburban eating up the miles as we headed east. Henry was in the passenger seat, having changed into a fresh set of clothes, the laptop on the console between us casting pale light against his fresh pink skin.

He watched through the window as we passed town after town, nearing the Indiana border.

"Feeling better?" I asked

His head was pressed against the window, leaving a damp trail of oozing clear liquid. "It still hurts," he said through clenched teeth. "More than you can imagine."

"I wouldn't bet on that," I muttered. I hurt, but I also felt numb inside. Hollowed out. Driving provided me a sense of purpose, something to occupy my mind, something to keep it from the slaughter at Warren's house.

I wanted to scream, but I knew it wouldn't bring Katie back. It wouldn't help my daughter. It certainly wouldn't help stop Jack.

I checked the laptop. The tracker Henry had placed on Jack's truck showed the truck in Tangier, Indiana. It hadn't moved in an hour. I remembered Jack's story. "He's gone home," I said.

Henry nodded. "It's all he's thought about over the years—what happened to him and what Silas became. Makes sense."

"What are you going to do after he's—after you've—"

"Return to Wyoming," he said, before I could stumble over the words again.

"Just like that?"

"It's my job, Sam. It's my home. It's where my wife, Alma, is."

I thought about that. "How long have you been the sheriff?"

"The sheriff? Or the Sheriff?"

I wanted to ask about the Sheriff, but I sensed that was information that could make me a target.

"The sheriff in Wyoming."

There was a long pause. "Going on twenty-five years."

"Don't people notice you don't age?"

A smile played across his lips. "I dye my hair with a little gray. If anyone asks questions, I give them a mental push. They chalk it up to good genes and clean living."

"That will only work for so long, won't it?"

He nodded. "Yes. I'll leave, then word will go around in a few years that I've died. Then I'll wait a few decades, come back as the old sheriff's son, and start over again."

I watched him out of the corner of my eye. "What about your wife?"

He turned back to the window. "She's the only woman I've ever loved. In a thousand years, I've never felt for anyone like I do for her. I don't know what I'll do this time. Alma means the world to me. I'd do anything for her. Isn't that how you feel about your wife?"

He was hitting awfully close to home. "She's feeding from our daughter. If I don't stop her, Lilly will die. She may already be dead. Plus, Katie's sister is in a coma. If I kill Stacie, it should save her sister. The only reason Callie is in that coma is because she saved my life. Katie gave her life to save her sister. I have to kill Stacie. Don't I?"

"There's one other option," Henry said. "You could ask your wife for the gift. Turn, and you'll be together forever. Or, until someone comes to kill you."

I shook my head. "That's not an option. What about my daughter?"

He shrugged. "There's very few things that vampires won't stand for, but turning a child is one of them. Oh, they'll feed from a child or even kill them, but turning a child is abhorrent. They would be trapped forever, their mind growing older but their body never aging. Children have been turned before, but they're soon dead, either from a hunter or another vampire."

I shook my head. "I have to protect my daughter. She's all I have left." The thought occurred to me then. "What about your wife? Have you thought about giving her the gift?"

The silence stretched on. I turned north and headed for Rockville, and finally Henry spoke. "Alma's never asked. I watch her growing older. It breaks my heart. She will wither and die—even turn to dust—and I'll keep on going. I made a vow when I first conquered my hunger, to never give anyone the gift. I've kept that vow."

He turned to me. His hair was gone, but pink skin now covered his scalp. It was various shades of yellow and purple, but the skin was growing back at an accelerated rate. The look on his face was unpleasant, and it wasn't from the burning skin. "For her, I'd reconsider."

CHAPTER FOURTEEN

Monday

We wheeled into Tangier just past midnight. The town wasn't much, just a small collection of worn out houses and crumbling foundations. I followed the GPS through town and headed west, through the rolling hills.

The headlights sliced through the dark, and it made me wonder. "Should I turn off the lights?"

"No sense in it," Henry said. "He'll hear us coming. Lights won't make a bit of difference."

A few minutes later we found Jack's truck, next to a crumbling barn and a brown and white mobile home sitting on concrete blocks.

I parked the truck and got out. The mobile home was dark and the gibbous moon, while not quite full, was bright enough to cast a pale glow. The air was damp and chilly, and only intensified the smell of the corn in the nearby field.

I turned as Henry shut his door. He carried the sword, point down, as casually as I would carry a newspaper. I checked the Colt strapped to my leg and was reassured by the heavy weight tugging at my side.

I waited, but the only sound was the breeze rustling through the corn.

Where could he be?

"Jack?" I called out. "Are you here?"

There was no answer, but I heard a noise from inside the barn. It was a quiet whimpering, followed by a racking cough, the sound wet and bloody. I closed my eyes and reached out with my senses. I felt the pressure against my mind, radiating from Henry's direction, pounding against my brain. As strong as it was, I felt an even greater presence nearby.

I opened my eyes and nodded at Henry, who motioned for me to follow him.

We entered the barn and my eyes strained to pick out the details, until my foot slipped in something wet. I slipped, catching myself before I fell, the muscles in my back pulled tight.

My eyes were sharp, much sharper than before, and I could make out the outline of something on the crumbling cement pad. A light bloomed around me as Henry turned on his flashlight and shined it my way. I looked down and was sickened by the crimson pools that covered the floor.

My mind struggled to piece together what I saw. It didn't make any sense. There were hands and feet and trunks of different sizes. It occurred to me that I was looking at bodies.

Two adult bodies and a child's were strewn about. My stomach lurched when I realized there were no heads. The smell finally washed over me, like a physical blow, and I stumbled out of the barn where I retched spit and bile over the deep grass in long heaves.

There was a sound to my left, a rustling in the grass, and I turned to find Jack watching.

"Sam."

I spat out the foul taste in my mouth and turned to him. He was still, no sign of emotion, no hint of humanity. "Jack. What happened?"

He didn't speak, just watched me with dead eyes.

Henry approached from behind. "Jack?"

"Henry. Glad to see you survived. Figured you might come after me. Shouldn't have brought the boy. Where's the girl?"

"She—she didn't make it," I said, and left it at that. "Where's Silas?"

Jack nodded toward the barn. "He's inside."

I glanced back at the doorway. "What happened here?"

"This was my home," Jack said, ignoring my question. "They tore down the remains thirty or forty years ago. Put up a cinder block foundation and put that metal home where my house used to sit. This old barn is all that's left. Looks like it might not have too many years left in it, either. Funny how everything changes."

"They lived here," Henry said quietly.

He was talking about the bodies. I watched Jack's face, waiting for him to refute it.

"They did," Jack said, matter-of-factly. "Don't know their names. A family, I think. I brought Silas here. The man came to investigate."

"You *killed* him," I said.

Jack shrugged. "He interrupted me. Then, I figured the woman might call the police, and I couldn't have that."

"You killed her, too," Henry said. "And the child?"

"Couldn't leave a child without her family. That's just cruel," Jack said, turning away. "I finally get it. I understand the hunger. The lack of control."

A cold pit settled in my stomach. "Oh, Jack. Please tell me you didn't."

He turned back, puzzled. "I was hungry. It wasn't hate or revenge. I needed to feed. Henry should understand. Of all people, he should know how I'm feeling."

Henry stepped forward, sword at his side. "I *do* understand. Even after all these years, I remember. It doesn't excuse it. The old Jack would never do this."

Jack's eyes narrowed, and I went numb under his gaze. "I'm *not* the old Jack. Not anymore."

Before I could blink, Jack moved. One moment he was a dozen feet away, then he was in front of us, standing so close that Henry didn't have room to lift his sword, his duster snapping as it caught up to his movements. "Let's talk to Silas."

He brushed past me. I glanced at Henry, and saw something on his face that made my stomach sink.

He was afraid.

We followed Jack into the barn. He stood in a doorway that led to the abandoned horse stalls. "He's right through there."

I navigated the mess on the floor, trying not to step in the gore, and my eye caught the child's body. I recoiled and my foot slipped in the slick mess. I felt Henry's hand on my shoulder, steadying me.

I peered through the doorway, struggling to make out the details in the darkness. I could barely see the remains of a wooden manger in the middle. The wet racking cough started again and I glanced about, trying to determine the cause.

The cough came again. I had to know what caused it. I stepped down, into the darkened room, and Jack followed.

I heard Henry reach in his jacket, then a snick. Light blossomed from his Zippo lighter, the soft glow exposing what lay within.

Silas was bound tight against a wooden post in the middle of the room. The post stretched up to the ceiling, a support for the hay loft above, and it was thick weathered. He was naked. Silver chains sparkled in the light and smoke rose from his skin, a slow smoldering fire where the chains burned him.

That didn't horrify me. What horrified me was the damage Jack had done to his son.

Silas looked up and I realized his eyelids were missing. They'd been cut off. Bloody stumps on the side of his head were all that remained of his ears. His hands were missing fingers—all of them. Cuts covered his body in a crazy jigsaw, the puckered skin gaping open as his vampire essence tried to heal the damage Jack had wrought.

Without fresh blood, the wounds weren't closing.

Silas opened his mouth and blood poured out. He choked and coughed again, and I realized Jack had cut out his tongue. Just when I couldn't imagine it any worse, I noticed the bloody stump between his legs.

He stared at me, long past madness. There was nothing left of the confident monster I first met in Arcanum. He'd been reduced to a crazed animal.

Henry cleared his throat. "You did quite a bit of damage in such a short time."

"His neck healed on the way here," Jack said. "By the time he could move, I had him chained up with silver. He wasn't going anywhere. I tied him down, like the beast he is, and commenced to work on him with my knife."

"Jack?" I said. "This is *wrong*. Killing him I understand, but this? This *isn't* you."

Ghostly shadows danced across Jack's face, outlining the sharp angles of his face. He shrugged. "It wasn't his fault. I understand that now. Once you turn, nothing means anything. Your mind…well, it's hard to keep things straight in your head." His eyes caught the reflected light from Henry's lighter and I felt that heavy weight, but stronger this time, threatening to submerge me. "Someone has to pay. Whether he was in his right mind or not? Doesn't matter. He *deserves* this."

I nodded before I could stop myself. I didn't agree, but something about Jack convinced me otherwise. "Yes," I said. "He *deserves* this."

"Sam?" Henry's voice came from a tunnel a mile away. "Snap out of it."

I shook my head and like that, Jack's eyes lost their depth. "No. He *doesn't* deserve this. Kill him, but don't do this."

Jack frowned. "I *said*, he *deserves* this."

This time his eyes were just eyes. No pressure inside my head. No weight.

"You've been subverting his will," Henry said. "You've been controlling him, changing him."

Jack turned to Henry, puzzled. "What's that?"

"I wonder," Henry mused, "how long have you been doing it. Even before the change, I'm sure."

"I don't know what you're talking about," Jack said, looking from Henry to me.

In a flash of insight, I realized what it meant.

"I think you do," Henry said. "You pushed Sam to come with you. I think every time he started to waver, you pushed a little harder. Just enough to keep him with you."

Could it be true? Had I only gone with Jack in Arcanum because he did something to my mind? What about abandoning Lilly? Why didn't I push harder to find her? Why was I so willing to go along with everything Jack said? "Is that true?"

"He may not have realized he was doing it," Henry said. "It might have been instinctual."

"I wasn't doing *anything*," Jack growled.

Henry raised an eyebrow. "If Sam was just a human, you could have overwhelmed him. But after his first kill? After the change? No. You can push him, but you can't change him permanently. He's too strong for that. You had to keep pushing."

I thought back to all that had happened in the past week, the decisions I made, the things I agreed to do. I temporarily put that all aside. "It doesn't matter now," I said. "You can't torture Silas. You're *better* than that."

Silas grunted, eyes bugging out of his head, and spat a mouthful of blood my way. I took a step forward and Jack followed me with his eyes. Something about his face froze me in my tracks.

I stopped. "Why are you doing this?"

Jack swept his arms around the room. "Poor Sam. You want to do the right thing. Surprise! There *is* no right thing. There's no point to any of it. Silas killed his own family. Why? What is it you kids say? Shit happens?"

"Then why does it matter?" I asked. "Why torture him like this?"

"Because I *like* it," Jack said. "Because I can. Because he means *nothing*."

"Could you do this to Sam?" Henry asked.

Jack hesitated. "Yes."

The word knifed into me. No, this wasn't the Jack I knew. The Jack I knew was long gone.

In his own way, he is now as much of a monster as Silas.

Henry put his hand on my shoulder. "You had to hear it yourself."

I nodded. *Henry was right.* "You said I should kill you if you turned. That you didn't want to be like this."

"That was before," Jack said. "Turns out, I really don't mind."

I turned to Silas. "I'm going to kill you. Understand that right now. For Stacie. For Katie. For Warren. For every one of our family you've hurt over the years."

I felt the tension rising in Jack and I hoped that he wasn't as powerful as Henry feared. My hand moved, lightning quick, to the holster. The Colt was slipping out when Jack struck.

It surprised me. I barely had time to think before I flew through the air and slammed through the barn wall, shattering the old wood like toothpicks, splinters flying everywhere. I struggled to sit, my legs tingling, and I realized I had come close to having my back broken.

I hadn't even seen Jack move.

My lungs couldn't get enough air. Slamming through the wall had knocked the wind from me. I panicked as my vision swam, then I managed to take a breath and immediately started coughing from the dust.

I looked around. I was in a storage room. An old anvil mounted to a wooden stump sat in the corner. Other tools, dirty and rusted, littered the ground. I heard the ringing of steel on steel from the stable, then a grunt and the sound of breaking wood.

I struggled up on rubbery legs and looked through the hole in the wall, trying to see what was happening in the horse stalls.

Silas huddled down like a frightened deer. Jack and Henry were gone. I reached down to my Colt, but it was missing. I saw a glint of metal on the stall floor and realized it had fallen from my holster when I hit the wall.

Or, before Jack knocked me through it.

I struggled through the hole in the wall and was reaching for the Colt when Henry blasted through the wooden wall to my left. He hit the floor and slid to a stop. Jack came after him.

Jack's fangs gleamed white, even in the dark, as if lit from within. His face was drawn back, the skin tight against his skeletal face. His eyes glowed—literally glowed—with an electric fire, even though they had gone a solid black.

It was the scariest thing I had seen. There was no question. Jack was now a monster.

Henry still held his sword and barely managed to stand before Jack reached him. He slashed with the sword and Jack stepped back as I fired the Colt. The bullet whizzed past Henry's arm and through the spot Jack had just occupied.

Jack grabbed a broken piece of wood from the floor and chucked it at me. It streaked across the room like a missile. I turned and it smacked into my left arm, right in the bicep. My arm went numb and I staggered back against the wall.

I blinked and my eyes focused in time to see Jack kick Henry in the chest, knocking him senseless and sending him in an arc through the air and into Silas.

Silas shrieked, but it came out as a bloody wheeze, then he spun sideways and attempted to grab the silver sword from Henry's hand.

Jack hissed and moved to stop him. Talons erupted from his fingers and he raked Silas across the stomach.

Silas glanced down as the claws on Jack's hand sliced through the skin like butter, his intestines dropping out in bloody pink loops onto the dirty floor.

Jack laughed, delighted, and I realized Henry was right. Jack was strong and fast.

I don't know if we can stop him.

I shook my head. I had to try. I fired the Colt and Jack easily sidestepped. The bullet went wide, and I fired again. Jack sidestepped it, too, but he was now a step closer. There was a piece of wood on the floor and I kicked it up and into Jack's face. He knocked it away, and I fired again.

This time, Jack wasn't fast enough. The bullet caught him in the side and it tore a smoking hole through his blood-soaked denim shirt.

He staggered and came at me like a madman. I tried to fire the Colt, but he yanked the gun from my hand and crushed it like a toy, dropping the pieces to the floor. He glared and I wilted under his gaze, then he grabbed me by the throat and lifted me from the floor. "You shouldn't have come, Sam."

I choked, trying to breathe, then managed, "It's my job. I'm a vampire hunter."

He threw his head back and laughed. *"You?* You're a *cook* in a *diner!"*

I saw Henry moving and I twisted away before Henry's sword rammed through Jack's back and out his stomach.

Jack roared in pain. He looked down at the sword tip now growing from his abdomen, then spun, twisting the sword out of Henry's hands. His talons caught Henry in the throat and he ripped away chunks of flesh and flung the bloody chunks against the wall.

Without thinking, I grabbed a piece of wood from the floor, a piece of Jack's old barn, the tip pointy-sharp, and lunged forward as hard as I could, pounding it through Jack's back, all the way through his heart.

Henry's eyes widened and he pulled away as Jack started to burn. Jack fell to his knees and turned to me, eyes blazing with fire.

I wanted to tell him I was sorry, to thank him for saving my life. Nothing came out. I watched the flames spread, faster and faster, casting long shadows down the horse stalls.

Jack stopped screaming and glared at me, and in that glare I read the hurt, the anger, the betrayal.

He collapsed as the flames finally engulfed his body. His skin dribbled away, becoming greasy black ash.

I wanted to scream. I wanted to stop the fire. I wanted the old Jack back. The man who loved me. The man who would die to save me.

Henry staggered up and yanked the silver sword from Jack's body. He stood with me as Jack faded a pile of smoldering ash.

I felt the electric arc as the vampire essence flowed into me. My body burned in agony , and I felt a surge of hunger like I had never known, and then everything that Jack could give was gone.

I don't know how long I stood there, but Henry finally turned to Silas, who watched us in horror.

Henry took a step forward, but I stopped him. "I'll do it."

He watched me, an unrecognizable mix of emotions on his face, then nodded and handed me the sword.

Silas waited, eyes focused on me, just like Jack's.

Of course, Silas couldn't blink or turn away. Jack had bound him and cut off his eyelids.

He tried to speak, at the end, to say something. Maybe he wanted to plead or beg for forgiveness, or maybe he just wanted to tell me to go screw myself. It didn't matter because I didn't give him a chance.

I swung the sword as hard as I could and it bit through his neck, cleaving his head from his body, which tumbled through the air before thudding to the ground.

Another surge of electric fire slammed into me, and before I knew it Silas was nothing but a pile of ash, just like his father.

"It's done." I handed the sword back to Henry, who clutched his throat, the bloody mess already filling in with pink new flesh.

Henry looked wearily around the room. "It is."

I accepted the pair of nitrile gloves from Henry, then helped him carry the bodies of the slain family into the horse stall. We piled the remains on chunks of splintered wood, then he doused the entire mess with gasoline, the same way he had arranged Warren and Katie's body in Decatur.

I eyed the remains skeptically. "Will this really hide their bodies?"

Henry shook his head. "You know how hot a fire has to get to completely burn a body? There's hardly any way gasoline will get that hot. The thighbone is too thick to burn. Someone will find this. They'll figure out the bodies were dead before the fire. They'll also find no evidence of tools used to dismember them. They'll wonder what kind of madman tore them apart and what kind of instruments he used. The fire will throw them off the trail, confuse them a little. You'd be surprised how many times authorities close out cases like this because they don't make any sense."

I watched him wind a long fuse through the wood and bodies, then stretch it across the floor. He flicked his lighter and lit the fuse. It sputtered, then sparked to life. "We've got about five minutes," he said.

He picked up the pieces of my Colt and handed them to me. "Don't forget this." He pointed to the pile of bodies. "When this catches, it'll take the rest of the barn with it. A fire like this will burn a good spell before someone investigates. We best be on our way."

I nodded. "Thanks, Henry."

"Don't thank me," he said, his face unreadable. "It's my job. Do you know where you're going?"

"I'm heading back to Indianapolis. Will you come?"

"I promised," he said. "Whatever you need."

Promises meant something to Henry, even though he was a vampire. I filed that away for future use, then nodded. We stood watching the fuel burn, the acrid smoke hanging in the air. "We should say some words for them."

"Yep." He bowed his head. "Lord, let these innocents find peace in your heavenly abode. Amen."

Surprised at his simple but heartfelt prayer, I asked, "You believe?"

"Yes," he said. "It took many a year for my faith to be restored, but I know he's there. I just don't know if he listens."

"You're not at all like I would expect you to be," I said.

He regarded me with the barest hint of amusement. "Same can be said of you, Mr. Not-A-Cook."

He left me alone with the dead. I wasn't sure what to do for them, so I crossed myself, then went to Jack's truck.

The keys were still in the ignition. Tears rand down my face as I started the engine. I wiped them away on my bloody sleeve. My body ached in dozens of places, and I was empty inside.

Jack was gone. Katie was gone.

There was only one thing left to do.

* * *

I stopped at the McDonald's in Crawfordsville and devoured half a dozen burgers on the way to Indianapolis, then stopped again on the west side for more coffee and burgers. The food did nothing to sate my hunger. When I parked the truck near Silas's house, it was still dark, but there was a hint of light in the eastern sky. I felt the coming dawn in my bones like a physical thing.

I would be a fool to say I wasn't worried about that.

I wasn't sure what I was anymore, after killing the vampires, after absorbing their essence. More than that, I was exhausted. My back and arms ached from the battle in Tangier, and my head felt like someone with a hammer was inside my sinuses, pounding their way out.

I wanted to stop. I wanted to rest, to sleep, and forget all the horrible things I had seen and done. The only thing keeping me going was the caffeine buzz from all the coffee. It made my heart pound, and I wasn't sure how much longer I could go.

The house was dark. Without lights, it looked ancient with its dark vines creeping up the brick. I got out of Jack's truck. Henry sat behind me in his Suburban, watching the house. He rolled down the driver's side window as I approached.

"You feel anything?" he asked.

I shook my head. There was a buzzing, a massive pressure in my head, but it was centered on Henry. "Nothing dead but you."

"You going to check it out?"

"Yeah. Wait here. If I'm not back in five minutes, come kill everything."

He raised an eyebrow.

"Right," I said, managing a sad grin. "Kill it again, I guess."

He grinned back. It was small and it was subtle, but it was there, the first sign of humor I had seen in the man. His hair had sprouted, maybe an inch long, between our departure from the farm in Tangier and our arrival in Indianapolis. His skin was losing its waxy, melted look.

He gave me a mock salute. "Be careful in there."

I walked across the football-field-sized lawn. There was a chill in the air and a cold drizzle soaked the grass.

I reached the door and placed my hand against it. I sensed nothing from the house. I tried the doorknob and found it unlocked. I opened the door, half expecting a vampire to attack me.

The front hallway was empty. I clicked on the miniature flashlight Henry had provided and cast the narrow beam down the right hall, then the left.

Silence.

The hall was clear, except for some ash and bullet casing. I stopped and picked one up. It was a .45 casing from Jack's Tommy gun. I dropped the casing to the floor and it clicked and clattered in the deathly quiet.

I continued on. The room where we had fought was wrecked. Ash lay everywhere, bullet holes pockmarking the walls. The smell of gunpowder still lingered, and there were gouges and scrapes everywhere, from Jack's silver grenades.

After a quick look around, it was time to investigate the part of the house I *hadn't* been to.

I found a sweeping staircase down another hallway. The banisters were made of some exotic wood and the stairs were carpeted in a rich, but tasteful red.

I shone the flashlight around and realized the carpet was the color of fresh blood.

I followed the stairs to the second floor and went room by room, but found nothing but elegant beds and tall wardrobes. Around me were the signs of wealth, gorgeous paintings on the walls, small statues displayed tastefully on pillars and shelves.

Silas had spent years accruing a fortune, it seemed, in addition to tormenting Jack.

As I came out of the bedroom nearest the stairs, I knocked against a table, dumping a figurine of a centaur to the ground. It shattered, the sharp sound echoing against the wood floors. I stared at the pieces, then deliberately stepped on them, crushing them to a fine white powder.

How dare Silas live in such finery, while feeding off the living like a parasite? I knocked a painting from one wall, then kicked over a dresser.

The anger rose, the farther in the house I went, until I came to the last bedroom.

This room was different from the rest. It didn't have a bed, just a collection of sleeping bags. I realized the younglings must have slept in this room, dozens of them by the count.

It was the final sleeping bag that sobered me, my anger collapsing. Under the flashlight's glare was a child's backpack.

I recognized the little girl on the orange backpack. It was Dora, my daughter's favorite character. My heart hammered in my chest as I picked it up.

It belonged to Lilly.

I spun, shining the light over the room, looking for another sign of my daughter, a sign that she'd been there not so very long ago, but there was nothing.

I retraced my steps through the house and out the front door to Henry's truck.

He saw the look on my face. "What?"

I held up the backpack. "This is Lilly's bag. She was here."

He looked around. "But not anymore. The place was empty?"

I held the bag in front, as evidence. "There's nothing but this."

"They felt it when Silas died," Henry said. "With his control gone, they are free to act to their nature. They're in the wind."

"She was here. She was *right* here!"

"She was," he acknowledged. "Now she's not."

I wanted to scream at him, but he was right.

The rain had increased from a drizzle to a heavy downpour, and it soaked my shirt, my hair, the backpack in my hand. Finally, I shook my head. "We'll track her."

"How?"

An idea came to me. "Leave that to me."

* * *

I bumped the truck door shut with my knee and turned to watch Henry pull his Suburban in behind me. He glanced around at the deserted street, then climbed out of the truck carrying his sword.

I shook my head. "You won't need that."

His eyes narrowed, but he grunted and put the sword back in the truck.

We walked across the street to the warehouse entrance where I knocked softly, then opened the red door and stepped inside. Henry followed, and I motioned for him to close the door.

We walked down the hallway and opened the door at the end, exposing another identical hallway beyond, another red door with frosted glass in the distance.

Henry jerked, then started back to the front.

"Don't bother," I said. "We're stuck until they decide to let us out."

He stopped, staring longingly at the entrance door. "Don't like this. You should have warned me."

"We're not in danger. They owe me." I thought about it. "They owe *us*."

The floor shuddered beneath our feet. There was a ripping, like tearing fabric, then the door opened and Milford Barlow stepped through. "Very good, Sam! You *did* it. Please, come with me. You too, Mr. Hastings. Where's Jack?"

I didn't say anything, and Milford nodded. "I see."

Henry grunted and followed us through the door and up the stairs to the living quarters. Milford's wife, Eva, hadn't moved from the last time I saw her, but her eyes were alive and bright and her ancient face lit up when we entered.

Henry took in the surroundings, then his demeanor changed. He stood straight and I realized he had been slouching. The man was big, maybe six-four. I could only imagine how he had looked to the peasants a thousand years ago. He bowed to the old woman on the couch, surprisingly formal, a courtly acknowledgment from an ancient time.

She lifted her hand in response and bowed her head. "Thank you," she croaked.

I watched their exchange. "You know, then."

"Of course," Milford replied. "I felt Silas die, like a cord snapping. I'm free of his influence. I'm finally free of *him*."

I approached, then stopped and knelt in front of her. "Mrs. Barlow. I need your help."

She smiled, and I could see the spark in her eye, the thing that gave Barlow the strength to fight his vampire nature. She was old, but she wasn't dead. Not yet. Those eyes watched me, appraising, then she nodded. "Anything."

"I need to find my daughter. Can you help?"

* * *

The old woman pulled me closer. She smelled of the infirm, but there was a hint of some spice underneath, a faint whiff of sweetness, some essential oil. She held out trembling hands and I took them. They were shriveled and sandpapery, but they still contained a fierce strength.

Her eyes were dark blue and the whites had yellowed with age, but when she looked at me, I felt her staring all the way to my soul. I shivered.

"Don't think," she said. "Allow yourself to feel."

I exhaled and nodded. She closed her eyes, brow furrowing.

Seconds dripped by and my mind wandered to the fight with Jack. He had been so quick, so strong. Henry was stronger and faster than the other vampires, but Jack manhandled him.

If Jack hadn't stopped to talk, we couldn't have stopped him. Even a second longer and we both would have died. It was a miracle we survived.

No, not a miracle. Henry.

If not for Henry, Jack would have killed me as easily as squashing a bug. I shuddered at my naiveté, thinking I could stand up to Jack. I almost got myself killed.

Eva opened her eyes and frowned. "You're still thinking."

I couldn't help but smile. "I can't seem to stop, Ma'am."

Her lips lifted in the ghost of a smile, then she squeezed my hands. "Focus on your daughter."

I closed my eyes and tried to picture the last time I saw Lilly, the way she looked, the sound of her voice, that long-ago Tuesday before she was taken. My mind struggled as I realized it hadn't even been a week.

I thought back to Stacie, how she looked in St. Louis and Indianapolis, the cold emptiness in her eyes, and then to Silas, the anger and frustration he felt toward Jack.

I remembered Katie, how she looked when we rescued her in Peoria. How she pressed against me in the old motel after Indianapolis.

I remembered the blood soaking the floor at Warren's, her eyes empty, and the smell of her as she died.

Eva's hands squeezed harder. I took a deep breath and focused. I pushed down all those memories, buried them deep inside, and summoned an image of Lilly. It was near the end of August, the start of school. Stacie asked if I would take her for her first day of second grade.

She was at the kitchen table, eating cereal from a chipped white bowl. She liked Lucky Charms, and she attacked the bowl with gusto. Her arctic blue eyes were alive with excitement. She kicked her sneakers against the chair leg, barely able to contain herself. I was usually at the diner, serving breakfast, but I agreed to open later that day, just so I could sit across from my daughter and enjoy watching her prepare for school.

She smiled. "I'm going to be in second grade. I'm a big girl!"

I laughed. "Second grade means you're a big girl? What happens when you reach third grade?"

She pursed her lips and frowned. "I don't know, Daddy. But, I'm a big girl now!"

"Yes, you are." I checked her backpack with her new school supplies. "Do you like me taking you to school?"

"Yeah! You're always working, I don't ever get to show you my friends. Oh, I've got a new teacher. I'll show you to her."

"I'm show and tell now?"

She smiled and it was like a ray of sunshine. "Yeah. I'm gonna show and tell you to *everyone*."

I laughed at the memory of that August day and felt a cool breeze wash over me. The wind tickled my face, then my skin began to crawl, like a thousand tiny ants walking across me. A surge of energy took my breath away and my eyes snapped open.

Instead of Eva, I saw my kitchen, light streaming through the windows. Stacie was at the table, hunched over, and Lilly sprawled across the tabletop. Her golden skin was pale and she stared at the ceiling, face blank. The back door opened and I saw myself walk through the door, carefully stepping over the trail of dried blood.

And, like that, the image was gone.

I stared into Eva's tired face and took a deep breath. "What was *that?* I thought you were going to help me find Lilly?"

She blinked. "You *found* your daughter."

"That was my house! That was me going in the kitchen door. Stacie and Lilly are in Arcanum?"

Eva smiled sadly. "That's *when* you found your daughter."

CHAPTER FIFTEEN

I blinked. "I don't understand," I said.

Milford and Henry watched us, alarmed. Eva lay still, then finally exhaled. "That was a vision. You *will* find your wife and daughter."

"In Arcanum."

"Yes."

Somehow, I knew she had seen more. "What else?"

The old woman blinked again and her face fell. "You are so young, Samuel Fisher. You've seen much these past days. I'm so sorry. Thank you for saving Milford."

"Wait, you saw something else. What? What did you see?"

I turned as I felt Milford's hand on my shoulder, his soft and portly face full of concern. "She can't tell you, Samuel. Whatever she's seen, it's *your* future. There will come a time when you will have a choice. She cannot influence that choice, else she might create a future worse than she already sees."

I felt my anger growing. "I'm supposed to go to Arcanum and hope my wife and daughter are there?"

He nodded. Even with seventy years as a vampire, his face still radiated compassion.

Henry cleared his throat. "Time to go. She's given you what you need."

I looked down and my hands were trembling. "I don't know what I'm supposed to do."

The old woman looked up at me. "Samuel. You're strong, like your kin. Do what you must. For your daughter. There is no wrong answer. No mistakes. Just pain." She held her hand out to me and I took it. She squeezed tightly. "Be good, boy."

I nodded as the tears flowed from my eyes. I was afraid of her vision and the choices I had to make, but I was even more afraid of what might happen to Lilly if I didn't attempt to save her.

I bowed, a sad imitation of Henry's. "Thank you both," I said.

"Don't thank us," Milford answered. "Find your daughter."

* * *

I drove through Arcanum, the afternoon sun casting a stark light on the town. The rain had passed, and the sunlight was reflected in puddles in the potholes and gutters. I was headed north on Main street, a DeKalb Seed cap that I found in the back of the truck on my head, and I pulled the brim lower as I cruised past the hardware store, the post office, and finally my diner.

It was dark inside the diner. There were no signs of life. No activity. No cars or trucks parked in front.

I kept driving north. Henry followed behind. I took a good look at my house as I pulled up and noticed for the first time how dilapidated it appeared. The asphalt shingles were curling, the brown hardboard siding chipped and peeled. The loose gravel driveway had weeds in it, and the leaves from the trees were still damp from the morning shower, carpeting the lawn like a soggy wet blanket.

The house looked in rough shape and then it hit me. The house *was* in rough shape. I had rarely looked at it with a critical eye. Now it was glaringly obvious.

Is this what Stacie had seen? Was the town dying? Was our marriage dying? Had she continued to live in Arcanum, well past the point she wanted to leave, only staying because of inertia?

I saw a glint of sunlight reflected through the garage door window. I got out and checked and found a silver BMW with Indiana plates parked next to Stacie's Taurus, probably stolen when she fled Silas's house.

Henry parked his Suburban in front. I went to the driver's door and he rolled down the window.

He nodded toward the house. "Think she's in there?"

I reached out, with my mind. Standing next to Henry was an assault to my senses—but, besides the blast furnace of his thousand years, there was another presence, oily and unclean. I nodded. "Pretty sure. There's another vampire near."

"How do you want to play this?"

"Stay here," I said. "I'm going in alone."

Henry raised an eyebrow. "You sure that's a good idea? You're stronger than a human and she's a youngling, but she's still a vampire."

184

I wanted to tell him no. I wanted him to go get my daughter, but I couldn't ask him to kill Stacie. She was my wife and Lilly was my daughter. It was *my* responsibility. I swallowed heavily. "Yes."

"Suit yourself."

I turned to go, then stopped. "Henry?"

He tipped his head. "Yeah?"

I wanted to say a million things, but I stuck my hand through the window. "Thanks."

He shook my hand and smiled. "Good luck."

I nodded and headed for the front door. I was ready to walk up the front steps to the porch when I remembered Eva's vision. Instead, I went around the house to the back door. I reached out, slowly, then remembered that Stacie probably heard the truck so there was no sense in stealth. I opened the door and stepped inside.

Stacie sat at the kitchen table, Lilly sprawled in front of her, unmoving. I entered, stepping over the dried blood trail that Stacie left just days before. The blood was now a dried brown stain. It was crazy to think that Stacie was alive and sitting at the table.

Only, Stacie wasn't. Not alive, anyway.

She looked up as I shut the door behind me, no hint of expression on her face. That was beyond her.

"You *finally* came home," she said.

I glanced down at Lilly. Her golden skin was pale, her face ashen. Her pink shirt was stained with dirt and blood, and her jeans were filthy. I shifted my gaze from my daughter to my wife. "*What* have you done?"

She ignored my question. "You killed Silas, didn't you? I felt a weight lift. I'm free now. He can't control me anymore."

I waited for her explanation. I hoped she would have some excuse, some reason for what she had done, but she just sat, still as the dead. "Did Silas tell you to feed from your daughter?"

Her eyes flicked downward. "No, that was me. Where's Jack and that little Catholic whore?"

"Gone," I said. "It's just me. I've come for my daughter."

Stacie stood in a rush, the old kitchen chair crashing backward into the cabinets. "Don't you mean *our* daughter? I own fifty-percent."

"You can't *own* a person, Stacie. The woman you used to be would know that, but the thing you've become doesn't understand."

She growled, and her fangs popped out, bright white in her mouth. "I owned fifty-percent of the diner. That's what you used to tell me.

And this house? Half mine, too. Only, they aren't worth anything. But our daughter is worth something. Her taste? It's indescribable. It's liquid gold that warms me all the way down."

I felt my pulse quicken. "Is that what this is about? You didn't like Arcanum? Or was it our marriage you hated?"

She edged closer, so smooth she almost floated. "Finally you understand, you *condescending prick*. I *wasn't* happy. With this town? In the ass-end of nowhere? What life did I have? I didn't have time for friends. I had to be at the diner. Rundown cars and a rundown house. When did I ever get a break? A vacation?" She practically spit the last part out. "When do I get what's coming to me?"

I smelled her, and it wasn't the sweet smell of her skin or shampoo, like I remembered. She smelled like a slaughterhouse, and I gagged in the back of my throat. The smell was something long ago forgotten by humanity. It was the smell of fear, of things that hunt in the night.

"What have you *done* to her," I repeated.

There was a flicker of uncertainty in her eyes. "I kept drinking from her. She tasted *so* good and I was *so* hungry. You've never felt hunger like this. You've never starved. That's what it feels like. Starving. Silas kept the rest from her, but I was her mother. He said I could take as much from her as I liked."

I took Lilly's hand in mine and her skin was too cold, too clammy. "You kept draining her."

Another emotion flashed across Stacie's face. Guilt. "I *tried* to stop. I didn't need so much. She kept getting weaker and I kept getting stronger. What was I supposed to do?"

I didn't let the anger get to me, or the guilt, or the sadness. "You almost drained her to death. She's on the edge."

Stacie took a step back. "She was dying. I can't have that. You may think I'm a monster, but I'm *still* her mother. I've given her the gift."

Oh no.

"Please, tell me you didn't."

She grabbed me by the shoulders. "You're going to do what I say. We'll be together soon."

I stared into those eyes and felt the heavy weight of them. Now that I knew what it was, I knew she was trying to compel me, to bend me to her will.

Either because I was now aware, or because I'd changed, I pushed back against the heaviness. "No."

She frowned. "You will *do* as I say."

I started to nod, spinning into those eyes. I was being dragged under, submerged against the force of her. I took a choking breath and pushed back harder. "I said *no!*"

I picked Lilly up from the table. She was light, just skin and bones, so little of her left as she was fading away. "Lilly? Can you hear me?"

She opened her eyes. The arctic blue had faded, the pupils dilated. She rolled her head listlessly, then tried to sit up.

"Daddy?"

When I heard her voice, so full of hurt and confusion, my heart broke. "I'm here, baby girl. I'm sorry I couldn't come sooner."

She tried to raise an arm but it flopped back uselessly. "Mommy hurt me. She *hurt* me, Daddy."

"I know, honey. I'm taking you away from here. I'm taking you someplace safe."

Stacie stood between me and the door, barring her fangs. "You're not taking her anywhere. I won't allow it."

"She can't turn, Stacie. Do you know what that would do to her? A child with no morality? No control? No limits?"

Stacie tilted her head to side and she spoke slowly, as if to an idiot. "I can give you the gift, too. If I turn you, we'll be together again, just like a family. We will watch over her, like parents should."

"Parents wouldn't allow their daughter to become a monster," I said, my voice rising. "You would know that, if you were still a human. She's just a *child*."

"She's going to die," Stacie snarled. "If you do anything to stop the change, she'll *die*. Would you *murder* your own daughter?"

Lilly looked up at me, frightened. "Daddy? Don't let her hurt me," she pleaded.

"I won't," I said, holding her tight. I turned my attention to Stacie. "You've *already* murdered her. Let her go in peace."

"I forbid it!" Stacie shrieked as she lunged at me.

I managed to protect Lilly from Stacie's grasping talon, but I had to dump her unceremoniously on the table as Stacie raked her claws across my back.

Pain blossomed like hot pokers across my skin and I knew that her claws had cut through my denim shirt, flaying the skin to the muscle, maybe even below.

I gasped in pain but I knew that I only had one chance. I yanked Jack's gigantic pistol from my waist.

I wasn't fast enough.

Stacie grabbed my arm and squeezed. There was a snap as the bones in my wrist broke, and I fell to the floor in agony. My legs banged the table and knocked Lilly to the floor. She landed with a thud, her body limp.

I tried to aim the Colt, but my hand wasn't working right. My index finger was still on the trigger, but I had no sensation in the finger tip. I tried to squeeze the trigger but my hand wouldn't obey. It had gone numb, maybe even suffered nerve damage.

Stacie came at me and I tried to scoot away from her. She grabbed me by the throat and whipped around, throwing me across the room. I slammed into the wall, the same cracked and dented wall where Jack had thrown Cassandra just the week before.

I hit and my vision went black as I collapsed to the floor.

Everything hurt. When I opened my eyes I saw the cracked wooden floor in front of my face. It was covered in flakes of dried blood, and I knew that if I didn't get up, my own would soon join it.

I made it to my hands and knees before Stacie kicked me in the ribs. There was a crack and I went sailing across the living room and smashed into the far wall.

When I hit, I didn't even have enough air in my lungs to scream.

I had never felt so much pain. Every breath was like a knife in my side. I saw black in front of me, and I tried to make sense it, then realized it was actually a dirty gray tweed fabric. I was looking at the back of my overturned couch. I gasped for air and a spasm of pain shot through my side.

I had never broken ribs before, but I knew Stacie had just broken mine with a single kick.

I heard her footsteps against the wooden floor as she came for me. I managed, "Wait. Please wait."

She lifted me easily with one hand and stopped beating me to death long enough to say, "You think you can stop this from happening? I'll keep pounding away at you until you're dying, and then I'll give you the gift."

I winced as I tried to get my air back. "We—we can't live like that. It's not right."

She eyed me curiously. "Why not? Why the *hell* not?"

In that moment, I realized I wasn't a brave man. Or, a moral man. I wanted to save my daughter, but I didn't want to die.

And, for a moment, I considered it. To die. To come back. Eternal life with her and Lilly.

Could we have a life? Moving from town to town, feeding on blood? Would I be consumed by hunger? What of Lilly? Henry's words.... What was it he said?

Abhorrent.

Henry said a child vampire is abhorrent, that not even vampires allowed it. Plus, there was Sister Callie. She was in a coma because of me. Because of Stacie. She was going to die, just like her sister.

I didn't want to die, but life as a vampire was *no* life. "I'll *die* before I become a vampire."

Stacie's eyes widened and her lips drew back. Her fangs glistened, and there was a gleam in her eyes. "Oh, yes you will, Sam. You *will* die before you become a vampire. I'll make sure of it. And when you come back, you'll understand."

* * *

The last thing I remember before I went crashing through the window was Stacie slapping me across the face. Except, as a vampire, her slap could knock over a refrigerator.

I landed in the soft grass, which felt a hell of a lot better than the walls and floors she had been slamming me into. I knew I couldn't take much more. I was almost beaten.

She's going to kill me.

I looked up and found Henry standing in front of me, face bland. "Keeping it in the family?" he asked.

My neck hurt so bad I could barely nod. I spat blood from where I had bitten a chunk from my lip. The coppery taste made me gag, along with the snot running down the back of my throat. I coughed up as much as I could before I was able to speak. "Kinda...not doing...so well."

"How many fingers am I holding up?"

I looked at his hand, trying to stop the spinning. "Three?"

"One," he said with disgust. "You better end *this* before she ends *you.*"

I tried to smile. "No kidding."

He shook his head, then placed a gigantic silver Bowie knife in my left hand. "End this, or I will. She's too dangerous."

With that, he picked me up as easily as Stacie had and threw me back through the window. I landed on the floor and managed to roll, coming up to my knees, the knife behind me. Stacie was waiting and I saw her eyes dart to the window and her mouth formed an 'O.'

"Don't worry," I said, "Henry won't kill you."

She turned to me, satisfied. "I'm not worried, honey. Everything is going to be better soon." Her grin grew wide. "I promise."

I didn't doubt she probably thought it would be. After all, I was a bloody mess. I had so many contusions that I would have bruises on top of bruises. My right wrist was broken. I had cracked ribs and probably several cracked vertebrae, and from the way the pain shot up my jaw, I think she might have fractured it. My vision was blurry and suspected I had a concussion.

As she came for me, I thought of our marriage. The day we exchanged vows. The joy we felt when Lilly was born. Everything was scary and fresh and exciting. Our lives were unpainted canvases, just waiting for us to *live*.

I thought of Jack. Of Silas. Of the unfairness of life.

As she grabbed me, I felt the love and anger and sadness fade, and my mind went still as she tilted her head and came for my throat.

I finally felt relief.

Then I plunged the knife into her with all my strength.

She was so close, so ready to bite. She didn't even see it coming.

The knife penetrated her chest, right through the bone, like butter. It shouldn't have been that easy. It should have taken more effort.

But, I had changed and it *was* silver.

Her eyes widened in shock. Before there was only anger and lust. Now there was only fear. "Sam?"

That was her last word. Fire erupted from her chest, from her heart, and she released me.

My legs buckled as I hit the floor. I couldn't have stood if I tried. She dropped to her knees, like she was praying, but her eyes never left mine. She opened her mouth and blue flames shot out.

Her lips worked, and the fire spread to her face, her hair. She convulsed, shaking and rolling across the floor, then she went still. Cold tendrils of fog inched across the floor and I felt the electric shock as it rushed into me, the sick nauseating feel that I'd recently experienced.

What finally settled on the floor was already less than human, a lump of melted flesh and fat. It smoked heavily, and the flames leapt higher.

I managed to get to my hands and knees and crawled to the kitchen. Lilly was still on the floor, but her eyes were open. Even though she was dying, I knew from her face that she had seen the entire thing.

Her eyes watched me as I approached. "Daddy?"

I wrapped my left arm around her and lifted her, clutching her tightly. My right arm hung uselessly by my side, and I coughed as I tasted the blood in my mouth. "It's okay, sweetie. Everything is going to be okay."

"You hurt Mommy." The words weren't accusatory, just matter-of-fact.

"I had to stop her from hurting us."

She nodded, accepting it. Then, "I'm cold."

"I know, sweetie."

Henry entered through the back door. His eyes focused on the remains of Stacie's body in the living room, slowing being consumed by fire, turning from woman into greasy ash. His eyes swept the room, then finally rested on Lilly. His eyebrows raised.

"Lilly? This is Daddy's friend. His name is Henry. He's going to take you outside."

She nodded weakly. Henry picked her up, being careful of my wounds. "Hello, Lilly. You're a good little girl, aren't you?"

She smiled at him and nodded wearily. Henry left with her, then returned shortly after. He gave me several moments, then, "She's been given the gift."

I continued watching my wife burn. "Stacie wanted to turn us into one happy vampire family."

Softly, he said, "Can't happen, Sam. A child made into a monster? I don't claim to know God's plan, anymore, but I'm pretty sure that goes against it."

I turned to him. "She's my daughter. What am I supposed to do?"

He paused, then shrugged. "You look like shit."

I spat blood on the floor. "I'm tired, Henry. I'm just so tired."

"You've been through something most people wouldn't have survived. What's your plan?"

"I have to get to Peoria," I said. "There's someone there who can help. She should be awake."

He looked me over. "Can you drive?"

I nodded. "I'll have to drive with my left hand, but I'll manage."

He shook his head with a frown. "You're an idiot. I placed Lilly in Jack's truck. We better get going. You have until midnight before she passes."

I prayed it was enough time.

* * *

I looked around the remains of my house. Ash and blood and pieces of broken furniture littered the floor. Broken plaster and lath were piled in heaps near the wall.

I sighed. My shabby home, the home that I *had* loved, was destroyed. I almost laughed at how little it meant. In the grand scheme of things, it was an unnecessary attachment.

I poked around in the kitchen cabinets, between the good plates and coffee can full of pennies, until I found the old bottle of lighter fluid my Dad had set aside for cleaning and degreasing.

I shook the bottle. It was almost full. More than enough.

I squirted the lighter fluid over the hardwood floor, soaking it, then made a trail through the wreckage to Stacie's still burning body.

The lighter fluid ignited, and a lick of flame followed the trail across the floor. I turned to leave, then remembered something. I quickly opened the wooden cabinet in the living room and grabbed Stacie's photo album, tucking it under my arm.

The living room was awash in flames and it was quickly filling with billowing black smoke. I took one last look at the remains of my former life, then kicked open the back door.

I came around the corner and found the Arcanum police car stopped in front of my house. Henry stood, leaning over, talking to Officer Elbert Morrison. I saw Elbert nod, then the car started and drove away.

I caught up with Henry as he was getting in his suburban. "What was that?"

"Neighbor called the cops. I took care of it. He'll be back in ten minutes and won't remember he was already here."

I didn't know if I should be happy that Henry compelled someone to forget, especially Elbert. He'd been a friend to my Dad, and was considered both a nice man and a dedicated cop. On the other hand, there was no way I could explain what happened to my house or my wife.

Even if I told Elbert the truth, there was no way he would believe it. Until a week before, I wouldn't have.

"That should be enough time," I said. "I set the house on fire."

Henry nodded. "You're learning, kid. It's not like they'll find a body. Let's get going."

I threw the photo album in the floorboards of Jack's truck. Lilly was curled up in a fetal position in the passenger seat, either asleep or unconscious, I couldn't tell.

I backed the truck out onto Main and headed south. I saw smoke pouring from the windows through the rear-view mirror. The Arcanum fire department was an all-volunteer force. By the time they put the fire out, there wouldn't be anything left.

People would wonder. What happened to the Fishers? The Coffee Crew might ask. Ralph, Bob and Earl had known me since I was a child.

I knew better. In the end they'd get their coffee at the gas station, then soon enough that generation of farmers would be gone. The diner would sit vacant until the city board used some legal means to get ownership. They could raze the building, but more likely appropriate it for storage.

In a few years, no one would remember the Fishers. They would forget all about the young man, Samuel, his beautiful wife, Stacie, and their wonderful daughter, Lilly.

* * *

My mind drifted on the long drive to Peoria, somewhere between Arcanum and Indianapolis, so I rummaged around the glove compartment until I found an MRE. I tore it open and used my good left hand to spoon the cold chili mac into my mouth while steering with my knees.

There was an instant pack of coffee in the bottom of the MRE, and I dumped the powdery contents in my mouth and swigged it down with a bottle of water from the floorboards.

I almost gagged at the taste, but managed to keep it down. The coffee helped focus my mind. As I navigated through the eternal traffic construction hell around Indiana, I no longer felt like I was dying.

Breathing caused a sharp stabbing in my sides and my kidneys felt like someone had tap danced on my back for an hour. I tried to clean my face with the wet-nap from the MRE, looking in the rear-view mirror as I wiped the bloody cuts. It stung, but I managed to get most of the blood off. There was blood drying on my back, and I stuck to the vinyl seat, a squelching noise every time I moved. There was going to be some hideous scars on my back, but I didn't dare take time to stop and clean them.

Lilly didn't move the whole trip. I kept glancing at her, checking to make sure she was still breathing, her tiny chest rising and falling so slowly that I almost thought it might have stopped. Then, a little movement as she took another breath, and I would sigh and relax a little, before I remembered she was dying.

I tried not to think about it, but it kept replaying in my mind. I had killed my wife. My beautiful wife. The last twenty miles on I-72 near Peoria, up the winding hills and over the Illinois River, took an eternity.

When I pulled into the parking lot across from the diocese, I felt I might scream. I kept reminding myself that my daughter was my only concern. The traffic near downtown was light, and as I got out of the truck, the deep cuts on my back screamed in protest. I felt wet and sticky, and I knew the wounds had reopened, but I didn't have time for that.

I grabbed a light brown coat from behind the seat, one that belonged to Jack, and picked my daughter up and headed for the front door.

Lilly didn't move. I could feel her heart beat slowing, much slower than normal, and the fear hit me. Without help, she would die.

I entered the building, Henry close behind. The old warhorse nun behind the reception desk glanced up.

I wasn't prepared for the giant semi-automatic pistol that appeared in her hand, like magic.

Her face blazed with anger. "Take one more step and I'll paint the wall with your brains," she said.

I stopped. I felt Henry behind me, so close he was almost touching me.

"I'm here to see Lewinheim."

The nun held the gun with a practiced grip. She pulled off her headphones with her free hand. "I know *who* you are. I know *what* you are. I even know *what* he is, though I don't know it can *be* here, on consecrated ground."

Henry said nothing.

I felt Lilly shift in my arms. "It's okay. He's with me."

The nun's eyes narrowed. "This is a Desert Eagle, fifty-caliber, silver ammo. You may think you're fast, vampire, but there's still a few minutes of daylight. I guarantee I will blow you away before you move. Don't even think about trying any vampire tricks. Do we understand each other?"

I nodded. "Yes, I think we do."

"I want to hear him say it."

Henry cleared his throat. "I swear on my honor, Ma'am."

The nun harrumphed, then hit the call button. "The Fisher boy is here."

Moments later, Callie opened the door. "Sam? Thank the Lord."

I smiled. "I'm glad to see you're okay."

"I woke early this afternoon. That was your doing?"

I nodded.

Callie noticed Lilly, then her eyes went wide when she saw Henry. "What is *it* doing here?"

"He's helping me. Lilly's been hurt."

Callie's eyes darted from me to Henry. "Where's Katie? Where's Jack?"

I didn't know how to answer that, but she must have guessed from the look on my face. As she made the mental connections, I saw the hope leave her eyes. "Oh no. Please Lord, no."

I looked down at my little girl, then back to Callie. "They didn't make it. I'm so sorry, Sister. You can't believe how sorry I am."

"Did *he* have anything to do with it?"

"No, he helped us. This is Henry Hastings."

Her eyes widened. More interesting, I saw the old nun's eyes widen. "Henry Hastings?" Callie asked. "The sheriff from Wyoming?"

Henry removed his hat and bowed slowly. "Pleasure to make your acquaintance, Ma'am. Sorry for your loss."

The Sister swallowed. "How can you even stand here on holy ground? The Father blessed it himself."

Henry shifted uncomfortable. "Frankly, Ma'am, it's like my eyeballs are being fried in a skillet. But, I made a promise to the boy. If you know anything about me, you know my word is good."

The old nun watched this exchange, then lowered the massive gun. "He speaks true, Sister Callie."

The Sister continued staring, then inclined her head, gesturing for us to follow. "Please. Father Lewinheim is waiting."

* * *

Father Lewinheim rose to greet us as we entered the chapel. "Good job, my boy. You saved her. Where's Katie?"

I couldn't meet his eyes. "She didn't make it."

The old man staggered, almost falling, then sat heavily on the oaken pew. His face was a play of emotions—anger, guilt, and mourning raced across it, then his eyes turned red and I watched uncomfortably as the tears welled up. "She was my responsibility," he said to himself. "Katie and Callie both." He wiped at his eyes with his long-sleeved shirt, then looked around. "Where's Jack?"

This time, I felt my own tears well up. "He didn't make it, either. He sacrificed himself to stop Silas," I said.

It was true, in a way. Jack's entire life was a sacrifice, watching his family die, trying to stop Silas. I prayed that wherever his soul was, that he finally found peace.

He deserved it.

The Father shook his head, blinking. "Who is this?" he asked, gesturing toward Henry.

Henry nodded. "Henry Hastings, sir. I'm here to help the boy."

Lewinheim's eyes lit up in recognition. "The vampire sheriff?"

Henry held his hat in his hands. "Yes, sir," he said, his voice slowing, growing deeper. "I promise I will make no war on you and yours, that I bring only good intent to your people, and that I will abide by good manners. I promise on my honor that I won't break that faith."

The Father nodded his head. "Then let us be bound by hospitality."

Henry nodded. "Sir, I believe we understand each other."

Callie closed the door to the chapel. "How can he," she said, pointing to Henry, "even be here?"

The Father eyed Henry. "It hurts?"

Henry nodded, and for the second time in a day I saw him smile. "Life is all about pain. I'm sure you understand that by now."

"A thousand years lets you walk on consecrated ground?"

Henry shrugged. "Can't stay long, that's for sure." He shook his head. "It hurts inside, but I made a promise to the boy."

The Father turned his attention to my daughter. "You saved her."

"Not yet," I said.

"Tell us what happened," Callie said.

I thought about all that had happened since Decatur, Illinois. "It's a long story and we don't have much time."

Henry placed his hand on my shoulder. "There's time enough for this."

I glanced at Henry, his face resolute, then to the Father, who looked every bit his age. Sister Callie's eyes were full of anguish. Henry was right. They needed to hear the story.

I carried Lilly to the altar and placed her on the worn gray carpeting.

"Good Lord," Callie said, "you're bleeding."

I looked down at my daughter. Her skin was so gray. The last thing I cared about was myself. "Don't worry, it only hurts when I laugh."

I started to turn and the room spun. When my vision steadied, I was looking at the high vaulted ceiling, my head numb against the thin carpet. "How did I get down here?"

I heard a scraping as Callie brought a chair close. She helped me up into the chair and then left. She returned carrying a brown leather bag. "Take your shirt off," she said.

I looked at the three women who danced in front of me. "Sorry, Sister, seems a little inappropriate in the house of the Lord."

"Son," the Father said, "there's nothing the Lord hasn't seen of you. Let Sister Callie tend to your wounds. You look like you're on death's door. You can talk while she works."

I sighed. "Okay."

I peeled my shirt off, the back in bloody tatters. Henry took it, folded it, then placed it under Lilly's head. He stood for a moment at the altar, then crossed himself.

He took a seat in a pew near me, but motioned for the Father to sit closer.

I told my story to Callie and Edmund. I told them of finding Barlow. I told them about the confrontation with Silas in Indianapolis.

I winced as Callie cleaned the wounds on my back with alcohol pads.

"Hold still," she said. "You really need stitches."

I remembered Jack's first lesson. "Got any superglue?"

She sucked her breath in, over her teeth. "No."

"Can you tape it, at least?"

"I *can* do that," she said.

I went back to my story, about our disastrous attempt to kill Silas. Then I told them of Henry's appearance.

"There really *is* a vampire council of ancients," Lewinheim interrupted.

"Yes," Henry said. "They try to keep the population under control, but things have a way of popping up. What Jack was becoming? He had power to rival their own. They hate the unpredictable. They're happy with the world just the way things are. It's good for them and it's good for humans. *That's* why I serve them."

"You care," Father Lewinheim said. "I wondered why a man like you would willingly serve *anyone*."

Henry snorted. "Not much choice, Father. They're old and they're vain, but they're also terrifying. I might stop any one of them, but not if they band together. That's their strength. They only trust each other. There's no way they would trust Jack. He was too unpredictable."

"I had grown quite concerned about Jack," the Father said. "Church records show no sign of a vampire hunter ever achieving that kind of success. I worried about what all those kills were doing to him."

"I don't think he really had a choice," I said. "It's *who* he was."

"Quite right," the Father said. "Continue."

While Callie taped the wounds on my back closed, I told them about my great-uncle Warren and the trap we laid. I told them about how Silas escaped. I told them about Katie's death at Pearl's hands, and I felt Callie's hands stop.

I turned and she was sniffling, tears flowing freely down her face. "I'm sorry, Callie. If I could do anything to bring her back, I would."

"She knew the risk," she said through the tears. "She wanted to save me."

I nodded. "She blamed herself for your coma. She blamed herself for being captured by Timm."

Callie shook her head. "Did she tell you she was older than me by one minute? She always thought she should protect me, even though she was the one always getting into trouble."

Her fingers worked brusquely against my back. I wanted to say something comforting, but the words escaped me. I continued with my story, about Warren's death and Jack's transformation. When I got to the part about how I helped Henry escape Warren's trap, Callie and the Father both looked at him. "How could you possibly have survived?" the Father asked.

Henry shrugged. "I'm old. Rugged. Hard to kill."

"Anything can be killed," Callie said, glaring. "Anything."

"Callie," the Father scolded. "He's here under the banner of peace. He's not the one who killed Katie."

Callie shook her head, chastened. Her emerald eyes were so much like Katie's. "Please forgive me."

"Sister, I *am* sorry for your loss," Henry said. "I didn't chose to become a monster, but know that while a monster I may be, I remain a man of peace, a man who begs for God's mercy and understanding for my actions over the centuries. I *can* feel."

Callie bowed her head. "My mistake, Mr. Hastings."

I continued with my story, Callie now cleaning the wounds on my face. I glanced down at my chest. It was a mass of yellow and purple bruises, the cuts now clean. I continued with my story, how we tracked Jack and how we confronted him. I told them about the monster he became and the family he slaughtered.

Father Lewinheim crossed himself. "Who would have thought such a thing possible?"

"There's never been a hunter like Jack," Henry said. "When he turned, he had the same bloodlust as a youngling, the same twisted mind. He was strong, stronger than me. It was a miracle that Sam distracted him long enough for me to...well...you know what happened."

"What about Silas?" Callie asked. "This is all his fault."

I shook my head. "It wasn't, really. The whole thing was just one long tragedy."

"You killed him, though."

"Hell, yes, I killed him," I said. "Pardon my language, Father. Sister. I may understand what happened to him. To Jack. That said, Silas needed to be put down."

Callie's hard eyes locked onto mine. "Good," she said.

I told them about Eva, Milford's wife, and how she helped track Stacie. I told them about confronting her. I told them how she had drained Lilly, then gave her the gift. Then I told them how I killed her and set my house afire, leaving nothing behind.

CHAPTER SIXTEEN

As I finished my story, I looked to the altar. Lilly was curled up, unmoving. "How can I save her?"

The Father stood on shaky legs and approached the altar. He bent, slowly, and touched her face. "Callie, can you perform the ceremony? She hasn't killed a vampire. It should be safe."

Henry cleared his throat. "She won't survive, Father. She's been drained. She walks the edge between life and death."

Callie shook her head. "There's got to be a way. Can't we get her to a hospital? Maybe if they gave her a blood transfusion?"

My heart leaped at the thought. "Why didn't I think of that?"

"Won't work," Henry said. "It's more than just blood. Or, blood is just a part of it. Blood feeds and sustains us, but there's another part. We can feed on a person's essence. Their...soul, I guess you call it. A youngling like Sam's wife, she had no control. She didn't just drink the girl's blood. She fed from her soul. They could pump blood back in the girl, but it won't change anything. She's dying."

My heart sank as the momentary hope was dashed. "What am I supposed to do, just let her die?"

Henry stood, his hands gripping the edge of the pew, wood creaking beneath his fingers. For a moment, I wondered if he might shatter the oak like balsa wood.

"I hate this," Henry said. "Even after all these centuries, it still hurts to watch innocents suffer. I wish there was another way, Sam, but if the Sister performs her ceremony, your daughter will surely die."

I slumped back in my chair. "So that's it, then. She's going to die and come back as one of them. One of you," I amended.

His face was as hard and unforgiving as granite. "If there were a way, I would do it. When I was a boy, my father taught me to protect the innocent and punish the wicked. When he died, I ruled the land. I was a fair man, but I quickly found my limits. I found that power alone cannot change the way of things. Some things are not for man to change."

"But it's not her fault," I said. "She doesn't deserve this."

"Of course she doesn't," he said. He turned from the Father to the Sister to me. "I don't know God's plan. I only know that what is, is."

Callie bit her lower lip. "What happens when she dies?"

"She comes back as a vampire," Henry said. "Only, she won't be a normal youngling. A young mind like hers, undeveloped, full of childish thoughts and needs and wants? She'll be nearly as strong as a full-grown vampire. It will twist everything. She won't ever mature, or grow old, or grow up. She'll be wild, no control, and she'll never control her bloodlust. She might look like your daughter, Sam, but she won't be. You might hold her hand and forget for a moment, and she could rip your arm from your body, tear your throat out, and kill you before she even realized what she was doing."

I let that image sink in. I saw it then, my beautiful young daughter, blood dripping from her mouth, shock and horror in her eyes as she stood over me, watching me die.

"It's worse even than that," Henry continued. "When she kills? She can't cope with murder, with bloodlust. She will lash out. At adults. At children. Imagine a child with a psychopathic mind and preternatural strength."

The Father and Sister watched me, faces guarded, and I saw it in their eyes.

They didn't want my daughter to come back as a vampire.

I kept watching my daughter, waiting for her to spring from the altar, to tell me it was all a prank. I waited for Stacie to emerge from the side door and tell me this was an elaborate joke.

I half-expected to wake from a nightmare, still in my bed in Arcanum.

As the seconds ticked by, I knew that this was no nightmare.

"Abhorrent. That's what you said?" I asked.

Henry nodded.

"There's no other options?"

He started to speak, then caught himself.

"What?" I asked. "There's something else? Tell me."

He hesitated. "There's a vampire. She lives in the mountains. She's over a hundred, but she has control of her hunger. It wouldn't be much of a life, but we could place your daughter with her. She could control Lilly, keep her away from humans. No deaths. No feedings. I take her blood bags. Make no mistake. Lilly will always be hungry. Starving. You won't ever be able to see her. Once she turns, you can't have any contact. She could kill you."

I pondered that. "Would this woman go for that?"

He nodded. "She owes me. I helped her, once. She would keep your daughter hidden."

"She wouldn't hurt her?"

He hesitated again. "I don't think so. No one has ever tried to keep a child vampire. There's very little that vampires find offensive, but a child vampire? I'll have to talk to her, but I think it would work. God help me, but I think it *would*."

I felt a surge of relief. It wasn't much, but it was something. My daughter could still live.

"I don't think that's a good idea," Callie said.

I turned to her, and my mouth dropped. "How can you say that? How can you tell me to let my daughter die?"

She frowned. "I know what you've been through, and I know it goes against everything you want to hear, but saving her at all costs isn't right. She's going to die. What comes back? She *won't* be your daughter."

"I'll take it. Any chance I can."

The Father cleared his throat. "You must consider what you're proposing. I know you love your daughter. No one doubts that. But, what Callie says is true. Physically, Lilly will remain your little girl. The rest of her will be an unholy thing, with no regard for human life. No chance for heavenly redemption. No relationship with God."

Henry winced. "They've got a point. It's not a life I would chose for *anyone*, let alone a little girl. She's your kin, it has to be your decision." He nodded toward Lilly. "Best decide soon. Her time is near."

How was I supposed to make such a choice? I'd lost so much, sacrificed so much. How could I let my daughter go? Hadn't my family suffered enough?

A nagging voice in the back of my head kept asking, what would Lilly be, after the change? Was Lewinheim right? Would she be a soulless monster?

How can I choose?

"I can't lose her. She's all I have left." I stood and staggered to the altar. I stood over her, the only thing I had left in the world. I was exhausted. My body was weakened, my soul crushed. "It's *not* fair," I said. "It's just not fair."

The Father spoke softly, "Sam…"

"Don't even start, Father. There's no right or wrong in this. God doesn't love us or care about us. He's abandoned us to the monsters. We're completely on our own."

Callie walked up next to me, so quietly I barely noticed her presence. "You're not alone, Sam. Don't ever say that. God is with you. *We* are with you."

Henry stood next to the Father, a remarkably similar expression on their faces. Sympathy. Anguish.

And reproach.

They disagreed with me.

It's my decision.

I knelt by Lilly's side and stroked her hair. "It's going to be okay, Lilly. I promise."

Callie snuffled, fighting back tears.

I picked my daughter up from the altar, holding her in my arms. Her skin was cool to the touch, the warmth fading fast. I held her against my chest, as close as I could, willing her to live, willing her to get better, even though I knew it was in vain.

I knelt so long my legs went numb and my back ached. A warm trickle down my back informed me that the taped wounds had opened again, and that I was bleeding through the bandages. I wondered how close I was to collapse, but I knew I couldn't leave her there. I couldn't let her go.

I felt her heartbeat against my chest growing slower.

Henry joined me. The Father, too. Callie joined in and they formed a protective circle around my little girl. Callie and Lewinheim prayed for her soul. They prayed for mine. They prayed for Jack and Katie. They prayed for God to help us through this time, all the while my daughter lay dying.

I don't know how much time passed. Maybe it was just minutes.…

I felt it when her shallow breathing slowed. I felt it as her heart slowed. I felt it as her body relaxed and as her life ebbed away.

Her last breath came almost as a surprise. I waited, but there was no more. Her heartbeat skipped, then beat, then skipped, and then her heartbeat was no more.

I looked to Henry and his face held no sorrow or regret. He was ashamed, and in that moment of insight, I knew he didn't grieve for

Lilly. He knew she was dead, the moment he carried her from my house in Arcanum.

He hadn't stayed for her benefit. He'd stayed for mine. He'd stayed because he hated what he was and what Lilly would now become.

Callie placed her hand on my shoulder. "She's gone."

I nodded.

The Father sobbed as he performed last rites, intent on giving her soul a chance to enter heaven.

Maybe he had a point. Maybe her soul would leave her body. Maybe that's what a vampire was, once they had changed. Just a body without a soul.

I kissed Lilly gently on her forehead. The skin was no longer cool, but cold.

Then I felt it. A pulse of ice radiating from her. I placed her gently on the carpet.

"She will wake in a moment," Henry said. "If I'm to take her, I must leave. Now."

I nodded. He was right. If she was to live as a vampire, Henry had to get her out of the chapel. If she was to continue, she had to go.

"Just a little while longer," I whispered.

"She doesn't *have* much longer. It's for your own good. I have to take her."

"I know." I stood. My little girl was about to rise from the dead as an inhuman killing machine. When her eyes opened, I'd be nothing but food.

I looked to Callie, whose eyes were bright and shiny, to Father Lewinheim, who looked as if he was ready to be sick, then to Henry, now concerned. "I loved her more than I thought possible. I would have done anything to save her. I would have given my life for her."

Henry nodded and as he bent down, I pulled the silver knife from my side.

Henry's eyes went wide and he stepped back, just as Lilly's eyes opened, the blue eyes deeper and darker than I'd ever seen.

"Daddy?" Her voice was hoarse. "I'm cold. And...hungry."

I said the only thing I could. "I love you, Lilly."

I repeated it over and over as I plunged the knife in her chest.

She convulsed, her mouth opening wide and as she began to burn, her eyes locked with mine. I saw the hurt there. The betrayal. She gasped and the flames erupted from her mouth, but her eyes never left mine.

I'll never forget that look. It will haunt me as long as I live.

Callie jumped back and knocked Lewinheim to the ground. They were both sobbing hysterically. Callie fell to her knees and the Father wrapped his frail arms around her to protect her from the sight.

Only Henry was silent. He stood with me, watching her, until soon there was nothing but a greasy pile of ash and burnt carpet in the chapel, the only remnant of my little girl.

God forgive me.

* * *

I didn't expect warm goodbyes from Father Lewinheim and he didn't give any. He avoided looking me in the eye as he shook my hand. "Good luck, young man. May God go with you."

Several snide remarks ran through my head, but I said, "I doubt it. Take care of yourself, Father."

We were in Father Lewinheim's apartment. Henry waited outside while I said my goodbyes. I turned to Callie. "See you in another life, Sister."

She chewed at her lip, then nodded as if coming to a decision. "I'm coming with you."

It was the last thing I expected. "You're joking."

"No, I'm not. You're going to continue Jack's work, aren't you? You're going to hunt vampires?"

"Absolutely not. I'm already responsible for Katie's death. Throwing my life away is one thing. I won't risk yours."

She clasped my hand. I tried to pull away, but she held fast. "*None* of it was your fault. You've been through a transformation. You've changed."

I felt the anger rising inside. "I've changed? I was happy in my little diner. Before Jack came. Before I found out about vampires. Now my wife is dead and I've killed my daughter Changed? The world sucks, Sister, and someone has to hold the line. Someone has to fight, so why not me? It's all I'm good for."

Callie's eyes filled with tears. "You're hurting. I get that. I've helped the Father, and I know more about vampires than anybody you're likely to meet. I can help."

Father Lewinheim grabbed Callie's hand and pulled it from mine. "Listen to the boy, Callie. He's heading down a dark road. You've seen what became of Jack."

She yanked her hand away. "You fought against them, Father, and you did what you could. Your time has passed. We have to do something. I'm a grown woman. I make my own decisions."

He eyed her mournfully. "What about the church?"

"I've not lost my way, Father, just found a different one. It's my place to go with Sam."

"You're not going," I interrupted. "I told you, I can't risk your life."

She swiveled to face me and her green eyes blazed with fury. "It's not your life to risk. It's mine. I'm being called. Go downstairs and wait, I'll gather my things and join you soon."

She stormed out and slammed the door on the way. I winced, then turned to Lewinheim. "This wasn't my idea."

He shook his head sadly. "She was never as *wild* as Katie, but she was always more *determined*. There's no arguing with her now." His eyes finally found mine. "Try not to get her killed, young man. I want you to watch her, keep her safe...protect her. Promise me, Samuel Fisher."

"It's Sam Harlan, Father. Turns out, I've always been a Harlan. It's time for the world to find that out. I'll do my best to protect her along the way."

He held my hand and bowed his head and his lips moved, but I couldn't understand the words until he reached the end. "Go with God, my son."

I nodded and gave the old man my best handshake.

Henry waited downstairs. He kept watching the nun. Her eyes were glued to him, her hand close to the desktop. He looked up as I came through the door, then flashed the nun an honest smile. "It's been a pleasure, Ma'am."

She blinked. "Don't ever come back to this place, sheriff."

He nodded. "Didn't plan on it."

We left the building and he followed me to Jack's truck. "What now?" he asked as I got in.

"Jack left me his place in Iowa. I'm going to go claim it, then I'm going to join the family business."

He raised an eyebrow. "Hunting vampires."

I didn't respond. I searched his face, but he betrayed nothing. "Did I do the right thing?"

He turned away, shrugging. "I'm the wrong person to ask. Been around a lot. Seen a lot."

"That's *exactly* why I'm asking."

He turned back to me, then shook his head. "It was a hard thing. The hardest. You made your decision. No idea if it was right or wrong." He paused. Then, "It was necessary. When you start to doubt yourself—and you will—remember what I told you about what she would have been." He stood back and slapped the side of the truck. "You going to need help?"

As he spoke, Sister Callie came through the front entrance, a tattered brown duffel bag slung over her shoulder. She spied us talking, then walked across the parking lot and tossed the duffel bag in the back of the truck.

Henry smiled and shook his head sadly. "Looks like you already got you some." He handed me a business card with his name and the Thermopolis sheriff's department number on it. "If you *do* run into trouble, call me."

He walked to his Suburban, got in, and drove away.

Sister Callie tossed her bag in the back of the truck, then heaved the passenger door open with a protest of screeching metal and got in. "He's not *that* bad," Sister Calahane said. "For a monster."

* * *

Tuesday

I found an envelope on Jack's roll-top desk with my name on it. I tore it open and dumped the deposit box key in my palm. I wanted to rest, to heal my wounds, both physical and mental, but I had one last piece of business to attend to.

The man at the State Bank of Toledo smiled pleasantly while he checked for my name in his ledger. His eyes flickered to my arm, held in its sling, a soft foam cast holding the bones so they could knit together, then his eyes darted to the scabs and scars on my face and neck. "Samuel Fisher?"

"It's Sam Harlan. I'm taking my mom's family name."

His eyes narrowed, then he shrugged. "Sign on the line."

I signed right above Jack's last check in date, just months before. The man led me to a vault that smelled of musty paper and lemon disinfectant. He opened the first lock while I used my key to open the second, then withdrew the long box and led me to the viewing area. "Find me when you're ready to leave," he said on his way out.

I nodded and took a seat at the table. The lockbox contained Jack's will. It was a single typed page, and left everything to me. I examined the other contents: a deed, a key, and a letter.

The letter was as short as the will.

Sam,

If you're reading this, I'm dead and gone. Nothing wrong with that. Dying is a part of living. I've had my time.

My house is yours, and everything that goes with it. The key will open my vault.

I wish I had more time with you. I hope that I told you who your family was, and how much you were loved. If I didn't, I'm telling you now.

You're a good boy. You were my kin. I loved you.

Go and live your life. Don't waste it like I did.

But if you do?

Good hunting.

Jack

PS. Don't forget to file the will at the courthouse.

* * *

Sister Callie was waiting at the house. I had claimed Jack's room as my own and she had unpacked her meager possessions in the spare bedroom, the one I slept in just a week before.

She glanced around the kitchen. "Plain. Like Jack. Functional."

I agreed. "I don't think he cared about appearances."

I took the key from my pocket.

"What's that?"

"I'll show you." I led her down the basement steps to the steel door set into the basement wall, inserted the key, and swung the massive door open.

She squinted at me, her face puzzled. I reached inside and found the light switch, flipping it on.

"Dear Lord," she whispered as she stepped inside, her eyes darting around the room. "There are *so many guns.*"

I followed her. "He didn't do things by halves."

In the corner, I noticed a safe the size of a small refrigerator, and when I checked, I found the massive key in the door. I turned the key, unlocked the door, and opened it. I whistled softly. There were gold coins with Lady Liberty stamped on the top. Dozens of them. No, hundreds of them. They practically filled the safe, except for the bottom where a shoebox pile of hundred-dollar bills lay in neatly wrapped stacks. I had never seen so much money in one place.

"Looks like he left you everything," Callie said from behind.

I turned and found her awkwardly holding a sawed-off shotgun. "Do you even know how to use that?"

"You're going to teach me," she said, "if I'm going to hunt vampires."

"I can teach you what I know, but it's not much."

She placed the shotgun back on the wall, then reached up and took a handgun, trying to test its weight. "Do you have a plan?"

I thought about that. "I'm going to sleep for a day. Then I'm going to eat a couple of thirty-ounce ribeyes and drink a bottle of whiskey. After that, I'm going to pound out the dent on the door of Jack's truck."

She smiled faintly. "And then?"

I felt my face go hard. "There's a phone on Jack's desk. When that phone rings, I'm going to answer. When that happens, I'm going to hunt vampires."

Her smile faded as she fingered the silver crucifix at her neck. "When that happens, I'll be right there with you."

We stood, staring at each other. The silent understanding made any more talk unnecessary.

A cold pit settled in my stomach. Vampires were evil, and by the grace of God we would make them pay.

ABOUT THE AUTHOR

Kevin Lee Swaim studied creative writing with David Foster Wallace at Illinois State University.

He is currently the Subject Matter Expert for Intrusion Prevention Systems for a Fortune 50 insurance company located in the Mid West. He holds the CISSP certification from ISC2.

When he's not writing, he's busy repairing guitars for the working bands of Central Illinois.